T0346266

Ronald Knox and The Murder Room

》》》 This title is part of The Murder Room, our series dedicated to making available out-of-print or hard-to-find titles by classic crime writers.

Crime fiction has always held up a mirror to society. The Victorians were fascinated by sensational murder and the emerging science of detection; now we are obsessed with the forensic detail of violent death. And no other genre has so captivated and enthralled readers.

Vast troves of classic crime writing have for a long time been unavailable to all but the most dedicated frequenters of second-hand bookshops. The advent of digital publishing means that we are now able to bring you the backlists of a huge range of titles by classic and contemporary crime writers, some of which have been out of print for decades.

From the genteel amateur private eyes of the Golden Age and the femmes fatales of pulp fiction, to the morally ambiguous hard-boiled detectives of mid twentieth-century America and their descendants who walk our twenty-first century streets, The Murder Room has it all. **》》》**

The Murder Room
Where Criminal Minds Meet

themurderroom.com

Ronald Arbuthnott Knox (1888–1957)

It was Ronald Knox, who, as a pioneer of Golden Age detective fiction, codified the rules of the genre in his 'Ten Commandments of Detection', which stipulated, among other rules, that 'No Chinaman must figure in the story', and 'Not more than one secret room or passage is allowable'. He was a Sherlock Holmes aficionado, writing a satirical essay that was read by Arthur Conan Doyle himself, and is credited with creating the notion of 'Sherlockian studies', which treats Sherlock Holmes as a real-life character. Educated at Eton and Oxford, Knox was ordained as priest in the Church of England but later entered the Roman Catholic Church. He completed the first Roman Catholic translation of the Bible into English for more than 350 years, and wrote detective stories in order to supplement the modest stipend of his Oxford Chaplaincy.

The Viaduct Murder
The Three Taps
The Footsteps at the Lock
The Body in the Silo
Still Dead
Double Cross Purposes

Still Dead

Ronald Knox

An Orion book

Copyright © Lady Magdalen Asquith 1934

The right of Ronald Knox to be identified as the author of this work
has been asserted in accordance with the Copyright, Designs and
Patents Act 1988.

This edition published by
The Orion Publishing Group Ltd
Orion House
5 Upper St Martin's Lane
London WC2H 9EA

An Hachette UK company
A CIP catalogue record for this book is available from the British Library

ISBN 978 1 4719 0053 2

All characters and events in this publication are fictitious and any
resemblance to real people, living or dead, is purely coincidental.

No part of this publication may be reproduced, stored in a retrieval system
or transmitted in any form or by any means without the prior permission
in writing of the publisher, nor be otherwise circulated in any form of
binding or cover other than that in which it is published without a similar
condition, including this condition, being imposed on the subsequent
purchaser.

www.orionbooks.co.uk

To Dr Robert Havard

Note to Readers

In keeping with the spirit of 'fair play' apparent in his Decalogue, or Ten Commandments of Detective Fiction, the author includes a series of footnotes towards the end of this book – as the solution to the mystery unfolds – that point the reader back to a breadcrumb trail of clues.

TIME-TABLE

JAN. 7TH (EVENING). COLIN REIVER LEAVES DORN.

FEB. 5TH. "SQUANDERMANIA" TOUCHES AT MADEIRA.

FEB. 11TH (SATURDAY). COLIN'S LETTER ARRIVES.

FEB. 12TH (SUNDAY). DONALD REIVER DANGEROUSLY ILL.

FEB. 13TH (EARLY MORNING). MACWILLIAM REPORTS DISCOVERY OF THE BODY.

FEB. 15TH (WEDNESDAY: EARLY MORNING). BODY FOUND BY ROADSIDE.

FEB. 20TH (MONDAY). BREDON ARRIVES AT DORN.

CHAPTER I

THE REIVERS OF DORN

As THE IDEAL STATE slowly greets the eye of a bewildered
public, and we realize with ever-deepening assurance that all is
for the best in the best of all possible worlds, the draughts of
modern progress (it will be admitted) are inclined to make us
creep closer together for warmth. We like to live in smaller
houses, in which patent kitchenettes replace those long, chilly
passages, as if we would draw our homes close about our ears
against the wind. The clerk who once was content to be
semi-detached and pay rent now owns, on the instalment
system, a small bungalow out in a field where the buses pass ;
the gaunt mansions of the more fashionable suburbs advertise
their emptiness with rotting boards that appeal for an
imaginary purchaser, and their occupants live in dumpy
maisonettes, a quarter of the size, compensating themselves for
the loss with an undeniable garage and a few yards of crazy
pavement. Meanwhile, those greater householders whose,
once, were the dreaming parks and Georgian piles we have
all coveted, have abandoned the expense of their upkeep and
crowded into London flats, with a fine mews outlook and a
postal address which looks respectable enough if you omit
the 95B. All the more gratefully, once and again, you come
across old families in the country who still keep up, by hook
or by crook, the external appearance of splendour ; keep the
palings sound and the paths weeded and the roof tiled by
prodigies, sometimes, of self-denial, and make it possible for
the local guide-book, even in these days, to talk of " stately
homes." In a few more decades of land-taxation and death-
duties these, too, will have abandoned the struggle ; and the
fields will go out of cultivation altogether for lack of a
squirearchy, until we ride down the hedges with tanks and
cultivate it all, Soviet-fashion, by slave labour. Or will a few
of the old landowners be left, financed by public subscription,

1

to impress the American visitor—a delicate return for the reserves in which he keeps his surviving Red Indians? In Scotland, especially, you will meet with these inhabitants of the past. Perhaps the Scot has a larger share of feudal pride; perhaps Edinburgh has not the same metropolitan lure as London; perhaps it is merely that even in these days you may hope to let shootings. Of such were the Reivers of Dorn, the family which concerns us in this history. They lived where they had lived before Bannockburn, and gave themselves no airs about it. A family curse, perhaps exaggerated by local rumour, condemned the property, so it was said, to pass always by indirect descent. There was a story, too, that the death of the heir was always made known, by presentiment, to his family. Certainly an impressive majority of Reivers had died childless, or outlived their heirs. This very fact contributed, it may be supposed, to perpetuate their attachment to the soil; the property was entailed, and the head of the family was naturally disinclined to break or commute the entail for the sake of cousins with whom, as a rule, he was not on speaking terms. Donald Reiver, who piloted the estate through the perplexities of the Great War and the difficulties of the times which followed, had quarrelled thoroughly with his cousin Henry, so long since that the very causes of the dispute were almost forgotten. And the quarrel was kept alive by the fact of neighbourhood; the Henry Reivers were settled near by, in the same county, and frequent meetings on public occasions fostered the disharmony.

The estate of Dorn was no sinecure to its owner. It was inextricably associated with surrounding farms, so that he must have some tincture of husbandry; it had been thickly planted with woods, so that he must needs turn forester; there was a tangle of sporting rights, and it was undermined at one point by a sorrowful inheritance of coal. Besides this, laird after laird had introduced on to the estate whatever at his own date was latest in modern improvements; the little territory could have faced a siege, so resolutely had it aimed at self-sufficiency. The milk of its dairies overflowed into neighbouring towns, its hens laid their eggs for distant markets; no meat was carved in the house, no cheese was cut, but what its native vigour had supplied; it boasted not only a house carpenter but an estate blacksmith. Strange outhouses met the eye at every corner of the policies: here a water-tower, here an electric light power-station, here a miniature sewage-farm, here an ice-house, replenished cumbrously, each winter, with cartloads of ice, which every summer saw melted away or put to use. To own such a property is to be owned by it; you have scarcely the residuum of time you can devote to public service or to self-cultivation. You labour like a highly paid works-manager, turning endlessly the wheels of industry in a vicious circle of production and consumption.

For such activities, while his wife lived, Donald Reiver was sufficient, and took pleasure in the exercise. Yet those who knew him best realized that he worked with the mechanical dexterity of the accomplished juggler, and was consoled only by the tacit self-congratulation which accompanies success; his heart was not in it. To play the squire with conviction, you must have the prospect of handing over the inheritance to a son who will value it not less than yourself. At Dorn, it was no secret that the young laird was ill fitted to step into his father's shoes. Colin Reiver, " Donald Colin " by baptism, was intermittently an invalid; weakness of the lungs made him a bad life, and Cousin Henry might reasonably have hoped to stand at his grave-side, even had there been no family curse to fortify him in the opinion. But, even if Colin lived to inherit, it was impossible to imagine his inheriting with gusto. All the energies of the father seemed to have gone into his daughter, Mary; she was already married to a prosperous man of business, and the conditions of the entail ruled her out of the succession. Her brother was an insignificant creature, of whom you could only complain that he was exasperatingly undervitalized. A school-master who observed " That boy, Reiver, has no passions " was held to have written his epitaph. He was placid without being good-tempered, silent without being meditative, stolid without being reliable. He looked at you with eyes that hardly seemed to register human interest, assented to your observations with an indifference ruder than contradiction. He smiled rarely, and when he did so it was with the air of one amused by a private joke of his own. He was not ill-formed, not ill-looking; he had learned, at a good public school, the kind of superficial manners a good public school can teach. But it was impossible to like him; and, though the life of Dorn was outwardly peaceable enough, you could not spend three days there without perceiving that the heir was a constant source of irritation to his own father. The fondness of parental love may be blind to every fault of temperament, may excuse every

3

lapse of morals; it finds no pasture to feed on in the stony soil of indifference.

The offence was aggravated because Colin did not pretend to the least interest in his family or its estates. He could shoot, and did shoot intermittently; but the pheasants might have been starlings for all he cared about their history or prospects. He fished sometimes, but he could scarcely have told you where the rights of Dorn marched with those of its neighbours. And as for the business side of the estate, the farms, the stock, the timber, they meant no more to him than the intricacies of Tacitus' *Germania*, which he was supposed to be studying at Oxford, and that was little. Appeals to family pride and to self-interest were alike unavailing; he parried them with a few cheap Socialist sentiments, picked up at a college debating society, or a defeatist conviction that in ten years' time life would be impossible for the landowner. Did you storm at him, he looked back at you with the injured eyes of a cat refusing to be dislodged from its retreat under a sofa; " You may kill me," they seemed to say, " but nothing will ever make me understand."

Donald Reiver, a good-natured but quite unimaginative father, came at last to give up his son as hopeless, but without pardoning the inefficiency. Nor was it only that he feared what might follow when Colin succeeded him; if Colin never lived to succeed him, as many hoped he would not, the property would survive, but it would survive in the hands of strangers, and Donald's widow would be left portionless. The management of the estate left no margin for saving; he had no other source of revenue from which to provide for her. It tortured him to think of her living in some cottage on the grounds, the despised pensioner of Cousin Henry. Somehow, he must back himself against the event, otherwise desirable, of his son's predeceasing him; and he did not need the advice of his lawyer, Mr. Gilchrist, to tell him what that necessity pointed to. Colin's life must be insured heavily, and the future was safe. Let the family curse take its effect; it would be felt by the family as a blessing, hardly in disguise.

If I seem too persistent in calling the attention of my readers to the existence of the Indescribable Insurance Company, it is only because the activities of that Company are so ubiquitous, so far-reaching, as to make it crop up everywhere in the history of modern crime. Nor let me be accused of advertising it; you might as well set out to advertise the

Bank of England. All insurance is, in a sense, gambling; the Indescribable plunges, and makes plunging pay. The most incalculable events—whether a seaside resort will have a good season next year, whether a fashion in hats will survive the spring, whether a given film will be banned by the censorship—have all been reduced by its experts into terms of actuarial arithmetic. The most gigantic risks—those of a parachutist out to make records, or those of a police-spy in Chicago—can be underwritten, at a price. If the Company has a fault, it is that of insisting rather too rigorously on the letter of its bond; premiums have to be paid on the nail, claims lodged within a specified time, loss suffered under certain prescribed conditions, or it is no use. But an element of red-tape is inseparable, as we see, from big business; you do not expect a multiple store to let you pay " next time you are passing."

Cousin Henry's recorded comment, " What, insured him with the Indescribable ? No idea the little beast was as groggy as all that," expressed a legitimate surprise. The ordinary reason for insuring with the Indescribable was because nobody else would take you on. Colin, though his was a bad life, was no desperate case; but the estate had already had dealings with the Company, and it was thought politic to keep up the connexion. After a bewildering cross-examination on his history, habits, and tendencies, and the probable causes of mortality among his great-aunts, his life was insured for a royal sum, which added several hundreds a year to the existing charges on the estate. For the first time since his extreme youth, Colin was regarded as an asset.

The arrangement had hardly been in force for a year when the reason for it was suddenly removed. Mrs. Reiver died, and with her death the whole situation changed for the worse. It is the first art of motherhood to be a buffer-state between the husband and the children, and Colin's mother had done her best. Now, except for occasional visits from Mary Hemerton, the married daughter of the house, father and son lived together, at uncomfortably close quarters. Colin " went into the City " for a time, but a very few months sufficed to betray his want of aptitude; then he lived at home, with an almost insolent air of waiting for his unwelcome inheritance. He had nothing in common with the neighbours, who would have tolerated any other eccentricity than the absence of an enthusiasm for shooting. The result was that

5

he began, insensibly, to unclass himself in their eyes by a cynical fondness for low company; in Cousin Henry's unsympathetic phrase he "went native." In England, the fireside of the village public-house has a place, always, for the Tony Lumpkin; ale is a good leveller, and the intrusion of "the quality" into the public bar is not suspected as a condescension. But the Scot, when he drinks in public, drinks with more embarrassment; he has no *abandon* in his conviviality; and, though politically he is by nature a democrat, he expects more of the laird's family than the Englishman expects of the squire's. Colin, soaking whisky among the tenants and workmen of his father's estate, won no good marks for affability; his glass, from the necessity of keeping up appearances, wanted ever more frequent replenishing, and he sank before the year was out into the unlovely habits of the dram-drinker. The family curse, it seemed, would have an easy prey, and the Indescribable was due to lose its money.

But if Cousin Henry was unmoved when he heard that Colin had taken to drink, it was otherwise when news reached him that the laird, on his side, had taken to religion. "Feller just on sixty, when he gets religion like that, gets it bad; full-time job, that's where the trouble comes in. You mark my words, the estate will start going back from now on. Likely as not, he'll get to think the world's coming to an end, and then who's going to look after the coverts?" For a moment, indeed, it did look as if Donald Reiver was going to take an unhealthy interest in the measurements of the Pyramids. That lure he avoided, but did not fall back on a "safe" creed. Modern Presbyterianism, however satisfactory in meeting the needs of sensible men, is lean diet for the devotee. And the old laird, though he had ever been on good terms with the Kirk, had laid no foundations for a fanaticism; if he was to deflect his energies to the promotion of a cult, it must be something unmistakably dynamic. He ran into it quite accidentally, when visiting a spa for his health; a chance interview, a handful of introductions, and he was swept off his feet into the newest of all revivals. He came home with a new vocabulary, a new orientation, with all the fervours of a convert.

There is a story that an elderly Catholic, after enquiring minutely into the religious observances of a pious sodality, and finding them, evidently, more exacting than he had thought,

6

summed up his impressions in the formula, " It sounds to me just the thing for my boy Tom. "   Probably old Mr. Reiver had some idea that the movement he had embraced, cradled as it was among the youth of the universities and designed, evidently, to appeal to youth, might reach Colin and infect, for the first time, that sluggish nature with an enthusiasm. But this was not primarily intended ; nor did the bored indifference with which his ideas were actually greeted in the home circle daunt his ardour.   He surrounded himself with fellow-devotees ; and Dorn, while the universities were in recess, took rank among the recognized meeting-places of the movement.

There had been some doubt, after his wife's death, whether Mr. Reiver would continue to pay the premiums on the insurance policy—I am sorry to harp so much on this subject, but it nearly concerns our story.   Mary was provided for, and he had nobody else to think of, once Colin was gone ; those annual payments, now, seemed like throwing good money after bad.   But his interest in " the Circles " decided him at once to continue them ; he could look forward, if he lived long enough, to being a religious benefactor ; and nobody dislikes that *rôle*, however much we affect to despise the loaves and fishes.   The estate, which he had no power to will away, was neglected meanwhile, as Cousin Henry had predicted that it would be ; but the results of such neglect did not immediately become apparent, while departmental officials looked after woods and coverts, farm and garden, as before.   The coverts were still shot, dinner parties were still given, and the neighbours looked leniently on Mr. Reiver's enthusiasm ; after all, it was not as if he had gone over to Rome, like young Ogilvie at Malloch.

You must picture him as a fine old gentleman, not yet beginning to feel the weight of years ; a little behind the times in continuing to wear side-whiskers, that emphasized a slight touch of foolish benevolence in the look of him.   To see him at his most characteristic, you should watch him reading a chapter to the assembled household at family prayers, in the manner of last century ; or going round the house to lock up, the last thing at night, with hardly less of ceremonial in the performance.   A man not born to do great things, but kindly and blameless ; not deserving certainly, were the apportioning of merit and reward our business, to be involved in mystery and tragedy on the threshold of his old age.

7

CHAPTER II

COLIN GOES ON HIS TRAVELS

THE FIRST ACT in the story I will take leave to tell in the words of old Mr. Reiver himself; he described it in a letter to his daughter Mary, whom he was expecting (with her husband) for a Christmas visit.

MY DEAREST MARY,

This is to know whether there is any chance that you and Vincent could make it convenient to come here before the time we fixed on; indeed, as soon as possible. We are in great trouble here through Colin's reckless driving in that new sports car of his, which I always said (if you remember) was unsuited to these narrow roads. He went out driving yesterday with an Oxford friend of his, young Denis Strutt, who is staying here; and on the way back he was responsible for a fatal accident, one very tragic in itself and very difficult for me. I don't know if you will remember Robert Wishaw, Hugh's young son, a bonny boy whom you must often have seen playing round the lodge; a great favourite and, I fear, an only child. He must have been coming back from school by himself when Colin's car ran straight into him, dragging him along the road and killing him on the spot. What makes it worse is that Colin had been drinking, there is no doubt, at an hotel; though young Strutt says "not more than enough to keep out the cold; not enough to do anybody any harm." Poor boy, he was sobered enough when he came in, but I doubt what his state was at the time of the accident, and Strutt, I am sorry to say it, is not a reliable young fellow—good-natured indeed, but without any tincture of religion.

Colin lies open to the charge of homicide, and there have been so many accidents round here lately that it is difficult to take lenient views. If he is acquitted, there is some ground for hope that all will be for the best as far as he is concerned. You will understand what I mean when I say that the shock of this wretched business seems to have *woken him up*; he has come out of that lethargy of his we all have such good reason to know, and is full of horror at what he has done; I sometimes hope, of repentance. He talks very regretfully of his past, and of the misuse made of his opportunities; he faces the prospect of evil times with a resignation surprising in one who has had so little serious background to his life. And, to tell the truth, his manner towards myself has grown almost

8

affectionate. I could wish that the great difference in my own life had come sooner, so that I might have been able to help him against the repressions of his youth.

Wishaw has taken it hardly, and cannot be blamed if he does so. His manner is perfectly respectful, but he has given notice of resignation, and I fear that I shall not be able to induce him to reconsider it. He talks of going out to join his niece in America. What I dread is the ill-feeling which all this will create among the men on the estate; not for my own sake, but for Colin's when he comes to succeed—it may be, before long. That is where we so need your help; all the people on the estate cherish a great respect for you, perhaps more than you know; and your influence, radiating from here, will do all the good in the world just now. Pray ask Vincent if he cannot make it convenient to antedate his visit; or, if he is kept down in the South, let you come on ahead. There is much more to talk of besides; but this cruel news has driven everything out of my head. If one did not know that everything is *meant*, it would be hard to take these things in the right spirit.

Hugh Wishaw, it should be explained, was the head gardener at Dorn; a grim, morose widower, peerless at his craft and a pillar of the local kirk, but with little human contact save for the paternal love now wrenched from him. It was typical, you felt, of Colin's genius for doing the wrong thing that the victim of his recklessness should have been the son of a tenant on the estate, and such a tenant. The evidence looked black against him; no other vehicle had been on the road, the turning was an easy one, and the car remained undamaged, except for a mudguard bent against a telegraph post when he ran up, too late, on to the bank. His record gave colour to the suspicion that he was the worse for drink when he took the road home. Besides, as the letter shows, the public was expecting an example to be made, before long, of some careless driver.

But those who are expecting severe sentences on motorists expect, commonly, in vain. Colin had indeed drunk largely at an hotel, but it was out of hours, and no landlord could be produced to give evidence of the fact. As for Denis Strutt, his education at school and University had taught him to hate lying as a mean Continental practice, but to perjure himself cheerfully when a friend's convenience was at stake. The very wantonness of the accident lent credit to his assertion that the child had lost his head, starting to run first this way

9

and then that, till the car was actually upon him. Perhaps—who knows ?—some allowances were made for a family that dated back to the other side of Bannockburn. In any case, Colin was exculpated from all blame, and so thoroughly that he did not even lose his driving licence. Those who were expecting an example to be made of somebody settled down to their expectations once more.

Our ancestors, like the superstitious fools we know them to have been, long observed the silly custom of " deodands," known to their more· enlightened descendants only through the crossword. These were fines, destined for charitable purposes, imposed on the owner of any dumb beast that (without his fault) had been responsible for a homicide. Your bull had gored a man ; no blame attached to you, if the beast was properly under control, or lacked the reputation of ferocity. But, here was a man dead, and it was not a wild beast that had made an end of him. Some amends, therefore, were due, in recognition of the artificial state of society which made such things possible. Believe it or not, in the early days of the railway a Company had to pay ·deodands for a loose truck which had run over a passenger. And there was this at least to be said for the system—it did involve a kind of restitution, a readjustment of values which snipped off, though it were only by a legal fiction, the loose threads of tragedy. The regrets of the inculpable owner had been externalized somehow. To-day, we have no substitute except the brutal farce of " compensation." Hugh Wishaw was not the kind of man who accepts compensation. He touched his hat and kept his counsel for a time ; then, the very day after Colin (as we shall see) had left Dorn House, he suddenly went berserk in the village during an evening of heavy drinking, and committed various disturbances of the peace which lodged him, for three months, in one of His Majesty's prisons.

And if the sufferer in this tragedy found no suitable relief for his feelings, neither did the author of it. Colin had been acquitted at law, his offence had been formally condoned, according to the polite usages of society, by the injured father. But his conscience, a more exacting creditor, gave him no discharge ; he wanted to pay deodands. He had not been brought up to any religion which suggested a way of making one's peace with an external Order of Justice. His father's newly found creed, well as it might deal with hidden wounds

10

that rankled inwardly, had no plaster for an open sore. There lies an instinct deeply rooted in our nature, pagan before it was Christian, which demands expiation for the wrong done. Commonly we smother it with commonplaces; perhaps to our own injury. But running down a child, regarded by most people as a normal incident of adolescence, awoke a greater horror in Colin because it came on the top of so much else—of a life starved of human affection through his own fault, of degenerate habits in which he had already seen danger. A clean sweep, turning over a new page of life, was what he called it to himself; what he meant was expiation. Soon after his acquittal, he announced his intention of joining the French Foreign Legion.

The ambitions of the young are sometimes generous, but not often unselfish. Colin, after many days of self-castigation, felt that he had been visited with a kind of inspiration when this solution occurred to him. (We owe it, presumably, to the works of Mr. Wren, and the shadows which they have thrown on the screen, that this form of earthly Purgatory suggests itself, now and again, to the undergraduate imagination). What did not occur to him was that he had duties towards others which he was proposing to shirk in a glow of self-congratulation over his own heroism. It really came to him as something of a surprise, so fully had he warmed up to the prospect, when the family council went into the idea of the Foreign Legion, and pronounced it utterly preposterous.

His father said the idea did him credit, but after all there was the property to think of. He himself was getting to be an old man; there was no saying how long he would be spared. Surely it was not wise for the heir to commit himself to a career on which it was so easy to enter, from which it was so difficult to draw back. His sister said it might be an easy career for some people to enter; but had Colin considered his health? Presumably there was some kind of medical inspection, even for the Foreign Legion. Why not go and see Dr. Purvis, and ask what chances he was likely to stand before a medical board? His brother-in-law said he had always said the Army was the best possible thing for a young fellow, but why go and live among foreigners? It was still possible to get into the British Army by applying to be attached to a regiment. He had a friend, a Colonel in the Rutlandshires, who would be willing enough to smooth the path towards a commission. His father said if

11

it came to that, why not the Coldforths? The Scottish regiments were always complaining that they got too many officers from the South. Colin sighed, and began all his explanations over again.

When at last he made them see something of what was in his mind, they fell back on the practical objections, health especially. Colin allowed himself to weaken, and finally proposed as an alternative that he should go to sea before the mast. He did not know much about going to sea, or which mast in a ship came where, but his reading assured him that it was necessary to be in front of the mast if one was to be properly uncomfortable. Once more the floodgates of unacceptable suggestion were let loose. His father said there was no denying it, after all, sea-air was the best possible thing for you when you were run down. Why not visit South Africa? He had seen one or two of these fellows belonging to the " Circles " who had gone out there on a mission—a wonderful mission it was, too—and they said there was scenery in South Africa to which you wouldn't dream of comparing anything in the home country. His sister said a great friend of theirs had been out on one of these Hellenic tours, and had found it extraordinarily restful ; only she wasn't sure whether there were any in the winter ; she could easily find out. His brother-in-law said, if the idea was to get right down to it and look at the sea through the eyes of the common sailor—and there was a lot to be said for that, mark you ; it was all experience—much the best thing was to sign on as a sort of honorary purser on one of these cargo-boats, and mess with the officers. He had a friend in the City who could, he was sure, arrange for Colin to go out to Mexico on an oil-tanker. His father said you had to be careful, though, about tinned meat.

In the end it was not the family council, but a long private conversation with his sister, which turned the scale. Woman-like, Mary realized that their father was a much better asset in argument when you removed him from the scene ; you could then appeal to his difficulties, his hopes, his grey hairs, the likelihood of his death. She talked to Colin with a frankness bordering on severity, such as elder sisters use ; told him that he had never been a comfort to his father as he ought to have been, especially since their mother's death ; that if he wanted to make good—and she admitted it was quite time he did—he ought to think first of those who had the first claim on im. It looked more heroic to go off fighting sheikhs or stoking engines, but the real path of self-abnegation lay in facing up to the facts; let him console the old gentleman's declining years by taking a decent interest, at last, in the family estates, and live down the evil reputation he had acquired among the tenantry by showing himself capable of better things. If women saw the faults of their children as they see the faults of their brothers, there would be less spoiling in the nursery.

In the end, all that remained of Colin's grandiose schemes was the agreement that he should go off on a sea-trip. His health was plausibly alleged as an excuse; the reason, barely concealed, was that the memory of his recent exploit might have time to grow fainter in the country-side. Nor was his journey to be made on an oil-tanker; with the cowed resignation of the man who has allowed himself to be beaten in an argument, he consented to be an ordinary first-class passenger on one of the well-known *Squandermania* cruises. This boat, built originally to cross the Atlantic in record time, ceased to be a commercial proposition when fewer people wanted to travel, and less expensively, between England and the United States. Thenceforth, with an appearance of majesty in exile, she was destined to cruise slowly around the shores where warmth is to be sought in winter—the Balearic Isles, Tangier, Madeira, sometimes as far as the West Indies; but always with a complement of valetudinarians; always with the express object of taking a maximum of time between ports, since it paid the Company better if passengers spent their money on board. It was now well on in January, and the trip would mean an absence of nearly two months, unless indeed Colin tired of the leisurely occupation before that, when it would be possible for him to return from Madeira, the mid-way point of the journey. An Oxford friend had arranged to go with him; but at the last moment (it appeared) he was prevented by illness, and it was too late to find another travelling companion. Colin professed himself indifferent; no doubt he would come across some passable people on the voyage.

" It's a pity young Hawkins couldn't go with you," said his father. They were sitting, the four of them, at dinner on the evening of the departure. Conversation was difficult; the family council eager to disguise its triumph, the laird showing a tendency to indulge in Polonius-maxims, which his daughter did her best to check.

" I don't know," said Colin. " He tells me he's a rotten
bad sailor, and it isn't much fun going abroad with a man
who is going to stick in his cabin half the time."

" Mistake to be in a party on board ship," observed Vincent
Hemerton, who had theories about the right way to do
everything. " Prevents you getting to know the rest of the
passengers ; and of course the really restful thing about a
cruise is chumming up with a whole lot of strangers you'll
never meet again in your life. That's what I've always found."

" I shall go with you next time, Vincent," protested his
wife. " And I don't like to think of poor Colin as the prey
of the ship's vamp, which seems to be your idea of a jolly
cruise. Dad, what would you say if Colin came back engaged
to an adventuress ? It's always happening, you know, on
these long cruises."

The laird permitted himself a scandalized teehee. " Eh,
Molly, you shouldn't put these ideas into the boy's head.
We'll have him getting wrecked on a desert island next, and
taking up with one of these beach beauties they show you on
the films. You must look after the company you keep, Colin.
Find some good, respectable heiress to rescue from drowning,
and I won't forbid her the door when you come back."

" There aren't many desert islands on the route the *Squandermania* is taking," objected Hemerton. " If Colin does get
cast away, he'll be picked up by one of these South American
boats and come home to us with the frozen meat."

" Let him come home," said his father, " and all's well.
Some more port, Colin ? "

" I'll just buzz the bottle if I may, Dad. No, no more ;
I ought to be starting. It's a grand wine, this ; I wish I were
going to find it on board ship. Makes you feel as if you
were prepared to meet your worst enemy and fall round his
neck. Well, I must be off ; the car's all ready at the door."

" What car are you going in, lad ? "

" I'm driving the garden-car in ; I'm to leave it at the station
garage, and one of the men will retrieve it to-morrow."

" Well, send us a post card when you get to Southampton.
Have you a pencil on you ? No ? Here then, take mine ;
it won't matter your losing it, for it's got my name written
on it. I'll just see you to the door."

" No, don't come out, Dad, or you'll catch cold ; it's a
perishing night. You must sit here and keep the hearth
warm for me."

CHAPTER III

DONALD REIVER MAKES HIS WILL

IT WAS NOT often Colin had given his father good advice ; but the warning just recorded might well have been taken to heart. Donald Reiver was a healthy man, but his chest was his point of weakest defence ; and soon after his son left he developed a chill, somehow, which seemed more than ever difficult to shake off—February, like January, proved to be a month of frost. Mary was so worried about his condition that she gave some hint of her alarms in writing to Colin at Madeira, one of the few ports of call at which you could be certain of reaching the *Squandermania* by letter. She did not actually suggest his returning, since it would be selfish to cut short his holiday for what might prove to be a false alarm. But she tried to write the kind of letter which would make it impossible for Colin to complain, if things went wrong, " You never told me." The desire to save our own faces accounts for more of our actions than we generally admit.

For the best part of a fortnight Donald Reiver was confined to his bed. He recovered, only to go down with a still more dangerous set of symptoms. On the 12th, a Sunday, Dr. Purvis used the word pneumonia, and hinted to the other members of the family that it might be a good thing if the laird were encouraged to put his affairs in order. He was already sinking, now and again, into delirium, and there was no saying what the end might be. His lawyer, Mr. Gilchrist, was notified by telephone, and agreed to come out from Edinburgh and sleep the night. Dr. Purvis himself would drive him out from the station, when he came for his evening visit. By the special request of the sick man, Henry Reiver was persuaded to come over at the same time ; it was not clear whether this arrangement pointed to a merely business transaction, or to a personal reconciliation such as the solemnity of the occasion might justify. Anyhow, Henry was prevailed upon, though he would not accept a lodging for the night ; he would come over after dinner, and would drive himself back.

It was a night of uneasy comings and goings. Mr. Gilchrist pottered to and fro between the sick man's bed-side and the business room downstairs ; Dr. Purvis was giving severe

directions to the night-nurse, or foraging for sick-room comforts
in the servants' quarters; Mary and her husband drifted into
the drawing-room and out of it, took up books and put them
down again, began conversations which were interrupted by
long pauses and ended with staring helplessly into the fire.
They chafed at their own uselessness, contrasted with all this
legal and medical energy. At half-past nine a fresh car was
heard on the drive, and they addressed themselves to the
embarrassing task of entertaining Cousin Henry. This was a
little, spare man, military in his bearing and his antecedents,
brusque in his manner, and finishing off every sentence he
uttered with a little interrogatory grunt, very disarming to his
audience. He had married, some years back, a lady whose
respectability did not come up to the standards of his Cousin
Donald, and criticisms had been made which Henry found
himself unable to forgive. In return, he treated himself as
heir-presumptive to the estate with an assurance galling to the
pride of Colin's father, little though that pride was fed by
illusion.

" Not at all; 'course I came over," he protested gruffly, as
if to vindicate himself against a charge of sentimentality.
" Hope it's all a false alarm, though; Donald's always lived
carefully, that's one thing. Eh? Yes, 'course I know
Gilchrist; in the business room, is he? I'll go and see him
now; and you'll send in word if Donald would like to see
me, huh? Mind, he's not to worry about it if it will tire
him; no use doing that. You'll tell me, huh?" Mary,
accustomed from her youth to profane farmyard imitations of
Cousin Henry's manner, found the little man unbearably
tragic in this unexpectedly melting mood of his. They found
Gilchrist busily grubbing in the piles of the laird's unopened
correspondence. " Oh, Mrs. Hemerton—how do you do,
Major Reiver, how do you do?—it's about that notice from the
Indescribable Company, about the premium, you know. Your
father says it always has to be paid in at the beginning of the
year, and now, you see, not being able to look at his letters,
he's done nothing about it. I thought perhaps you might be
able to lay your hand upon it. . . . Ah, that's more like it!
Yes, their name's on the flap of the envelope. I'll just draw
out a cheque for him and take it up for him to sign, that will
put his mind at rest; dear, dear, how folks will leave things
to the last moment! Then I'll come back and see you, Major;
or bring you word if the laird would like to see you first.

There! We'll soon have the Indescribable people settled."
Donald Reiver did see his cousin, and there was evidently
some kind of reconciliation, though neither was communicative
about it afterwards. Henry had his interview with the lawyer,
and then took the road, refusing renewed offers of hospitality.
He consented to take with him, and entrust to the late post
at Pensteven on his way home, the precious envelope which
was going to "settle the Indescribable people"; Donald's
mind kept recurring to it and worrying over it, as a man's
mind will when he is on the verge of delirium, and it was
something for his daughter to be able to say that it was actually
on its way to the post. There remained the signing and
witnessing of his will, for which the doctor's signature and that
of the butler were called into requisition. As those who knew
the laird best had foreseen, the bulk of his personal property
—and that meant little more than his expectations from Colin's
life insurance—was to go to the sect he had so recently
embraced. Dr. Purvis, who had his own views on the subject,
frowned, fidgeted, shrugged his shoulders in resignation, and
traced the familiar hieroglyph. His business was to tide the
patient over the crisis if possible; and it was certain that any
attempt to cross his wishes would be a kind of murder.

But when he proposed to follow the example of Henry
Reiver and go home for the night, he was confronted with a
clamour of dissuasion. A bed was there all ready for him;
if he was wanted for any other emergency, the night-nurse
would get the telephone call, and it was quite as easy for him
to start out from Dorn as from his own house in Blairwhinnie.
"That's quite true, Mrs. Hemerton," he explained; "but
you see, I must get back. I've told the night-nurse that your
father is to have an ice-pack; we must get that temperature
down somehow. So I thought I'd knock them up and tell
them to send some ice over from the fishmonger's." "But,
doctor, there's really no difficulty about that. I'll give you the
key of the ice-house here, and you can get some in your car.
You can't miss it; it's among those trees on the left, half-way
down the Blairwhinnie drive." "Eh, that's true; I hadn't
thought of that; it will be quickest that way. But it will
fuss him, you know, to think that the doctor is still about;
much better be able to tell him that I've gone home." "Of
course I'll tell him you've gone home," replied Mary, with the
simplicity of her sex; "but that's no reason why you should
go." "If I only had my things for the night!" "Nonsense,

17

Vincent will fit you out quite easily. What kind of razor do
you use ? There, you see, it's perfectly simple ; that's the
kind he uses, and it's only a matter of putting in a fresh blade.
Honestly, doctor, I'm not trying to make you comfortable ;
I'm trying to give Father every chance. And I shall really
feel you've let us down if you don't stop."

In the end, it need hardly be said, Dr. Purvis submitted, and
carried out the programme his energetic hostess had outlined.
We must not pass him over without a word of description.
He was a local oddity, and something of a local treasure ; a
character like his enriches the district. " We are a small
township in Blairwhinnie, but we are not so uncultured as you
suppose ; sprain an ankle, and you may find yourself being
attended by a man like Dr. Purvis." Not that he was of the
great world, or that his name figured in the records of scientific
congresses, such as fill up newspaper space in the early autumn.
But he had written in medical journals ; and it was thought
that if the views he expressed had been less heretical, his fame
would have travelled wider. Blairwhinnie, which had no idea
what his theories were about, had no doubt either as to their
value or as to the misrepresentation which had dogged the steps
of their author ; however, the ill wind which had frosted his
laurels had blown good to the township, in leaving such a
doctor to vegetate there. That he was a clever doctor, there
was no doubt ; every child born in that district bore witness
to that, and the abundance of rosy octogenarians completed the
picture at the other end.

About his conversation and his attitude towards life there
was, to be sure, something a little uncanny. He was, or
represented himself as being, a pessimist through and through.
He was all for sterilization and for lethal chambers ; not only
the feeble-minded, by his way of it, but the cripples, the topers,
and the idlers would all be the better for a swift end and a
home in the ugly cemetery on the hill-side. Familiar paradox
—you would see the man lavishing prodigies of attention and
medical skill on some chronic drunkard, rescuing him from
the consequences of his excesses, and then telling him that
he would have been happier unborn ; lamenting the surplus
population, while he fought desperately against some epidemic
that threatened to decimate it ; twitting the aged with their
eagerness to sit on over the embers of life, and then prolonging
that life beyond all reasonable expectation. For all that, there
was a cold-bloodedness about him which made you shiver

18

sometimes ; he raved against the anti-vivisectionists, and it was common talk that he had put a bullet through his favourite dog on the spot, when evidence was brought him that it had been running sheep. Some said he had no heart ; some, that his heart had once betrayed him, and that he had devoted the rest of his life to ignoring it. He was a widower, with an unmarried daughter to keep house for him.

The doctor knew his way about at Dorn well enough ; he often came over unprofessionally, especially when Vincent Hemerton was there, a keen chess-player like himself. To-night, Hemerton was tired, and had no heart for the game ; he and Mary both went off early, apologizing for leaving their two guests to each other's company. But indeed, no apology was needed—a doctor and a lawyer, Scots both of them, keeping late hours over a bottle of whisky belonging to a third party, what more promising material could you have for a *sederunt* ? The doctor was tall and wizened, with bushy eyebrows that seemed to be always questioning ; the lawyer short and round and red-faced, with merry eyes peering out through his spectacles seeming to herald a frivolity which was in fact strange to his nature. The clock stood at eleven before they sat down to their entertainment ; no matter, the night was young.

" It's a remarkable thing," said Mr. Gilchrist meditatively, " what a lot of money changes hands in the world, or doesn't change hands, just for want of a drop of ink—forms filled up the wrong way, cheques with no signatures, and God knows what else. Here's poor Reiver, you see, in arrears with his insurance premiums, and I wonder how many men there are in Scotland that honour the demand by return ? And if young Mr. Colin had killed himself, instead of the bairn "—he swept his cigar round in a graphic semicircle—" no insurance."

" That was two months ago, though," the doctor pointed out. " Still, as you say, people are careless. I tell you, Mr. Gilchrist, I wish to God this piece of carelessness had gone on a little longer. Oh, I know you lawyers, you don't mind what the money goes to as long as it's all drawn up in legal shape. But here am I, merely to oblige a friend, putting my hand to an instrument that wills away Colin's insurance money out of the family, out of the estate, to a religion I've no kind of use for. Tell me, oughtn't I to have refused my signature ? "

" Save us, that's not a question for a doctor to ask a lawyer ;

19

it's a question for a lawyer to ask a doctor. You know well enough you'd do anything to humour a dying man, and give him a better chance of recovery."

" I know ; but why would I ? It's my trade to be for ever interfering with the designs of Fate, or Providence, or whatever your theology likes to call it, by adding on a week here and a month there to men whose lives are no more matter to the world than a weevil's. Oh, I know the laird's family are fond of him, some of them. But is there anyone who can say it's to his advantage that Donald Reiver should die late, rather than soon ? "

" Yes," said Gilchrist unexpectedly. " Major Henry."

" Henry Reiver ? How's that ? "

" It's to his advantage to have Donald die late rather than soon. Or, if you like to put it that way round, it's to his advantage to have Colin die soon rather than late. You see, there's the double death duties. It'll cripple the man, taking over from Donald ; it would fair break him, taking over from Colin, if Colin lives just a year or two to inherit, as it's likely he will. Oh, you may trust me, Major Henry didn't come over here just for charity ; he wanted to see how his cousin really was, and he wanted to see whether any of that insurance money was to be set off against the death duties, when the time came. He'd be a troubled man if he knew, would Major Henry."

" So he ought to be. I'm not for keeping up these old estates myself ; they create a parasite class. But I tell you, if that will's disputed, you won't get me to go into the witness-box and testify he was of sound mind. He's been all soft since his wife died, that's well known ; and here he is waking up out of coma to make a will, and sinking back into coma before the last witness has dried his quill on his coat-tails. It's not sense."

" It's good law, for all that. You know as well as I that that will will never be upset, unless Donald Reiver lives to change it. Mr. Henry's made his own bed, and he must lie on it. *Scienti et volenti non fit injuria*, that's our tag ; he knew what he let himself in for when he quarrelled with Dorn. I'm not a very religious man myself, you'll observe, but I like to see a man remembering the next world when he comes to make his last will and testament. *For that shall bring a man peace at the last*—you're all for wanting to see the world tidied up, doctor, and organized on the principles

20

of common sense, but there's feelings in all of us that'll beat you yet."

"Well, I'll tell you this, then; I'm going to try and keep Donald Reiver alive till I can knock more sense into 'him. And if I could' keep Colin Reiver immortal—well, we won't talk of that. This is good whisky, Mr. Gilchrist. The laird didn't empty his cellar when he turned religious, that's one thing to be thankful for."

"I'm thinking you'll have a job to keep Mr. Colin immortal, if all they say's true," observed the lawyer, going through the pantomime of raising a glass to his lips, and then, on second thoughts, turning the pantomime into reality.

"Oh, it's true enough; you could have seen it coming any time these three or four years. The boy oughtn't to have been born, that's the trouble. Well, let's not talk of him, with his old father sick and perhaps dying in the room upstairs. Are you for another, Mr. Gilchrist?"

"No, thank you, Dr. Purvis; I've had my allowance. *Jus suum cuique* is good in medicine as well as law. Well, we'll see which of us is first down in the morning. By the way, Mrs. Hemerton was telling me that Colin may be here by breakfast time; if he's come up by the night train, that is."

"Colin Reiver back? But. . . they've heard from him, then?"

"They have and they haven't. There was a letter from him yesterday, and she took it up to the laird and read it to him. Only it seems it must have been written before he got the news his father was ill; he says nothing about that. All the same, when he did get the news he will hardly have stayed away. And he'd catch the same boat as that letter, you see, if he wanted. They were half expecting him to-day, as it was."

"Well, I shouldn't be sorry to see him back. Good night, Mr. Gilchrist, and walk softly upstairs; the laird wants sleep now, if ever a man did."

21

CHAPTER IV

THE MAN WITH SECOND SIGHT

IT IS A vice of the English mind to suppose that the whole of Scotland is divided into two parts by a horizontal line running across its waist; that the southern half is quite flat, with a population of Bolshevik coal-miners and a few weavers who argue about theology over their hand-looms, whereas the northern half is made up of hills and precipices, and populated only by gillies, who say " whateffer " at the end of each sentence. More intimate acquaintance with the country reveals the fact that large tracts of the Lowlands are very hilly, and the Highlands are partly made up of valleys; that the dividing line is not parallel with the Equator, but slopes, roughly, from the south-west to the north-east; and finally that it is not possible, without provoking angry contradiction, to say that the division between the two comes just here or just there. Dorn House, for example, belongs technically to the Lowlands; but on a first visit you might be pardoned for imagining that it stood on the southernmost slopes of the Highland country, looking out over a broad Lowland plain. You would be wrong, but you would not be many miles out.

The great feature of Dorn, anyhow, so far as scenery goes, is the broad, rich river-plain they call " the Carse," with Pensteven Castle standing up nobly as sentinel over it. The hill on which it is built is in reality quite small, but gains the illusion of height from its neighbourhood; the rugged lines of the castle building harmonize with, and seem to grow out of, the rugged lines of the rock itself. It has more of elevation than Windsor, more of isolation than Durham, more of definitiveness than the castles of the Welsh Border. It fills the eye. Look down from the terraces of Dorn on a summer's day, and you will see the shadows chasing each other across the plain so that they play hide-and-seek with the castle, now gilding it, now obscuring it; or, better still, towards evening, you will see it half gilded and half obscured. In autumn, the river mists will throw a veil of fine lawn over it, like a glass case over a clock; or they will carpet the floor of the plain all round it, and sweep up to the foot of the hills, leaving the castle rock isolated in the middle, for all the world like an island in a sheltered bay. But perhaps it is at its best in the pale sunshine of a morning in winter or early spring, when

22

the chill, sharp air and the hoar-frost on the terraces make your perceptions the more eager, and the clear outlines of the view harmonize with the brisk edge of the oncoming day.

Dorn has two drives, one of which slopes down towards the town of Pensteven, the other bends round towards the left and the north, offering more direct communication with the postal town and railway station of Blairwhinnie. The two lodges are set about a quarter of a mile apart on the Blairwhinnie-Pensteven road, a well-made road from south to north with a busy traffic of cars. The Pensteven lodge was occupied by the head keeper, MacWilliam ; the Blairwhinnie lodge had been Hugh Wishaw's, and stood tenantless since the tragedy. We must give some account here of MacWilliam, who is the next character to figure in our story. His manner and his speech were those of a Highland Scot ; but his ancestry was in fact mixed ; his mother had been a dark woman from one of the loneliest of the Outer Islands, ont the fringe of fairyland. From her the keeper had inherited a religion which had never heard of the Reformation, and, so it was averred, a gift familiar in the Outer Islands, that of " second sight. " Where he was born, it was said that the priest was never sent for when man or woman lay dying ; he knew and came.

MacWilliam was also an early riser, as men are whose work lasts the length of daylight. And only the first grey hint of dawn had come over the hills, the morning after Donald Reiver had disposed of his earthly goods, when this conscientious servant left his wife and his children (all too numerous for Dr. Purvis) at home, and made his way along the road towards Blairwhinnie. It was his intention to visit a covert close by the Blairwhinnie lodge, but he never reached it that morning. Only a hundred yards short of it he saw, lying by the road-side, that which sent him crashing through the hedge and running up by a patch across the fields towards Dorn House. The night-nurse observed him from an upper window, and made haste to intercept him at the door, lest his evident agitation should disturb the household with its alarm. To her, then, he stammered out his news—that Colin Reiver was lying cold and stiff beside the great road, the colour of death on him, and his heart not beating.

The night-nurse had no hesitation at all about her duty ; she went upstairs at once and reported to the doctor. All nurses lived in a holy terror of Dr. Purvis. He said, " Where was this ? " and, without further question, carried the news to

23

Vincent Hemerton and the little lawyer. Mary Hemerton, the better to watch over his needs, was sleeping in a room close to her father's; and her they did not disturb till they should have satisfied themselves about the report. " We'll all go in my car," said the doctor. " What about the police ? " asked Hemerton. " We shall have to fetch them in sooner or later; it will save time if I go and fetch them in my car, from Pensteven, while you take Mr. Gilchrist and have a look at the poor fellow. MacWilliam may be wrong, and there may be life in him." The doctor hesitated a moment; then he said, " If you like; go straight to Pensteven. But here's another thing ; keep a good look about you on your way, and if you see anybody working by the road, ask him whether any cars have passed in this last hour or two. There may be a watchman where they are mending the road, just before you get into the town. We'll ask at our end too, when we've seen what can be done." A few minutes later, Hemerton had whipped off the rug that was swathed over the front of his big Tarquin, and thrown it impetuously inside; he left the doctor still having slight trouble with his engine, chilled by the cold night, and set out at racing speed for Pensteven.

The doctor was not more than two or three minutes later in starting. " Jump up, man," he cried to MacWilliam, who stood looking on as if stupefied, " we may want you." As they turned into the straight stretch of the Blairwhinnie drive, they saw that the gaunt iron gates at the end of it were shut ; MacWilliam had to get off and open them. They swung out into the main road, their eyes peering anxiously through the half-darkness. " Which side of the road ? " asked the lawyer. " The right, sir, next the Park ; just resting against the further side of that heap of stones beyond the telegraph post." They heard the grind of the brakes as Dr. Purvis pulled up short. Mr. Gilchrist was the first to leap out, and race round to the further side of the stone-heap. There was nothing there.

" What's this, MacWilliam ? " asked the doctor, turning and clutching the keeper by the arm. " What have you done with him ? "

MacWilliam bent over to take one look at the ditch close by the hedge. Then he stood erect, crossed himself, and stammered out his apologies. " Before God, I never touched him. Twenty minutes since, he was here, and now he's gone from here. The Lord pity us, that's not a chancy thing."

24

" The thing's not possible," said the lawyer. " Man, you've given us all a fright. God knows, these mornings are dark enough, and you might easily have deceived yourself, do you see, with that black shadow on the further side. But you might have looked twice before you came up to the house rousing us all out of our beds, and after a late night too. Come. away from here, Dr. Purvis ; you see for yourself it's just a hallucination."

But the doctor was not so easily convinced, for all his customary scepticism. " That's just like a lawyer, Mr. Gilchrist ; you think all witnesses are alike, and all untrustworthy. Don't you see that MacWilliam here is a gamekeeper by profession, and when he looks at a patch of grass he knows whether there's a body there, and what like a body it is. It may be somebody's come by and moved the thing."

" Eh, and it might be the wrong heap," suggested Gilchrist.

" The heap'll be right enough," retorted the doctor inconsequently ; you could see that his nerves were all on edge. " Just walk up this side of the road, and see if you can see nothing in the grass ; I'll take the right-hand side, and Mac-William can stay by the car here. There are poachers about here most nights ; and we've got some unconscionable scoundrels in Blairwhinnie."

Before they had conducted their fruitless search for ten minutes, they heard the sound of a horn passing the Pensteven lodge, and Hemerton's great Tarquin was almost on the top of them. " What's up ? " he asked as he climbed out from the car, with a melancholy police inspector at his heels. " Can't you find him anywhere ? "

The situation was breathlessly explained. Vincent Hemerton looked grave, seemed to hesitate ; then he said, " Of course, I don't know what it's possible to believe about these things. But I expect you know, Purvis, that the people round here all say MacWilliam has second sight. Do you think it's at all possible—I know it sounds absurd—that he really saw something which . . . which wasn't there ? "

The inspector, who had opened his note-book, shut it with a snap ; to him, clearly, the preternatural was not evidence. The lawyer, who was thoroughly unconvinced, tried to look judicial, because he thought it would be more broadminded. It was Dr. Purvis who scouted the suggestion. " Talk sense, Mr. Hemerton," he urged. " The man says he *saw* the body lying there, he didn't just *think* of it. He felt it, too, to see if the heart was beating still. Ask him, if you like ; here he is."

And MacWilliam, though he seemed thoroughly scared by the disappearance of the body, was positive enough that it had really been there ; he had touched it, and felt it cold to the touch. The inspector put him through a rapid catechism about his movements and the position in which the supposed corpse had lain. No, it had not the look of a man lying asleep, for a man lying asleep will crook his arm under his head for a pillow, if it lies against something hard. Was it like a man drunk ? asked the inspector, who believed in directness of speech. No, that would not do ; a drunk man makes himself comfortable where he lies, but this was a body that had fallen all loosely, as if it had been thrown down when already dead. Gilchrist recognized the truth of Purvis's contention, that in such matters a gamekeeper is a good witness. Finally, MacWilliam was sent back to his lodge, but with strict injunctions to say nothing about what he had seen unless and until the facts became public. (Actually, the secret was never kept ; it leaked out almost immediately, up at Dorn. It was thought that a servant had overheard what was said ; though Dr. Purvis, on mere suspicion, sent the night-nurse back to Edinburgh. Anyhow, it was all over the estate by breakfast-time.)

The four men left in the road continued to scratch their heads over the mystery. Gilchrist still hankered after the idea that the keeper had been mistaken. Purvis held that the body must have been moved, by some person or persons unknown. The inspector suggested, but with diffidence, that there was no evidence except his own to clear MacWilliam from the charge of having tampered with it. Hemerton had struck out a new and more hopeful line ; if MacWilliam really saw Colin lying there, he argued, he must have been mistaken about the fact of death. After all, he was no doctor. What if Colin had been there, asleep, perhaps even the worse for drink ? He had plenty of time, while the keeper was making his way up to the house and while the search-party was being organized, to wake up and take himself off somewhere—privately, he suspected the Blairwhinnie Hotel. The inspector's suggestion that he should be advertised for by wireless was coldly received ; in the circumstances, nobody connected with the family was anxious to court publicity.

" By the way, Doctor," said Hemerton, " I found that man watching at the place where they're mending the road, as you suggested. We asked him about cars passing, and he said that he couldn't remember any within the last half-hour or so. But that doesn't help us much, because of course there were a good many lorries and two or three cars that passed during the night, and naturally he couldn't give any account of those. Is it worth asking, I wonder, at Blairwhinnie ? There aren't any turnings to speak of between that and here."

" We'll do that all right, sir," said the inspector. " I've a couple of my men coming on behind, and of course we'll look out for all tracks of cars, and make enquiries too. But there's not much hope in that, with these dry roads especially."

" Well, I think we'd better be getting back to the house," suggested Hemerton, as he backed his car a little towards Pensteven. " I'll turn round, I think, and go by the other lodge, so as to have a word with MacWilliam and make sure he understands about not saying anything. You'll be going up the other way, will you ? Breakfast ought to be ready before long now ; see you up at the house." He backed on to the grass, turned adroitly, and left the three men together.

" There's one thing, sir," said the inspector, " that I didn't quite like to ask with Mr. Hemerton about, knowing they have their troubles up at the house. Was Mr. Colin at Dorn at all lately ? It was in the paper that he had gone abroad for his health, only a month or so back."

" We were both at the house last night," Gilchrist explained, " and there was no word of his having been back since he left for his trip. But they were half expecting him, you see, because they had written to tell him the laird was poorly, and he'd just have had time to get back to England yesterday or the day before. But if you ask me what he'd be walking the roads for like this, and at night seemingly, it's more than I can tell you, or anyone up at the house either."

The inspector was now joined by his two subordinates, and the guests from Dorn went back to their breakfast. But activity still reigned at the house ; when they reached the front door, they found Hemerton and his wife just getting into the Tarquin for a fresh expedition. Mary Hemerton was full of apologies : " I'm so grateful to you both," she said, " for all you've done, and so sorry you should have come in for all this trying time. Now you must really go in and get something to eat ; you'll find it all ready. Vincent and I are going off to Blairwhinnie ; we both feel we can't rest until we have made enquiries at the hotel there, and at the railway station, to know if anything has been heard of Colin. We shan't be long, and we shall certainly be back before you've finished seeing Father, Dr. Purvis. I hope you'll be able to stay on too, till the eleven o'clock train, Mr. Gilchrist ; but if you want to catch the earlier one, you've only got to tell Sanders ; the car will be quite ready for you. I'm afraid you'll think us dreadfully rude, but I really can't rest till we've probed this story to the bottom. Of course, I think it's all a mare's-nest ; MacWilliam must have been brooding over that dreadful motor accident—so temperamental, these Highlanders. Get in and drive, Vincent ; I'm too rattled to sit at the wheel this morning." And they disappeared down the drive, still shouting apologies.

So the *sederunt* of the night before was resumed, but in a more chastened mood. Indeed, the two men said little at breakfast, and it was only over their pipes that Mr. Gilchrist became more communicative. " Well, now," he said, " you've been very silent about all this, you that's well known to have theories about everything. What do you really make of this morning's business ? "

The doctor smiled curiously. " No, I'll have no theories," he said ; " I just have my plain instincts. And they tell me there's a tragedy here, and the curious thing is, it's a Greek tragedy, Mr. Gilchrist. But I'll leave you to guess which."

CHAPTER V

THE BODY REAPPEARS

THE SCENE IS once more laid at breakfast ; but time, place, and *dramatis personæ* are different. The time is three days later ; the place, a house at Burrington, in Surrey ; the *dramatis personæ*, Miles Bredon, private enquiry agent to the Indescribable Insurance Company, Angela, his wife, and Francis, their son, who is a *muta persona* as far as the exigencies of the breakfast-table allow.

" See what you can make of that," suggested Miles, " while I take turns at picking up Francis's napkin."

" That " was a rather scrubby-looking periodical, the kind of sheet which always proves to be the organ of some philanthropic or progressive movement. You felt certain that it was privately printed, and at Droitwich. It was headed in large letters *Survival* and devoted itself exclusively to Psychical

28

Research. Above the title was scrawled in pencil, "Read marked article on page 6 and keep by you."

" It must feel jolly to be so famous," mused Angela. " Asking himself what is wrong with the movement, the editor sees at once that it is a wash-out until it secures the adherence of the great Bredon. So he sends it along. The marked article on page six is rottenly printed, but I'll have a shy at it. Some butter first, though."

The article may as well be given here in full. It ran as follows :

At the moment of going to press, we have received from a correspondent who prefers to remain anonymous, although we can vouch for his reliability and critical discrimination, a remarkable record of recent events at the little town of Blairwhinnie (Scotland). Many of our readers will have seen accounts in the daily press of the death of a young resident there, Mr. Colin Reiver, apparently from exposure. What interested the news-paper public was that the young man was found lying dead in the road, only a few hundred yards from his father's house. It now appears that all these accounts have been censored, and that the story as it has been told to the public at large is a story violently torn out of its psychical context.

The discovery was made on February the 15th, that is, last Wednesday. The body of the young man was found lying by the side of the Blairwhinnie-Pensteven road, propped up against a particular heap of stones about a hundred yards from the lodge of Dorn Park, where his father resides. He had been dressed in ordinary walking clothes, but without stick or great-coat. He must have returned suddenly from a foreign cruise, having been last heard of at Madeira. And (the importance of this will emerge later) nobody, except his sister and his brother-in-law, had the least reason to suppose that he was not still in foreign parts. How he came where he did, or in what circumstances he died, can only be a matter of speculation.

To those, however, who believe that the only really important thing in our present life is its interpenetration by spirit-life, the following facts will present much more interest. On Monday the 13th, at half-past six in the morning, *the exact hour* at which the young man was found dead two days later, Hector MacWilliam, head keeper at Dorn, was passing by *the exact spot* where the discovery was to be made. He is definitely psychic, the mother having come from the Outer Islands, where such gifts are notoriously common ; but he has never practised as a medium, or taken any interest in spiritual manifestations. Yet he alleged, and was prepared to swear, at half-past six on Monday morning, that he had just seen the body of his young master lying against the identical heap of stones by which it was in fact found two whole days later. MacWilliam's experience was of the most vivid kind; he even speaks of having "touched" the body, but he is not able to explain exactly what he means by this—he has never even heard of ectoplasm. It is not surprising, therefore, that in his simplicity he imagined the whole phenomenon to be on the sub-astral plane, and went up to Dorn House to report his disco-very. When he returned to the spot, accompanied by others whose atmosphere was hostile to psychic influence, the condi-tions were of course disturbed, and the phenomena no longer presented themselves.

The recent correspondence in these columns on the existence of Time brought to light several instances in which our readers had received retro-active impressions from events that were "about to" happen. But the Blairwhinnie manifestation is perhaps the most striking instance so far recorded of an event being foreseen in the fullest possible detail, with such an exact correspondence of circumstances, and being communicated to other persons in all its detail before the actual occurrence. It is becoming increasingly difficult——

◆

But the rest of the article was in the vein of propaganda, and there is no reason why I should inflict it on the reader.

"Do you see the curious point about all that?" asked Bredon, as his wife threw the document back to him.

"I should have thought it was all pretty curious. Oh, bother, of course you meant me to say that."

"Well, the editor of *Survival* doesn't seem to think it curious. And indeed, if you believe in that kind of thing, I suppose there is nothing odd about it at all. Whereas if you don't believe in that kind of thing, to call it curious would be an understatement. No, I pass all the spook stuff, if it was really spook stuff. Don't you see what makes it a curious story, merely as a record of common human events?"

"Cough it up. You won't catch me solving your snappy little problems at breakfast."

"I will humour your evident curiosity. No, don't you see that it's a bit of a coincidence almost too good to be true, that the body should be found twice over at exactly the same time of day, and that such a very early time of day? That on each occasion, I mean, there should have been somebody wandering about at that precise moment at that precise spot—not even half an hour before or afterwards? Oh, it's perfectly possible; but I'm dashed if it isn't a coincidence. Spiritualism or no spiritualism, MacWilliam was really there at half-past six on

Monday, and XYZ was really there at half-past six on Wednesday—not exactly the time of day for a stroll. If this were any of my business, which thank God it's not, I should be very much interested to know who it was who persuaded XYZ to follow so accurately the time-schedule of Mr. MacWilliam. Since it's no business of mine, let us address ourselves to the subsidiary problem—What harmless lunatic can be responsible for posting on these jottings about the future life to me ? "

" If it was a lunatic, we shall never be able to find out. A lunatic acts without motives, and therefore you can't get a line on him. You needn't think you're the only person who can say that kind of thing."

" Quite good, for a beginner. As you say, we shall probably never know. Give me the *Daily Distress*, and let me glance through the Bootlegger column before we start on the serious idleness of the day."

It proved, however, that they were to hear more of the article in *Survival*. It was only a few minutes later that Bredon was rung up by Sholto, a friend of his in the Indescribable office, who wanted to know if there was any chance of getting a pick of luncheon on his way through ? It was a Saturday, and Sholto often looked in on his way to week-end golf-courses ; so the arrangement was ratified without surprise. But Sholto added, before ringing off, " You see, I want to talk to you about that thing I sent you yesterday. You got it, I suppose ? "

" No, I'm dashed if I did. Nothing by this morning's post, anyway."

" Not the thing about the Phantom of Strathbogle ? "

" Good Lord, that wasn't you, was it ? I never knew you'd taken up that kind of thing. Look here, you won't turn the luncheon-table, will you ? "

" Don't be a fool. This is business, this is. Explain when I see you. Keep that rag, though." And the telephone relapsed into silence.

During most of luncheon, the conversation went over ground with which the reader is already familiar. It was borne in upon Miles Bredon, and finally conveyed to him point-blank, that the Company wanted him, as its representative, to go up and enquire into the circumstances of the young laird's death.

" You see," explained Sholto, " the Company is involved in all this, up to the hilt. The old man took out a whacking insurance policy on the son's life while his wife was still alive, and has gone on paying up his premiums good and regular

31

ever since. *But* at the beginning of this year the new instalment never arrived; the old man, it seems, went sick early in January. Well, of course, we always give 'em a month's grace, as a matter of decency, though it only says a fortnight on the card. After that, the man remains uninsured unless and until the instalment rolls in. Well, if Mr. Colin Reiver really died on Wednesday, he just saved his bacon, if one may put it that way; because the payment of the premium reached our Perth office on Monday morning. But if he really died first thing on Monday, he was uninsured at the time of death, and I don't see the Reiver family touching us for a farthing. You know what the directors can be when it comes to a thing like this; specially, of course, if there is any suspicion of hanky, not to mention panky."

" Suspicion ! Why, it's a trout in the milk. You've only got to find out who was the beneficiary . . . "

" Yes, but it ain't such plain sailing as all that. The immediate beneficiary is the old gentleman, and he was lying in bed all the time, with a certified temperaturer anging between 103 and 105. And, even if you could prove the motive, you've got to get the facts. The Company has a reasonably good reputation, but it can't start refusing to pay up claims on the unsupported evidence of one gamekeeper, probably a bit cracked."

" M'yes, it'll want looking into. And that means, curse it, being on the spot. One or two other things, though, you might be able to tell me off-hand. Let's see, Angela and I were puzzling over something this morning; what was it, Angela ? "

" You were wanting to know what harmless lunatic had sent you the copy of that paper."

" Well, that's all right; we know which now. No, don't get insulted about it; you see what I mean. Oh, by the way, though, that does raise a further point, which might be a dashed important one—who sent that rag to the Company in the first instance ? It's not the kind of thing the directors read on their way up from Brighton, is it ? Not much zip about it, when all's said and done. But if some unknown party forwarded it to the Company's offices . . . "

" No, that's a dead end, that line of argument. You'd hardly believe it, but I thought of it myself. Only this paper came in the regular way of business, from our press-cutting agency. They sent the whole issue, I suppose, because no man on God's earth could possibly want the rest of it."

32

" But the Indescribable wasn't mentioned in the article at all," Angela pointed out.

" The Indescribable wasn't, but Colin Reiver was. And we regularly subscribe for cuttings about any of our clients who's above the ten thousand level. Comes in useful, sometimes. You remember the Razzi business, don't you, Bredon ? "

" Do I not ! And this is a fresh score for the system, because in the nature of things there's no reason why the Company should ever have heard that Colin Reiver makes a habit of dying like this. And I suppose they'd have paid up like lambs, while the family kept MacWilliam continuously drunk to prevent him blowing the gaff. Yes, it all seems rather exciting. Oh yes, and now I've remembered the other question I was going to ask you. Who was it that found the body the second time, on *Wednesday* morning, I mean ? "

" That's a queer thing, too. Early on Wednesday morning, it seems, there was an alarm of fire on the estate ; the remains of a straw-stack towards the Blairwhinnie end of it had got alight somehow, and of course they called all hands to the pumps. On his way to it, our old friend MacWilliam . . . "

" . . . Came across the now familiar sight of the young laird lying about on a stone-heap. What did he do ? Take the pledge ? "

" Don't be a fool. He went and told them up at the house."

" And they said they'd been had that way before ? "

" No, but this time Hemerton, the brother-in-law, was down at the farm putting the fire out. The butler went down, and the odd boy ; and Mrs. Hemerton telephoned to Pensteven for a doctor. Their own man, at Blairwhinnie, was out on a sick call."

" And how long did the corpse stay put, this time ? "

" I told you, curse you, that it was taken up to the house and post-mortem'd and buried. So you won't be able to examine it for unnoticed bullet-holes without an exhumation order. The police weren't on at all in this thing, apparently. There's a chap called the Procurator Fiscal who does all the inquest work on his own ; and he was satisfied with the doctor's report, that the man died of exposure. "

" And died, you say, how long before the body was discovered ? "

" Four or five hours. Which is going to give you trouble, incidentally, in proving that it was dead on Monday."

" But I thought you said the police had been on to this thing ? "

" On the Monday, yes, not on the Wednesday. Hemerton himself went straight off and fetched them on the Monday. Dunno why. "

" You bet you don't. Look here, they'd no reason to think there was foul play; and they'd every possible reason for hushing the thing up. You told me yourself the young man was pretty apt to lift the elbow; naturally, then, they'd think he was just logged by the roadside; they'd probably had to put him to bed before. Why do they suddenly rush out and fetch the police ? It won't do, you know, Sholto; there's the devil of a lot behind all this. However, the police will know something about it. I wonder now, is there any hope I could get on to them through a man I know at Scotland Yard, chap called Leyland ? Would he have any pull with the Pensteven police, or is there a place called England Yard in Edinburgh ? No harm in trying, anyhow."

" I would if I were you ; you could ring up to-day. Can you be there on Monday all right ? They want you to stay at the house, by the way. I must say, they've been very decent about it. "

" Oh Lord ! Well, I suppose I shall have to ; one doesn't want to miss chances. The bother is, if I go up by car it's such a long drive ; if I go by train, I've no car to rely on."

" That's all right, precious," put in Angela. " You start by train on Monday, and I'll take the car, arriving Tuesday night, bar accidents. I can shake down at an hotel. Where's Bradshaw ? The Blairwhinnie Hydro Hotel, terms moderate, splendid view overlooking romantic scenery, and all the rest of it. Then when they shoot you out of Dorn House for being found listening at the keyhole, you can fall back on me. Meanwhile, I shall have got all the local gossip for you. A hydro—think of the amount of gossip one ought to be able to pick up there ! "

" You know," said her husband, " that isn't half a bad idea of yours. Tell the directors that I will be there. I suppose I ought to write to Mrs. Hemerton, by the way. Look here, Sholto, let me make certain I've got it properly mapped out so far. Colin went abroad on January the seventh. Old Mr. Reiver made his will on Sunday night, the twelfth of February, and it was on the same night he wrote out the cheque for the premium instalment, which reached the office on Monday morning. MacWilliam found Colin Reiver dead by the roadside at half-past six on Monday, February the thirteenth, and again on Wednesday, February the fifteenth. No doctor examined the corpse on Monday, because there was no corpse to examine ; the doctor who examined it on Wednesday said it had been dead four or five hours—in fact, not very long after midnight of Tuesday. Is that correct ? "

" Couldn't be better. By the way, you'll find the old gentleman still ill, apparently, but on the mend, so there ought not to be any difficulty about seeing him."

" Does he know all about this business ? "

" He knows all we know ; but, as you justly observe, that ain't much. Well, thank you most awfully for my nice luncheon. Bring me back a piece of white heather, if it's in season."

CHAPTER VI

YEW AND CYPRESS

DORN HOUSE DOES not throw open its secrets to the newcomer. Built at a variety of periods and without any appearance of plan, it is full of character, and its quaintness endears it to the *habitué*. But when you arrive just before dinner on a dark night, so that you have no external impression to go by, its odd corners and *culs de sac* are enough to daunt even the resourcefulness of a detective. You open what was once the door of your bedroom, and find yourself in a cupboard ; you come out of the bathroom, and find yourself suddenly surrounded by shut doors you have not the courage to try ; staircases wander this way and that, passages run across one another without communicating, nothing seems to be on the same level as anything else. This, even if you are a legitimate visitor ; the embarrassment of the experience is multiplied if you feel yourself to be a spy on the actions of your hosts, and nourish the suspicion that they regard you in that light. The first evening, Bredon confessed to himself, did not go with a swing. . Mary Hemerton was much in attendance on her father, who was now promoted to the dignity of not having a night-nurse ; and her husband, when he heard that the guest was not a chess player, seemed disappointed that a respectable insurance company could employ such an emissary. Bredon, however, managed to give him a game at billiards, and seized upon the first mention of the fatigues of his journey as an excuse for retiring, first to the cupboard and then to his bedroom.

He sat for a little before the whimpering flames of a wood-fire, indulging his impulse to speculate about the household. Nothing, if you came to think of it, was more curious than his own presence in it. The Insurance Company had not ruthlessly quartered him on a house of mourning; he had received, before setting out, a charmingly worded letter from Mary herself, apologizing beforehand for the sad welcome Dorn would offer him, and insisting on the advantages of his staying in the house while business kept him in the neighbourhood. They obviously wanted him to be there, at a time when the son of the house was only two days in his coffin. And the death, though it was commemorated by all the decencies of social convention, had not really (you felt) left any gap in the life of the house. There was no vacant place at table or fireside; there were no pathetic breaks in the conversation, no trace of " He would have enjoyed that " or " You ought to have known Colin." Rather, it was as if a situation had been eased, as if a family knot had been unravelled. Later, from his talk with Dr. Purvis and others, Bredon became aware of the temperamental differences which accounted, at least in part, for this seeming callousness; at the time, he found himself baffled.

You could not say, after all, that there was anything sinister in the atmosphere of Vincent Hemerton or of his wife. He was plainly a man of the conventional governing class, with clubs in London and a " good " school and university education behind him; he carried his riches well, and lacked neither modesty nor good fellowship. The only fault you noticed about him—it has been mentioned already—was a tendency to preach a little about the right and the wrong way of doing things; he had been a shade too anxious to lecture about the theory of billiards, too didactic about some obscure way in which Bredon might have saved himself twenty minutes of his journey, too pedantic about the advantages of home-made soda-water. His wife was capable and hospitable; she put you at your ease; she was well-read in common literature, without a hint of the blue-stocking. And yet, while their atmosphere was all right, their attitude was all wrong. It was as if they had never forgiven the dead Colin for being the boy, not the girl.

Bredon rose early next morning, to a day full of bright
sunshine and the pleasant tang of a light frost, that silvered
the lawns and gave them a buoyant consistency underfoot.
The house, as revealed externally and in daylight, was not
the complete labyrinth he had taken it for ; but there was a
pleasant shapelessness about it which recalled generations of
owners, each determined to leave its mark on it just so. The
mention of a large house in Scotland ordinarily conjures up
to the mind one or other of two pictures—that of a castle
which looks like, but is not, a habitation, or that of a habitation
which looks like, but is not, a castle. The former kind will
provide you with gaunt majesty, historical memories, and
perhaps a ghost story ; but windows and staircases and the
shapes of rooms will be uncomfortable, and you will be lucky
if you get a bath. The latter kind will give you all the
amenities, but with the consciousness that the architect has
ruined his plan by trying to graft them on to a building
synthetically mediæval. At Dorn, though parts of it date
back three or four centuries, there are no memories of troubled
times ; nor has anybody tried to make it look other than what
it is, the residence of a peaceable country gentleman. The
windows are honest oblongs ; stone and rough-cast live in
harmony side by side ; the roofs are steeply-pitched, as northern
roofs should be, but without any affectation of " the Gothic."
What is perhaps its most distinctive feature, narrow bushes of
Italian cypress climb up, or rather nestle against the walls,
as if whispering a secret to the second-floor windows, a portent
to the expert, a delight even to the layman's eye.

In conformity with the taste of such a building, the garden
in its main features is a formal garden in the Italian manner.
Irish yews, in regimented lines, spring from the ground with
their lowest branches so close that they seem rather to rest
upon it, like giant shuttlecocks balanced on their round ends ;
or the gardener's clippers have shaped them into cones and
round balls and long, square hedges ; variegated hollies edge
the paths, themselves too forced into shapes amid this realm
of orderliness. The sloping ground is cut away into terraces,
whose lawns and borders communicate by stone staircases ;
stone balustrades, recesses, and niches emphasize their outlines,
and a stone bridge completes the inviolable circuit of the
garden by spanning the whole width of the drive. There are
remoter walks, to be sure, where formality is forgotten and
nature allowed to have her own way ; but the first impression

made on the newcomer is one of triumphant regimentation.
I say triumphant, because the proper glory of man, after all,
is his success in the struggle with nature, and these formal
gardens are the enduring trophy of it, dragging nature, as it
were, behind the chariot-wheels of humanity. They speak,
too, of a long-settled civilization ; such trees and lawns do not
reach their maturity till they have had more than a century of
meticulous grooming. Yet, if they remind man of his great-
ness, they remind him also of his littleness ; yew and cypress,
so docile to his influence, are yet the symbols of his short-lived
tenancy ; *neque harum quas colis arborum te, praeter invisas
cupressos*—in so adorning your house you make, in some sense,
a tomb of it. Even in the fresh air of the early winter's day,
they suggested to Bredon something of a sinister atmosphere,
clinging to that house of mourning which did not mourn.

You are not to suppose, however, when I speak of a formal
garden, that the whole plan of it was exactly marked out in
accordance with some geometrical design, so that the ground-
plan of it would have looked like an illustration in Euclid.
The garden, no less than the house, intrigued and baffled the
detective by sprawling this way and that in mysterious shapes,
as if determined to make you lose your way. The secret of
it is, that you cannot reach the garden of Dorn, unless you
are an active climber, except by going through the house.
The park communicates only with the front and back doors ;
side-doors and french windows give on to an enclosure, of huge
extent and fantastic shape, protected everywhere by walls or
ditches against commerce with the outside world. It was a
fortunate thing, Bredon reflected to himself, that the body had
been found so far away from the house ; if it had been in
the garden, he might have spent all day drawing maps before
he had cleared up the first data of his problem. Actually, one
angle of the garden enclosure juts out and makes the sweep
of the drive take a sharp bend ; the drive, therefore, even
before it forks towards Blairwhinnie and Pensteven, is out of
view from the windows. This morning stroll might help him
to get the atmosphere of Dorn House ; it did not bring him
near the scene of the tragedy he had come to investigate.

Breakfast brought news to Bredon that Angela was sleeping
the night at Durham on her way north ; the car going
splendidly, and a good front room safely reserved at the Blairwhinnie Hotel. To the Hemertons it brought, among other
communications, an announcement from Henry Reiver that

he was particularly anxious to see them, and proposed motoring over about tea-time if this would suit them. " What on earth can he want ? " Mary exclaimed. " You'll be interested to meet Cousin Henry, Mr. Bredon. He's heir to the estate now, of course ; but to tell the truth we haven't seen a great deal of him. He made an unfortunate marriage, you know, and Dad didn't like it. And he's rather a peppery sort of person, isn't he, Vincent ? " " Silly ass, he's not on the telephone," supplemented her husband, as if this were in itself sufficient reason for breaking off all intercourse with a relative. " Do you know what I did, first thing we got married ? My father-in-law, you see, was rather old-fashioned about these things, wouldn't have a telephone in his house. So I installed the telephone here as a wedding-present to the bride. He couldn't refuse that, you see. Well, Mr. Bredon, what about a walk round ? And then I dare say they'll have cleared the decks upstairs, Mary, and you could take Mr. Bredon to see Dad."

Mr. Reiver's room was on the first-floor landing ; a wheeled invalid's chair identified the door. The old laird had picked up in health, and showed no signs of fatigue. " It's very kind of the Company to be so prompt in making its enquiries," he said. " We've never had any complaints against one another yet, the Company and myself, and I hope you aren't going to be hard on me, Mr. Bredon, if I was in default over a matter of technicalities. But I believe you don't make any trouble over the late payment provided it's made in the end."

Bredon realized, to his acute embarrassment, that when the Indescribable offered to send down its " representative " it had been understood, at least by the old gentleman, as being ready to make a business deal with him—perhaps to deduct some discount for late payment, and hand over the rest. He felt he was expected to bring out a large cheque-book and say, " There, there, we won't quarrel about trifles." He was not merely a spy in the enemy's camp, he had wormed himself in under false pretences. Stammeringly he explained that he held no responsible position in the business, that his visit was just a formality, occasioned by the discrepant stories which had got about as to the actual date of Mr. Reiver's loss. As to the Company, there was no doubt at all that they were legally bound to pay if they were satisfied that the death occurred after the receipt of the premium ; if not—well, he was in no position to say what the directors would or would not do ; but his visit must not be taken as implying that they had the intention of fighting the claim, in whatever event. He hoped he might be excused for intruding in this way on the hospitality of the family, when his mission was such an ungracious one, but . . .

"Dear me, Mr. Bredon," the laird broke in, "you mustn't think you are any the less welcome here, whatever your business is. Quite right that the Company should satisfy itself that everything's in order; they'd be bound to. Well then, you'll be wanting to see the people that can tell you more about what happened than I can. I dare say you've heard, Mr. Bredon, that my health's been very poorly, and they didn't even tell me the poor lad was gone till Thursday, that's the day after they found him; let alone that queer tale of Hector MacWilliam's. They didn't like to worry me with it; he was all the son I had, you see, and we were expecting him back, we were expecting him back. But if I can help you at all to get your mind clearer about the way things went, I shall be awfully glad. You believe in MacWilliam's story ? "

"I haven't seen him yet; I was hoping to this afternoon. Only he must surely have seen *something* . . . what I was going to say was, would you mind telling me all you know about what your son's plans and movements were ? I hate to bring all that into the discussion, but . . ."

"Don't apologize, Mr. Bredon. It's so different, you see, when one knows that all these things are *meant*. Twelve months ago, a thing like this would have bowled me over absolutely. You see, I hadn't got things straight then. Have you come across the Circles, Mr. Bredon ? "

"No, I don't believe I ever did. Well, what I was going to ask especially was this—your son left you a month or so ago to go on this cruise; have you any evidence that he did go on the cruise ? Or is it conceivable that, for some reason we don't know of, he really stayed behind, and so got into some kind of . . . trouble or other which led to this ? "

"Ah, that's a perfectly plain question, and there's a perfectly plain answer to it. I had a letter from my boy, addressed from Madeira and correctly postmarked; let's see, when did I have it ? It must have been the tenth or eleventh of this month; for if it had been later I should not have been well enough to read it. As it was, they kept my business letters from me, but seeing the handwriting was his, they thought that could do me no harm, and perhaps would help me to pick up a bit, getting word from him, you see. Yes, it will have been the tenth or eleventh. And the letter itself was dated on the fifth;

we noticed that particularly afterwards, when we came to ask ourselves what the poor lad was doing in Scotland at all. "

" And he said nothing in that letter, of course, about coming home ? "

" You couldn't expect it; for he said nothing about my illness either. So you see he must have written that letter while he was still at sea, and posted it the moment he got into port, before opening his mail and getting the news from home."

" And there was nothing since then ? He didn't write or cable about his plans ? "

" He'd hardly write, would he ? Because of course he would be coming back on the same boat that carried the mails, and he would expect to reach Dorn as soon as a letter, or very little afterwards anyway. Most people would have cabled; but then, Colin was always an unpractical sort of a lad, and he may have been hurried, changing his plans so suddenly and getting off; that's what we thought."

" I suppose he doesn't mention in his letter anybody else who was travelling on the boat, who might have known what his plans were ? Of course, one could get hold of the captain, but it's always a job running these sea-going people to earth. But if he'd made friends with somebody on the journey, who will be back home before long, it would be easier to make enquiries."

" I'll tell you what, Mr. Bredon. You're a discreet sort of man, anybody can see that; and Colin wasn't the kind of lad that was very intimate in the way he wrote home; a reserved sort of a lad, Mr. Bredon. Well, you shall have his letter and take it away with you, and look through it at your leisure; I'd like, of course, to have it back afterwards. There it is, do you see, on the dressing-table, with the foreign stamp on it, just peeping out from under the others. Then you can see for yourself what chance there may be of getting on the track of his movements."

" Thank you enormously, Mr. Reiver. It's only an off chance, but it might be useful. I'll be very careful of it. Now, if I might ask one more question—have you formed any opinion, in your own mind, of what your son did when he came home, or how he came to lie where he did ? "

" Well, we made enquiries, as you'd imagine. But we could get no word at the station or anywhere that he had been seen making his way here. Supposing he came by the same train as you came by yesterday, there's commonly a good few

41

people travelling; and it's possible that the man who took his ticket at the station wouldn't see who it was; you'll have noticed for yourself how dark the platform is. But then, you'll say, what became of his luggage? We've written to the railway, in case he should have left it behind him in his hurry, and they're making enquiries. If we don't hear anything about it . . ." He paused a little.

" If you don't . . ."

" Mr. Bredon, I've no doubt the Procurator Fiscal is an honest man, and knows his business, but if we hear no more, I shall begin to ask myself—is it possible that my poor boy met with foul play? "

CHAPTER VII

TRAVELLERS' TALES

THERE WAS NO opportunity for the laird to develop this line of speculation; Mary Hemerton came in at that moment to announce the arrival of the doctor—would Mr. Bredon mind putting off the rest of the interview? It is a convention of the sick-room that when the doctor says there is nothing much wrong and it would not hurt us to get up for an hour or so about tea-time, this is a professional secret which must not be overheard by profane ears. Accordingly, Bredon made way; nor was he disappointed in his hope of meeting the doctor on the stairs. Dr. Purvis, in middle life, still had the athletic frame of a young man, already had the lined face, full of character, which we are used to expect in the old; as Johnson said of Burke, if you had met him under a hedge you would have said, " This is a remarkable man." And Bredon was prepared to be interested in him—let's see, this wasn't the doctor who did the *post-mortem* when the corpse was found, but it was the doctor who went to look for it when it wasn't; he would be worth cultivating. It was, then, with a faint annoyance that he found his hostess made no attempt to introduce them. To be sure, they were not guests; they were only professional visitors; perhaps the doctor was a very busy man, and did not like being bothered with the acquaintance of strangers. Nevertheless, the detective was piqued; and that " contrariness " which lives in all our natures made him determined that he would beard the doctor after all. He settled himself in the front hall to wait, providing himself with a copy of *The Moor* to lend him countenance : from that organ he learned more in a quarter of an hour about the domestic habits of the ptarmigan than it would be possible to use (as they say) in a lifetime.

Sure enough, when the doctor came down, with Mary still in attendance, the introduction had to be effected. Nor did the doctor, on his side, seem at all unwilling ; his greeting was almost effusive, and they talked easily of unprofessional things for some minutes. Mary did not leave them, and it hardly seemed decent to talk about the finding of the body while she was present. After a little she said, " Oh, Mr. Bredon, we got MacWilliam, the keeper, to come up and see you. He's in the business room ; would you mind seeing him now ? " Then, as if conscious that she was breaking up an interview too abruptly, she turned to the doctor and asked if he couldn't possibly come up to dinner ? Vincent was longing for his revenge, it seemed, at the chess-table. Dr. Purvis accepted, to Bredon's great satisfaction ; he was beginning to feel he must see more of the doctor. At the same time, was he getting fanciful ? Or had he really any right to the faint suspicion that his hostess didn't, in the first instance, want him and the doctor to meet ; dind't, when they met, want them to be alone ; felt a guilty conscience about that unwillingness of hers, and so tried to save her face by organizing a fresh meeting at dinner, when it was very unlikely the two would have a chance of talking in private ? Oh Lord, he was beginning to imagine things ; it must be the fault of this labyrinthine house, with its suggestions of mystery. He turned, impatient with himself, and made his way first (by mistake) into a passage leading to the pantry, then into the business room.

MacWilliam was waiting for him there, as only a keeper and a Highlander can wait. He would fain have stood fingering his cap, in the approved attitude of feudal obsequiousness. But Bredon, who had no feudal instincts, prevailed upon him to sit down, and broke through, in doing so, the defences of his reserve. Poor MacWilliam had suffered a good deal in the last week. On Monday and Tuesday, there was no housemaid at Dorn who was not ready with a pert jest at his hallucination, and the question whether he had been seeing any more corpses had greeted him at the very entering-in of Blairwhinnie. Since the actual recovery of the body on

Wednesday, he had been treated with exaggerated respect, as a man from whom the future held no secrets ; there was awe in the faces of children when he passed, and one of the ministers had preached against him. He was naturally shy, and a little suspicious, after the northern fashion ; he was prepared to be impenetrably stupid. But Bredon got through his guard by merely being natural ; he did not try to play the gentleman, by talking to him about the birds and the coverts. He appealed to him for help very much as a traveller does who has lost his way ; and that appeal never goes unanswered.

"I expect you're tired of telling your story by now, Mr. MacWilliam, and being asked what your own explanation of it is, and all that. I'm only here to make a report to these insurance people, and if you'd just fill out the details of the story a little, it's all I want. I'm not interested in ghosts, you see." He permitted himself a slight smile, and the severity of the keeper's face was momentarily relaxed. "This is one thing I'd like to know, if I may call so far on your memory—was there any difference to be seen at all between the body as you found it on Monday and the body as you found it on Wednesday ? Any change in the clothes, for example ; or more of a beard on the chin ; or even any difference, though of course that's not so important, about the attitude in which he was lying ? You might not notice it in that light, but there's just the chance."

"If you'll excuse my saying it, that's the first sensible question anybody's asked me about this business. Now you mention it, sir, the two pictures aren't at all alike in my head. When I found the young laird on Wednesday, he will have had his shoulders and half the body propped up against the heap of stones behind him, not just the neck, as it was on Monday. And he was leaning a little more to the side, towards the road, on Monday than on Wednesday. But the clothes and the general look of the man were just the same ; that's the impression I have."

"Good. You don't mind if I take a note or two, do you ? And of course there was nobody in sight when you found him on Monday, naturally, or you'd have called out to him. But can you tell me this, was it likely there should have been anybody passing there just after you'd left, as early in the morning as that ? Any of the men on the estate, for example ? "

"I'm not thinking it very probable. But there are poachers

out on Sunday night often enough, and they wouldn't be just very anxious for me to see them, you may be certain of that. But what would such folks be doing with a dead body ? "

" I know ; it doesn't help much. And on the other hand, you'd satisfied yourself that the man was dead, naturally, or you'd have stayed with him ; you felt the heart, I suppose, or put something to the lips ? "

" I felt the heart, and it was not beating. "

" And when you bent down to do that—excuse my asking—did you smell any whisky on him ? "

" There wasn't a trace of it. Though the doctor said something about alcohol when he made the examination—but you'll have seen about that. "

" Yes, that's why I asked. Now, here's another point ; I meant to ask you before—would anybody have been expecting you to be out so early, and going out along that particular road at that particular time, either morning ? Or was it just a chance ? "

" On the Monday, I just went out in the usual way ; but it's not often I go along the main road like that. On the Wednesday, I was perhaps two or three minutes later, and I was still dressing when the telephone bell went. "

" Oh, they rang you up ? From the house, I suppose ? Or from the farm ? "

" From the house. It's just a private line, you see. "

" And told you there was a fire down by the farm there, and would you go over to help put it out ? That would be Mr. Hemerton, I suppose ? "

" It was the butler gave the message, but it came from Mr. Hemerton in the first place. I went on my bicycle that time, to be there as soon as possible."

Bredon asked a few more questions, not because he wanted the answers, but because he wanted to see a little more of MacWilliam and size him up, while there was still an excuse for it. The impression he got was that of a perfectly honest man who was concealing nothing and had nothing to conceal. But he remembered that he was dealing with one who came from a foreign race, and the races differ in their reactions. He would not leave MacWilliam altogether out of sight in his investigations. " I suppose I could always find you if I wanted your help over anything else ? " he said at last, and was assured that he would be welcomed at the lodge any evening he would be at the pains to call.

There was still an interval of time before luncheon ; what better way of filling it than to take a preliminary look, anyhow, at that letter from Madeira ? He carried it off to his bedroom, and laid it out carefully on the writing-table, envelope and enclosure side by side. It was postmarked Funchal, February the 5th ; the time, as often happens with postmarks, was unfortunately illegible. The less chance, then, of calculating whether it was sent before or after the receipt of his sister's letter, with its news of the laird's illness. The envelope and the enclosure were not of that thin, flimsy consistency you expect from people engaged in foreign travel, nor were they stamped with nasty little pictures of the *Squandermania*. Colin had evidently taken out a plain writing-pad with him, and a few plain envelopes to suit his modest needs as a correspondent. The envelope had been dog's-eared as if by long travel, and passed a good deal from hand to hand, not always clean ones. But it was well and truly stuck, and had clearly never given up its contents until it was opened by the recipient. It was addressed to " D. Reiver, Esq.," with the Dorn address, and had been postmarked at Blairwhinnie early in the morning on the 11th. So much Bredon noticed, mechanically scrutinizing the document in view of possible frauds.

None suggested itself here.

The enclosure was long—surprisingly so, when you considered how inarticulate most young men are on paper ; when you considered, moreover, that this particular young man had the reputation of being very reserved, and not on good terms with the home circle. Bredon was rather touched by the picture of this family failure, unaccustomed to the pen (there were some mis-spellings, which I spare the printer) and perhaps no great observer at the best of times, sitting down to compile a laborious budget of impressions about the scenery and the legends of the places he had passed, in the manner of our grandparents.

It looked as if he was really determined to make amends to his father for long neglect, and found it less embarrassing to do this on paper than face to face. Yes, on the whole it looked like the writing of a young man who loved his father sufficiently, in spite of everything, to break off a cruise in the middle and come posting back home at a hint that he was in precarious health.

But we will let Colin speak for himself :

46

My dear Dad,

This is written very late, I know ; but somehow although there is so little to do on a cruise one doesn't seem to want to write, and there are always people about in the writing-room. I expect you will be glad to hear that the weather has been good all through, and it is getting hotter and hotter now. As you will see, we are near Madeira as I write. We touched at Lisbon first of all, so it can't be said of me any longer that I haven't seen anything good—which is what the Portuguese proverb says about people who haven't seen Lisbon. It is really pretty good value, coming into the harbour especially. The hills behind are quite low, but the bay is enormous, and the town rises up in terraces, which reminded me of the terraces at Dorn. However, I dare say you touched there when you went out to India that time, so I won't bore you with guide-book stuff. And, of course, you must have seen Gib too, so I'll leave that part out. Majorca was the next place we made, and there we went ashore for two days, and stayed at a topping hotel. Palma's the name of the town. The cathedral there is any age almost, and the sculptures on the front of it are terribly good. There's a big clock-tower by the side of it, which is supposed to be very interesting, though one doesn't notice it much, because it's mixed up with all the other buildings in the street. The best thing inside was the tomb of some old king or other, all in black marble with bronze figures on it. But what they seem most keen about in the town is the clock-tower of the town hall ; it marks the way the sun goes or something ; I didn't quite catch on to the idea.

Minorca was less interesting, perhaps because it rather reminds one of England. Windmills, I mean, all over the place ; one doesn't go abroad to see them. Port-Mahon looks well from the harbour, but is dull when one gets to it ; the old capital, Ciudadella, is really more interesting—it's got rather jolly old walls. Then on to Naples, which was just like the picture-books, only Vesuvius wasn't functioning very well. And my word, what a dirty town Naples is ! I must say I bar that kind of thing. But Sicily is really worth while. Taormina was the first place we went to, with an old Roman theatre, all in ruins, of course, but as large as life, and the view from the hill above it beats anything I've seen. It's all way up in the hills, you see, and the quaintest old place, though there are lots of modern hotels there. Palermo's got some topping things in it, too, especially the Royal Palace ; walls and floors all covered with mosaics, you know, as old as anything, and the chapel is terribly impressive. I wish we'd spent even longer in Sicily, because I believe there's lots more to see.

I'm not ordinarily much of a hand at writing letters, as you know, but this travel business does give one lots to talk about.

My hand's quite tired of writing already, and I haven't got beyond Europe yet. I shall have to keep Algiers and all those North African places for another letter. There are some quite decent people doing this cruise, and everyone is very matey—you don't seem to have to wait to be introduced to people. I play backgammon a good deal with an old boy we call " The Colonel "; I don't believe he ever was in the Army really though. Please tell Mary I haven't found the Ship's Vamp yet; all the women I've seen much of so far are as ugly as sin and well over fifty. I expect there will be letters from you waiting for me at Madeira, but I shall stick this up and send it off as soon as I get the chance, because if I keep it till after we've gone ashore I shall probably put it in my pocket and forget about it. I hope you're all well at Dorn. From your affectionate son—COLIN.

" Well, that's that," said Bredon to himself. " And now, as it still seems a quarter of an hour to luncheon, there can be no harm in poking about in the library for a bit." He was still poking when his hostess called out to him to say luncheon was ready.

" Mr. Reiver very kindly allowed me to look through that letter from Madeira," he said. " I had been half wondering whether it would not be a good thing to cable to the *Squandermania* to know if your brother left the ship at Madeira; or possibly ask the passport officials at Southampton whether they remembered him—not that they would be likely to. But this letter seems to make it quite clear, doesn't it? Immediately after posting it he must have got your letter, and have started out for home at once. The letter will have arrived in England, and consequently your brother will have arrived in England on the tenth—that's Friday a week ago; if he had caught the mail train, he might just have been here, like the letter, on Saturday morning. I think it will be best if I try to find out, by private enquiries, of course, whether there is any trace of his movements during the week-end. He might conceivably have stayed at a hotel in Southampton, for instance. Supposing he'd gone straight to London, and spent the week-end there, can you think of any friends he would have been likely to stay with, or, at any rate, to call on? Because we might get a line on his movements that way."

" He generally came to us when he was in London, didn't he, Vincent? And I'm sure we should have heard from Mrs. Cripps if he had looked in at the house. I could write and ask, of course. And then there's that friend of his, Strutt, who was with him when he had the accident; he lives in London, and he'd almost certainly be in the telephone book. You might try him; I can't think of anybody else—though, of course, he had plenty of friends at Oxford that we didn't know."

" It all shows," observed her husband, " that a great deal of trouble is caused in the world by people grudging the penny stamp on a post card. I always send a post card when I arrive anywhere."

CHAPTER VIII

COUSIN HENRY COMES TO TEA

THE LIBRARY AT Dorn is the largest room in the house; the ground plan has the appearance of two rooms thrown into one, and half of it has the height of two storeys—in this an iron corkscrew staircase leads to a wooden gallery, lined all round with books. Everywhere, woven into the mouldings of the ceiling, into the tiles of the fire-place, you see the horse-shoe which is the emblem of the Reiver family. For all its spaciousness, it is a comfortable room enough even for a small party, and in winter it was the accepted *venue* for afternoon tea. Bredon, still " poking round " at half-past four, had Major Henry Reiver suddenly let loose on him, and experienced all the embarrassment of the unintroduced guest, with the added feeling that his presence was unexpected and unexplained. The little man had obviously hoped for a private interview with his cousins; and if he made any attempt to conceal his disappointment at finding an intruder there before him, it was quite unsuccessful. A piece of good fortune broke the ice between them. A copy of last Sunday's *Onlooker* was lying about; it led to the discovery that they both tried to solve the ingenious crosswords which appear every week, under the signature of " Topcliffe," in that paper. The arrival of their hostess was nevertheless welcome to both.

" Oh, Cousin Henry, how are you ? Vincent will be in in a minute. This is Mr. Bredon, my cousin, Major Reiver. So nice to be getting a bit more daylight at tea-time, isn't it ? We were so sorry you couldn't stay behind at all after the funeral, Cousin Henry; but we really shouldn't have seen

49

anything of you if you had, there was such a crowd of people in. It's much nicer to see you by yourself like this. Ah, here's Vincent " . . . and she devoted herself to the mysteries of tea-making as her husband took over the exchange of the banalities. It was clear, however, that Henry Reiver had not come to talk about the weather; he shifted this way and that, as if his chair was uncomfortable; looked at Bredon as if wondering whether there was any chance that he would go away, closured avenues of conversation with a grunt more than usually emphatic, and at last became explicit. " I came over, you know, well, I came over because I wanted to talk about something. Might I ask, is Mr. Bredon the gentleman you were expecting from the Insurance Company? Because, if not, I don't want to bore him; boring listening to other people's family conversation. And if he is, well, I don't mind, and he don't mind, I don't suppose; question is, do you mind my saying what I've come to say in front of Mr. Bredon? No use putting one's foot in it, huh? "

Bredon swallowed half a cup of scalding tea, and was just rising to excuse himself when Vincent Hemerton stopped him. " That's all right," he said; " so far as the insurance is concerned, Mr. Bredon's object is the same as ours, to establish the exact facts and the exact dates. I'm sure he's to be trusted not to wash the family dirty linen in public, if that's what you mean, except where loyalty to his principals is involved. Have another cup, Bredon, and settle yourself down. D'you like this tea? You don't get it everywhere; I have it imported specially. Now, Major, what's worrying you? "

" Murder; arson; sabotage," said the Major, in the machine-gun style of oratory, and was silent.

" My dear fellow," said Vincent Hemerton soothingly, " my dear fellow! "

" Well, I want to know what you're going to do about it? No use pretending I haven't got an interest in the property; another of these attacks might carry your poor father off, and then what sort of property do I come in for? Murder, arson, sabotage—all over the place."

" But, Cousin Henry, you don't mean that Colin . . ."

" I do mean Colin; how did that boy meet his death? You don't know, you don't ask. Well, I'm the next heir to the property, and I do ask. Look at that! " And he produced from his pocket a crumpled document, which he

50

flattened against the table. " You're connected with insurance, sir ; just you look at that, and tell me how much a man's life's worth who gets letters of that kind by the morning's post ! "

Bredon took it up, and read the following words, inscribed in a sprawling, spidery handwriting, such as is familiar to the recipients of anonymous letters : " Mr. Henry Reiver, sir, the curse is on your family again, you murderers, grinding the faces of the poor and knocking their children down with motor-cars ; how did Colin Reiver die ? It will be your turn next, you swine. The devil have mercy on your soul ; we shall all laugh." There was no signature.

" But that's surely a lunatic, Cousin Henry," suggested Mary, who had been reading over the detective's shoulder.

" There are more lunatics going about loose than were ever locked up," agreed her husband. " And they'll always get hold of the latest sensation that's been in the papers, and write mad letters to the principals in the affair. Your name was mentioned as heir to the property, you see, Major."

" Lunatic, was it ? Then d'you think it was a lunatic did in that poor boy Colin ? "

" But, Cousin Henry, nobody's even suggested that Colin was murdered. How could he be ? There was no sign of violence, no trace of poison, and the doctor was very careful about it. Poor Colin died of exposure ; you can't get round that."

" I dare say he did die of exposure ; what difference does that make, huh ? There's more ways of killing a cat—there's more ways—what's that proverb, sir ? " he demanded fiercely of Bredon, looking at him as if he were a dictionary of familiar quotations.

" Drowning it in milk, isn't it ? " suggested Bredon. " I'm quite with you, sir, up to a point. I do think that when you get dead bodies turning up at odd times and in odd places, it's difficult to explain the facts by accidental death, or even by suicide. But the trouble here, as Mrs. Hemerton says, is the manner of death. You *can* kill a person by exposure, if you maim him or tie him up or drug him, so that he won't be able to walk away. But maiming and pinioning and even drugging leave their marks, and no competent doctor, least of all one who is accustomed to police work, as I understand this one was, could possibly overlook those marks in a *post-mortem*. That's the difficulty."

" And what if you put a person up on a height, where he's

51

afraid to jump off? Or shut him up in an enclosure, where he doesn't stand any chance of climbing out? What marks are you going to leave then?"

"The difficulty about that, I should have thought," suggested Hemerton, "is persuading your man to accompany you without violence. Wouldn't he be likely to struggle?"

"Isn't that what I'm telling you, that Colin wasn't set on by a single man, but by a whole crowd of fellows; kidnapped, and then left to die somewhere? Shocking feeling among the men on the estate, ever since that unfortunate car business; ever since your father, Cousin Mary, left off looking after the estate. Who found the body on Monday? MacWilliam. Who found it on Wednesday? MacWilliam. Never trusted that man; a Highlander—not civilized. But heaven knows how many of 'em may be in it, with all this Bolshevism going about. Conspiracy, don't you see? First they murder Colin, then they start setting fire to your ricks. Same in India, same in Ireland."

"Cousin Henry," said Mary, with desperate calm, "do let's have your account of the whole business, exactly as it happened. We shan't get on any further with random suspicions like this."

"If I may put in a word, sir," added Bredon, "isn't the really salient fact about last week's events the disappearance and reappearance of young Mr. Reiver, alive or dead? And I don't quite understand yet how your notion of a kidnapping by disaffected men on the estate fits in with that. I don't mean it may not, but I don't yet quite see how, that's all."

"I'll tell you exactly how I work it out," said the Major; and to the relief of his audience dropped his voice for a sentence or two. "In the first place, the servants here have been talking. Stands to reason people outside the house couldn't have known Colin was coming back, or known when he was coming back, if there hadn't been talk going on. Mind, I don't say the servants in the house had any hand in it; may have been just gossiping; but they talked. Next, if you want to kidnap a man you must meet him with a conveyance; that looks as if one of these taxi fellows was in it; better keep our eye on them. You get him to go on board the taxi, with his luggage, and you either drive him out of his way without letting him notice it, or you have one or two people ready to get into the taxi and see that he doesn't jump out or make a noise of any kind. You drive him off—where to?

52

I've thought of that ; and I know what I'd do if I wanted to kidnap a man ; take him to the Devil's Dimple, see ? You don't know this part of the country, Mr. Bredon ; Devil's Dimple is only a mile or two up in the hills, but it's a lonely place, just a ledge on the hillside with a sheer drop underneath it, and a rather difficult climb to get up from it. People hid there in the '45, so they say. You only need one guard, or two at most, to see that he doesn't climb out. You give him just a little food ; you don't want him to die of starvation. You just leave him there, and on these cold nights it's only a matter of time before his strength gives out. Then you've got your corpse, and no one the wiser."

Mary gave a slight shudder ; to one who knew the Devil's Dimple, the picture was horribly real. " But you mean they took him there on Saturday, and he was dead by Monday morning ? "

" No, don't you see, that's just where they miscalculated. He was in a dead faint already, and they thought he was done for. So they took him off to a public place, where he could easily be found by a passer-by ; the side of the main road's good enough, that time in the morning. Then MacWilliam —he's the obvious man, he lives near—goes up to give the news at Dorn, while the rest clear out. But, when he's gone too far to be called back, your dead man opens his eyes ! That won't do ; he's got to be found dead when people come. So they whisk him away, back to the Devil's Dimple ; nothing else to do. Makes MacWilliam look a fool, of course, but they can't help that. Keep him two more nights, to make sure of him. Then down they come again, put the body on the roadside as before ; MacWilliam goes up to the house as before. The rest run off and set the rick alight."

" Why that ? " asked Hemerton.

" Sabotage, partly ; wanted to injure the property for all of us. Partly to create general confusion ; people don't notice how the dead man lies, 'cause they're rushing off to put out the fire ; don't worry about how the fire started, 'cause they're rushing back to the house to see if the young Laird's really dead. Military idea, creating a diversion. May be some ex-soldiers in the plot. You'll find that's what happened."

Bredon was the first to recover his powers of rejoinder. " Was it a large rick ? " he asked.

" Large ? " repeated Hemerton. " I don't see what that's got to do with it anyway."

" Fair-sized, I think," added his wife ; but without much conviction in her voice.

" Nonsense," put in the Major in correction ; " I know the farm, if nobody else here does. Why, it was only the tail-end of a rick ; not worth twenty pounds at the best of times. What's that matter ?"

" Only that if they were really out to injure the property, I should have thought they would have started with a more valuable one," suggested Bredon mildly.

" Still, that was the one they *did* choose," objected the Major.

" But that's assuming that it *was* arson. If the rick caught fire accidentally, the size wouldn't matter."

" I've always assumed it was an accident about the rick," agreed Hemerton. " It's the sort of thing that's always happening. Now, if they piled their ricks as we do in England . . ."

" Well," the theorist broke in, " if that's all the objection you can find to the explanation I've been giving you . . ."

" Oh, but it isn't," persisted Bredon amiably. " I think there are all sorts of objections. I mean, as you say, you want to make very sure that your man has really died, isn't going to come round under treatment, in a case like that ; therefore you would be inclined to keep the dead body for a day or so to make certain of the death ; here, the doctor said that life was only four or five hours extinct. Again, who knew what train would have to be met ? Mrs. Hemerton tells me she had no idea when to expect him, if at all. Again, if you are going to be at the pains of taking your man to the top of a precipice, why keep him there ? Why not throw him down, and allow it to be supposed that he fell off while climbing ? There are hosts of minor difficulties of that sort in your account, any one of which you might meet with fresh explanations, but collectively they are fatal to it. . . . I'm sorry, sir, I'm afraid I have been lecturing to you rather. But, you see, in an amateur sort of way I've always taken rather an interest in stories of crime, and my hobby is apt to run away with me."

Those who are acquainted with Miles Bredon's reputation already will know that this last sentence was a gross perversion of the truth. Or, at any rate, it was in direct conflict of the account he usually gave of himself—that he hated mysteries, and only tried to find a solution of them for the sake of his bread and butter. It seemed to him, though, that he was

54

showing his hand too much by posing before his present audience as an expert in crime.

Henry Reiver seemed slightly crestfallen. " Well, that's what I think," he said, " and it's what I'll think until somebody shows me a better way of getting round it all. Confound it, man," he added, turning to Hemerton, " d'you mean to say that you don't mean to do anything about it, huh ? Prepared to sit down and call the whole confounded thing a mystery ? "

It was Mary Hemerton who answered. " Yes, but, Cousin Henry, we don't think the whole thing is so extraordinary, Vincent and I. We have very little doubt, either of us, that Colin lost his memory and was wandering about, perhaps even *looking* for Dorn ; he can't have been in a normal state, can he, Mr. Bredon, or why should he have been found *between* the lodges ? That was no way to Dorn, wherever he was coming from. That's on Wednesday, of course ; as to what happened on Monday—well, it's always possible to take the hard-headed Britisher point of view and say that on Monday he was already wandering about like that, and had fainted from exhaustion when MacWilliam found him, but wasn't dead. If so, he must have come round and wandered away as he had wandered there ; if only we'd found him ! But for myself, I really believe that what MacWilliam saw was a warning to us of what was coming, given to him by some telepathic instinct ; I think it's so difficult to account otherwise for the *exact* correspondence of time and place between the two experiences. I sometimes think MacWilliam himself believes that, though, of course, he won't say so ; so proud, these Highlanders. Well, that's what I think happened ; and after all, these cases of loss of memory aren't so uncommon, are they, Mr. Bredon ? I expect you must have come across them before now. Do tell us, if you've any other suggestion to make."

" Who, me ? No, I think your account, one way or the other, seems much the most probable in view of anything we know at present. It's only the question of what happened to your brother's luggage that is worrying me ; if he simply left it behind somewhere, one would think it must turn up. But perhaps we shall hear about that from the railway before long. And his overcoat—surely a man doesn't get separated from that further than he can help, these cold nights. It *must* be found somewhere. Meanwhile, Major, I really don't see what can be done about it if there is any ground for your fears. It would be very difficult to get police protection for the property, or for yourself, without more evidence than that. No, I think the only thing to do is to make any further enquiries we can think of as quietly as possible. If the men on the estate are really responsible for a crime, the less we say about it the better; we should only put them on their guard—don't you think ? "

" I suppose you're right—police wouldn't do anything. Nothing ever *is* done in these cases till too late. Same in Ireland, same in India. I'll tell you what I'm going to do. Going to look all along the road, *both* sides of the hedge, see if I can't come across something. Carting a man about like that, alive or dead, almost sure to drop something. That's what I'll do. Don't tell Donald what I think, not till he's better. Only make him feel uncomfortable—no use doing that."

CHAPTER IX

THE DOCTOR DINES

IT WOULD HAVE been difficult to find a greater contrast anywhere than the guest of tea-time and the guest of dinner-time, at least so far as their conversational habits were concerned. The Major apoplectically threw all his cards on the table, and any hint of opposition only served to confirm him in the opinions he had arrived at about five minutes before. The doctor thought before he spoke, a quite sensible pause introducing his answer even to the most commonplace question; and he had that rare gift of good-breeding which shows unaffected interest in what the other man is saying. Conversation turned, almost inevitably, on the Major's lurid picture of disaffection among the tenants on the Dorn estate. " Now, Doctor," said Hemerton, " you've worked among these people all your life, and you know them better than any man alive. Would *you* say that Henry Reiver has any grounds for his suspicions at all ? I mean, I suppose we should all agree that he exaggerates ; my point is, has he any basis of fact to exaggerate from, or does the whole thing come out of his head ? "

" Well, Mr. Hemerton, I'd always say that it's a mistake to meet the arguments of a man who's generalizing rashly on his

56

side by generalizing on your own. I wouldn't say there are
no disaffected men on this or any other estate ; if by that you
mean men who think they ought to be head carpenter instead
of second carpenter, and second gardener instead of third
gardener, and all the rest of it. They will talk when they're
in their cups, those men, and if you listen to them you could
easily think that it all means something. But what the Major
says is moonshine, for all that. Especially, mark you, when
he tries to make you believe that a man like MacWilliam is
the head and front of this conspiracy of his. MacWilliam,
you see, is getting a very decent salary, though he's a fool to
try and make it do for twelve mouths when it would do better
for six. But besides that he's got a fine position, and it's the
best position a man like him would covet. And then he's a
Highlander ; and they're very independent folk, the Highlanders, but they've the feudal sense strong in them. Whatever's the truth of all this, you mustn't think MacWilliam
has been playing fast and loose with you. It's not in character."

" Then you don't attach any importance to the anonymous
letter ? " put in Bredon.

" I don't, Mr. Bredon ; and I'd give a good guess that you
don't either. I don't say that there aren't plenty of these
mining folks down Bantrie way that are out of work and have
a grudge against anybody that's a landlord. And there's been
overcrowding and overbreeding among that lot, so that you
get a good few poor lunatics who'd be better out of the way,
to my thinking. And here's this education we're all so proud
of that teaches them to write but doesn't teach them to think.
I tell you, they've got a regular itch for writing, some of these
lunatics, Mr. Bredon ; they can't see a piece of paper lying
about in the street without thinking that it's wasted if they
haven't used it by dropping a line to somebody. And because
they've very few friends to write to, they write to the last man
whose name they've seen in the paper ; and they generally
write something insulting, because it's the first thing that comes
into their minds, and they can't repress it. You have to be
a bit of an alienist, when all's said and done, if you've got to
doctor folks in Blairwhinnie."

" But there's a lot of lunacy in the Highlands, isn't there ? "
suggested Mary.

" Oh, there is, and it's the result of in-breeding ; you'll
always get that in lonely parts, Mrs. Hemerton. But Mac-

57

William, if you mean that, is as sane as you or me. All that story about his having second sight is foisted on him by his neighbours; he never claimed it, and he never showed any signs of it, that I could hear of. Now, of course, with reporters coming down from London, and all the silly wives clucking about him like a set of hens, he'd have some excuse for beginning to believe in it. But no, there's no sign of it; he's as plain and practical as ever."

"I must say I liked what I saw of him this morning," admitted Bredon. "But you'll admit, Doctor, that it's rather difficult for anybody who has got to deal with the subject judicially to rest a case entirely on the unsupported evidence of one man; especially people up in London, who don't know him."

"Do they believe in second sight, then, up in London?" asked the doctor.

"After all, what does it matter?" said Mary Hemerton, with a touch of asperity in her tone. "I think we are all much too fond of being inquisitive. Certain things about life we shall never find out. Far best leave them alone."

"Ah, but Mrs. Hemerton, you can't do without inquisitiveness," protested the doctor. "It's the birthright of humanity. Breed out inquisitiveness, and you make the world over to the white ants."

"People will always be inquisitive where money is concerned, at least," ventured her husband. "But we shall be making Bredon here feel nervous if we go on talking about that. I've never seen, myself, why you sceptics, Doctor, have such difficulty about believing in second sight. After all, it's only a question of time, isn't it? Ever read that book, *An Experiment with Time*?"

"Psychical research isn't in my line," Bredon put in; "but surely, Doctor, even if you don't believe in second sight you've got to allow for hallucination. And the experiment with time I would like to be able to do would be an experiment of any sort which would show that Mrs. Hemerton's brother was still alive on Tuesday. It seems to me almost incredible that he should have been wandering about all that time and left no trace of himself, met nobody who could swear to his identity. There *must* be traces left, somewhere."

"You're from the South, Mr. Bredon," said Mary Hemerton, "and you've probably no idea how lonely this country of ours becomes, once you get away a mile or two into the hills. Colin

was always rather a lonely sort of person, and he would often
go tramping by himself on the hillside when he was younger.
I wonder, if he came back from that cruise with some kind of
mental aberration, the result of all his worry over the accident,
isn't it possible that he'd take to the hills by instinct, and keep
away from human contact as much as possible ? "

" Yet he seems to have been on the main road when his
last weakness overtook him. I suppose that might be explained,
though."

" Isn't it possible that his brain cleared a bit, and he remembered, if only by a kind of instinct, the way home—turned
back in that direction almost as an animal does ? Dr. Purvis,
you tell us you're interested in these things ; doesn't that
strike you as a possibility ? "

" I'm not saying that wouldn't be the most natural explanation of his disappearing so suddenly, and of how he came
to die of exposure. But what I don't feel so certain about,
Mrs. Hemerton, is whether he could have lasted so long as
four days, from Friday night to Tuesday night, with nobody
to look after him and nowhere to get food from. The lad had
a very poor constitution, you see, Mr. Bredon. Now, if he'd
been found dead on Monday morning once for all, there'd
have been nothing surprising about it. But if you want me
to believe that he was alive till Wednesday morning, or rather
till Tuesday night, then I'm with Mr. Bredon here ; I'm
wondering whether he can have got on so long without having
a place to lodge or somewhere to get food."

" Oh, you're hopeless," laughed Mary. " It's well known
all over the country-side that Dr. Purvis, once he's made up
his mind, never changes it. And he's determined to believe
in MacWilliam, the whole MacWilliam, and nothing but Mac-
William. Well, I'm going to leave you gentlemen to your port,
because I just want to go up and make Dad comfortable for
the night. Don't be too long, though, or you'll never get that
game of chess finished by midnight."

There are few pursuits more fascinating for the first few
minutes, more unutterably wearisome afterwards, than watching
a game of chess. Here you have human figures turned to
brain ; they scarcely remember to avoid cramp by shifting
their attitudes from time to time, so thoroughly have they left
the trappings of the body behind in this ecstasy. Their eyes
are cemented as if by a fast balm to the ridiculous symbols in
front of them. Their actions, dictated by pure intelligence,

59

lose the semblance of human actions and might be mistaken for the jerkings of automata; or, rather, let us think of them as two Martians, all brain, without passions or impulses. They strive for sheer mastery—whoever heard of playing a game of chess for money?—and concentration of thought seems to radiate from them, till you can almost hear the units of brain-power ticking away like the register of a taxi-meter. In this case the combatants, evenly matched as far as their form went, were dissimilar in their style, since dissimilarity of style is possible even among chess-players. Hemerton was the more eager, the more demonstrative; occasionally he would whisper to himself " No, that won't do "; he would try out a move, with his hand numbly glued to the piece, for several minutes together, then withdraw it, frowning, and relapse into contemplation. When his opponent was playing, he would look from face to board, from board to face, as if he hoped to read the thoughts of his antagonist. The doctor, on his side, made every move with decision, letting go of the piece as soon as it was firm on its square—you could hardly believe that action so decisive was the result of thought so prolonged. When he was out of play, his eyes seemed fixed on space, as if he found it easier to work out plans on the image of a chess-board that was photographed on his mind than on the too solid chess-board itself.

Bredon and his hostess watched till it became tiresome; then they withdrew to the further side of the fire-place, and talked in those comparatively subdued tones which we use in church during weddings. When he found that she was beginning to make plans for the next day, he braced himself and told her he was afraid he would have to leave, as he had warned her in his letter. Was he not going to make any more enquiries? she asked in surprise. With still greater difficulty, he explained that he was going no farther off than Blairwhinnie. He did not produce Angela as his excuse; it would have looked like asking for a second invitation; and Mrs. Hemerton seemed so hospitable that he felt he would have been urged to send for his whole family, nurse and all, if he had tried the plea of home ties. He represented instead, what was no more than the truth, that the enquiries he intended to prosecute were such as to make the Blairwhinnie Hotel a better centre. He would be wanting to go this way and that at odd hours, interviewing now a railway porter, now a hotel-keeper, now a hairdresser; people would have to come and interview *him*, perhaps, and telephone calls would keep on coming for him ; he might want to make midnight expeditions. In a word, he must be free ; and in the end he managed to persuade the reluctant Mary Hemerton that this meant freedom even from the golden shackles of her hospitality. The compromise arrived at was that he was to regard Dorn House as his own, drop in to any meal, commandeer any assistance, feel quite free to ask what questions he liked of the servants or of the men on the estate. Perhaps he would bring Mrs. Bredon to luncheon or tea one day ? They would so like to make her acquaintance.

There was a brief pause, during which you could almost hear the brain-waves of the two chess-players. Then " Mr. Bredon," said Mary, " if you are really going to-morrow, there is one thing you may as well do while you are here—now if you like. Don't you think it would be a good thing if you took a look round Colin's room ? We've left it just as it was, the papers and all that ; and it does seem just possible, doesn't it, that the letters and so on which he left there when he went away might give you some help in finding out what became of him ? "

Bredon accepted with alacrity. They slipped out, unnoticed by the other two. " Wait one moment," said Mary when they were in the passage ; " I shall have to go and get the key." She carried it with her upstairs, and opened an uncharted door amid the labyrinth of doors on the first landing. As she did so, Bredon noticed that she blew on the key slightly, as if to clear the dust away. Where had it been kept, that it should have collected all that dust in little over a month ?

It was chilly in the fireless room, and Mary excused herself on the ground of evening dress ; Bredon assured her that he would find his way down, in half an hour or so. A careful housekeeper had swathed everything in dust-sheets or news-papers, and it was not without some difficulty that he identified and unveiled a book-case and a writing-table, the only pieces of furniture that were likely to yield any evidence. He turned to the books first, as we all do ; tried to conjure up, as we all do, some picture of the man who had inhabited this room from the silent friends with which he had surrounded himself. But the test is a precarious one, especially when you are dealing with the young ; for the most part, they accumulate books at haphazard, as the need or whim of the moment suggests ; there is no policy, and therefore no self-revelation, about their choice. Here were school-books, Oxford text-books, thrillers, illustrated Christmas-present books, one or two very modern novels, and even collections of poetry, as if at one time there had been an interval of self-cultivation ; there was the usual congeries of odd volumes which knit the brows of the searcher with the question " What on earth did he buy that for ? " You could hardly expect to get the atmosphere of the young man who had died so tragically from a library like this—Hall and Knight's *Algebra, Statuta et Decreta Universitatis Oxoniensis*, Pliny's *Letters* (selected), *Clubfoot the Avenger*, Dulac's *Arabian Nights, Angel Pavement, Wheels, Three Men in a Boat, How to Breed Rabbits,* Walsham How on *Confirmation, The Mysterious Universe*. Only one book seemed to call for special attention, because it was lying on the writing-desk, as if its owner might have been actually engaged in reading it just before he left home ; and it was, appropriately enough, Stevenson's *Poems*. A favourite book too, apparently, for faint pencil lines were drawn down the side of the page here and there, to record a preference or an enshrinement in the memory. The stub of a pencil actually held the pages apart in one place, and the poem thus singled out (it was copiously marked down the side) was the one written to the air of Wandering Willie. Yes, there was certainly appropriateness here.

> Now, when day dawns on the brow of the moorland,
> Lone stands the house, and the chimney-stone is cold ;
> Lone let it stand, now the friends are all departed,
> The kind hearts, the true hearts. that loved the place of old—

that might remind the reader of the precarious tenure on which Donald Reiver's branch of the family held their inheritance of Dorn. The house itself might have stood as a model for the line " Fire and the windows bright glittered on the moorland " ; and there was a pathos, presumably undesigned, about the final quatrain :

> Fair the day shine as it shone on my childhood,
> Fair shine the day on the house with open door ;
> Birds come and cry there and twitter in the chimney.
> But I go for ever, and come again no more.

But there were other lines which had no pencil-marks at the side, and the omission was perhaps no less significant.

Home was home then, my dear, full of kindly faces,·
Home was home then, my dear, happy for the child——

had Colin Reiver had the opportunity to echo such sentiments
as that ?
Yes, they were banal enough, these markings, and yet
perhaps they gave you a glimpse of a young Scot who had
cherished, more than those nearest him could guess, the love
of hills and open places.

Be it granted me to behold you again in dying,
Hills of home, and to hear again the call——

that prayer had been granted at least.   Or again :

This be the verse you grave for me,
Here he lies where he longed to be ;
Home is the sailor, home from sea
And the hunter home from the hill.

Bredon read through these passages carefully, whistling slightly
as he did so ; then turned to the letters, which presented no
feature of interest whatever.   He picked out a very unimpor-
tant one, and took the liberty of pocketing it ; the signature
gave the address of the Oxford friend who had been with
Colin Reiver when he ran over the child—just possibly it
would be worth writing to him.   Nothing remained but to
replace the dust-sheets, turn out the light, and start on a
voyage of rediscovery for the library.

CHAPTER X

ABSENCE OF MIND AND BODY

NEXT MORNING, BREDON had a second interview with Donald
Reiver, but only a short one.   The old laird said he was
improved in health, and looked it ; but he was ill at ease, as
though he interpreted Bredon's departure from the house as
evidence that he was going to report unfavourably to the
Company.   Not that any allusion was made to the money
question ; but he was plainly anxious to know what form the
" investigations " at Blairwhinnie were to take.   And while
assuring Bredon that Purvis was a " grand doctor," he complained, as Mary had complained overnight, of the man's pig-

headedness ; " don't you be too much moved by what Purvis says ; he's a great scholar, but he wants judgment—I never yet knew him admit he was in the wrong of a question." And so they parted, Mr. Reiver echoing, almost querulously, his daughter's offer of further hospitality.

To her, Bredon put a suggestion which had arisen in his mind as he thought over the pencil-markings he had found in the Stevenson book. " It does seem to me as if your idea was right ; I mean, about your brother having taken to the hills when he came back from his trip—I suppose, as you say, in some access of mental aberration. Well, obviously one can't search all the hillsides round here with a fine-tooth comb. But the Major, if you remember, was talking yesterday about some very lonely place round here . . ."

" The Devil's Dimple ? "

" That was it. He said, if you remember, that it was the kind of place he would choose if he wanted to kidnap a man and keep him away from all human contact. Well, wouldn't the same notion probably occur to the mind of a boy who wanted, on his own part, to avoid all human contact—to die, perhaps, among the heather and the hills ? "

Mary Hemerton knitted her brows and thought for a moment. " That's a clever idea of yours," she said. " Now I come to think of it, it's just the sort of place he would make for. I remember he and I used to go up there and picnic sometimes when we were quite small ; though we weren't allowed to, of course, because it's a frightfully dangerous place for children. Look here, Mr. Bredon, why not stay over to luncheon here ? Then we could make an expedition to the Devil's Dimple in the car this morning. It isn't more than five miles, even in the car—barely two miles, if you don't mind walking it over rather rough paths."

But Bredon was not to be diverted from his plan of action. " It's awfully kind of you, Mrs. Hemerton, but I really don't think I can afford the time for that just yet. I thought I would get through all the routine work of sending out enquiries to-day, and then to-morrow I could run up to the Devil's Dimple in the car. But I wonder, would you mind showing it me on the map ? Because I don't want to draw attention to it by asking people about it."

Bredon was driven down to Blairwhinnie by Vincent Hemerton, who had to go up to London for the night. Angela was the kind of wife who didn't expect her husband to enquire

anxiously after her health and that of the family ; or to say
how well she looked ; or to complain of the dullness of being
absent from her for a couple of days. This was as well,
because Bredon was the sort of husband who does none of
those things. They had hardly been together five minutes
before they were deep in discussion of the situation which
needed clearing up ; Angela as usual genuinely thrilled by
its complexity, Miles relieved to have an audience at last which
he could address without reserve. He did stipulate, however,
on this occasion that he was not going to tell Angela about
his suspicions. " You see, I want you to form your own
suspicions," he said. " It's no use expecting that, if I keep
supplying you with suspicions at second-hand. I'll tell you
what I've heard, and I'll tell you what I think, and I'll tell
you what I wonder, but not what I suspect. Partly because
so far I've only the vaguest suspicions, and they're probably
all wrong, so I don't want to have you laughing at me. And
partly, as I say, because I want to know how it strikes you.
Now, here goes." And he retailed his impressions of Dorn,
and of its inmates.

" Well, there's one thing," reflected Angela, " unless your
military friend is right about the local Jacobinism—and
I assure you there's very little of it in this hydro—we haven't
got to think about murder. You know, Miles, I sometimes
get rather worried about you, wondering what would happen
if you came across a murderer who turned nasty and tried to
hit back at you. But it doesn't look as if there were any
murderers about here. I don't mind telling you at once,
since you are so anxious for me to form suspicions, that I think
there is dirty work going on at the cross-roads. But it looks
rather, doesn't it, as if the dirty work were confined to playing
about with dead people, not murdering live ones."

" I know. You think because the medico said death must
have resulted from exposure that there couldn't be any violence
about it. I grant you, I don't very much believe in the
Major's notion that it's a handy way of murdering a man, to
keep him away from his great-coat at the point of the revolver
till he dies of it. But I want to see more of Dr. Purvis, and
ask him—I didn't like to ask him up at the house, for fear
of distressing the others unnecessarily—whether the verdict of
death from exposure is so certain as all that. I mean, isn't
it rather a declaration that you can't think of any other reason
for the death, than that you have found the true one ? I seem

to have read about ways in which one can kill a man without leaving any trace—hitting him a violent blow, for example, in the pit of the stomach, or just over the heart. I must get on to Dr. Purvis about that."

"Since you insist on discussing your suspicions, may I ask why you are so anxious for it to be murder? Just love of sensation, or is there any reason behind it all?"

"Yes, confound it all—the luggage. Colin Reiver set out from Dorn with suit-cases containing clothes and razors and things, with a great-coat, with money in a purse, with a passport (and remember that it is a frightful curse losing one's passport, because there is no end of trouble when you want it renewed). Colin Reiver was found lying by the roadside, with none of these things on him or near him. Now, you can produce explanations of why he may have lost them; as, that he had gone potty (his sister's theory); or that he had gone native and wanted to live the simple life; or anything of that kind. But if you lose your luggage you lose it somewhere; and almost certainly you lose it on the railway, which has special arrangements to meet such absent-mindedness on the part of passengers. I grant you, luggage does sometimes disappear in the most extraordinary way, and for long intervals of time—it gets sent off to odd places, Kingsbridge on the Great Western, and in these parts probably Fort William. But then, this business about Colin Reiver has been in the papers, and it's almost inconceivable that any porter reading the name REIVER on a label shouldn't at once start being officious about it."

"Dash it all, there's such a thing as stealing luggage."

"There is, but it's not done wholesale like that. You pinch a woman's bag, because it contains her purse, or a man's great-coat (if he is a fool) for the same reason. But you probably put back the great-coat, after you have been through it. You have to be a very clever thief to steal off with a great-coat and a couple of suit-cases and a stick and probably a travelling-rug, all together. No, I don't believe those things could be lost, and I don't believe they were stolen. It may be that Colin himself laid them by somewhere; if so, I'm going to make it my business to find them. But it looks to me as if their disappearance were part of the general mystery. And if that's so why should anybody want to dispose of them?"

"Well, if you're going to assume that someone is taking liberties with the dead man's body, I don't quite see why you should expect him to be squeamish about mislaying the golf-clubs."

" Yes, but the motive ! Was Colin Reiver lying dead by the side of the road on the Monday ? MacWilliam says he was, but MacWilliam saw no sign of his belongings anywhere in the neighbourhood ; nor did those other people, though they were at pains to search the hedgerow. Now, suppose you had some motive for dragging Colin's dead body to the light on that particular day, and were in the fortunate position of knowing where his body was to be found, all dead and ready for you. Wouldn't you at least put a stick by him, to make him look as if he had been walking ? Wouldn't you even have shoved a tooth-brush or something in his pocket, so as to give the suggestion that he was on the hike ? And a little money—nobody travels without money, even if he's lost his memory. Suppose you had some motive for dragging the body to light on the Wednesday and not before, the same considerations apply. But the instinct of the murderer—ah, that's different ! "

" If I murdered you, I don't think I should bother much about the stage properties. If I murdered you in the car, I should leave your umbrella in the car, and let on that you had left it behind—it would be like you. If I murdered you in a train, I'd cart your luggage off to the cloak-room and take a ticket for it. And . . . "

" The precise mistakes you would be guilty of if you committed a murder do not interest me at the moment. I am talking about the normal murderer, and I believe this is absolutely certain—that one leading element in the fear that grips him is the question of tidying up. What the devil am I to do with all these things ? he asks. Clues, clues ! shrieks conscience, and in a panic he determines to make all the dead man's belongings disappear somehow—throws them off a bridge, or burns them in his back-yard, or does some tom-fool thing which ordinarily lands him in the condemned cell. That's why I believe we ain't merely trying to find out how the corpse got where it did, but how it came to be a corpse at all."

" Any other reason ? It doesn't sound to me as if you'd get the police to sit up and take notice merely on a story like that. I suppose you'll begin to talk about coincidences. You always do."

" No ; at first sight it looks as if there were coincidences about this business, but they aren't really very startling.

February is the sort of month in which, you die of exposure if you sleep out much. It is also the sort of month in which people get pneumonia. And the Indescribable always likes its premiums to become payable on the first of January, I suppose for that reason—I always imagine them making quite a tidy income every year out of the people who get carried off by pneumonia before they have remembered to pay up. The only coincidence, as I've always told you, is that the two alleged discoveries of the body should have happened at exactly the same time in the morning. But it would be no good taking that to the police either. No, what seems to me rotten about the official view of the case, so to call it, is this idea that Colin Reiver suffered from loss of memory. That doesn't ring true, to me."

" But, dash it all, it's always happening, isn't it ? People found wandering about in country lanes and not knowing who they are. And this young man, apparently, had bad health from the start ; he had made it worse by soaking a goodish bit ; and he was a sort of ugly duckling at home. After that accident, he had come to think of himself as a complete failure, unwanted even at Dorn. Mightn't all that make him go soft in the head, in the long run ? "

" In the short run, yes ; in the long run, no. What I mean is, if he'd turned potty immediately after the accident, or soon after the accident, I wouldn't have minded so much. Or even if he'd turned potty on board ship, and started trying to lay out stokers with marlin-spikes, you could have pieced it together all right. But what we're asked to believe is something quite different. We're asked to believe that Colin Reiver did, for a short time after the accident, get into a sort of hysterical state in which he wanted to join the Foreign Legion and all sorts of foolishness. Then after that he was talked round, and persuaded to go on a sea-trip, like any ordinary young man who'd been overworking for schools. What happens to him ? Why, by his own account, given in that perfectly natural letter, he is quite cheerful and taking an interest in life. Then comes the news of his father's illness. Not, mark you, that he is dangerously ill, but just that he's got a cold which he can't shake off properly, and they are worried about his chest. Well, there's nothing much in that to make his son go off the deep end ; but if he had wanted to, why didn't he do it there and then ? Why didn't he literally go off the deep end—chuck himself overboard when they were out at sea? Lots of people do. But Colin Reiver seems to have made a dash for home—the act of a resolute man, not of a loony. On the way home, he must have behaved quite normally, or somebody would have noticed it, and they'd have communicated with his relatives. He starts out for home in the ordinary way; and then, quite suddenly, in the train, memory and reason desert him. He throws two suit-cases, a great-coat, a stick, his money, and his passport over a bridge, arrives at some station in this neighbourhood without being noticed by anybody—noticed, either as behaving oddly or as being Colin Reiver—and then takes to the road like a tramp. I put it to you, does that really work out?"

" N-no, not when you put it like that. It's too deliberate. I suppose he can't just have gone on the drink? That seems to be on the cards, though I suppose the family don't quite like to put it to themselves in that way."

" My good woman, have you ever tried to remain continuously drunk, without any money in your pocket, for a whole week-end, in the Lowlands of Scotland? And if so, have you managed to do it without anybody remembering having seen you while you were at it? When I say without any money, I don't mean that he might not have had a few odd shillings to pay for his drinks with; the point is he hadn't enough to bribe a policeman with. Of course, if one went to the police that's what they'd say—that he had got drunk and been robbed; and they'd comb out all the disreputable alleys in Pensteven, and watch the pawn-shops. But Colin Reiver had a perfectly good wrist-watch on him when he was found—rather an expensive one. And if he was laid out by a set of common thugs in the back streets of a town, how did he come to lie where he did, just outside his own home? If they knew who he was, what insolence! If they didn't, what a coincidence! No, there's design in all this; though, curse it it's a dashed complicated sort of design. The motive force comes from some stronger will, not from a habitual drunkard or a temporary lunatic."

" Well, all right, let's make it murder, then. You won't discuss suspicions, so I'll have to do that part myself. Let's suppose there is somebody due to benefit by Colin Reiver's life insurance, being heavily mentioned in Donald Reiver's will. He kills Colin, only to find that he has been premature ; the death is not covered by the insurance, because the premium hasn't been paid up. It therefore becomes necessary for him

69

to see that the premium *is* paid up, and thereupon he produces his corpse. Steady, though, I'd forgotten about Monday morning. Oh yes, he first produces the corpse on Monday morning, thinking that it is insured ; then, suddenly finding that it is not insured, he hides it for a day or two until Donald Reiver's cheque has been sent in. M'yes . . . "

" The operative word, for which I thank you, is *suddenly.* Dash it all, the murderer can hardly have satisfied himself about the position of the insurance in the interval between MacWilliam's running up to the house and his return, with witnesses, about twenty minutes later. It follows that he must have found out about the position of the insurance in the course of that night, the night of the twelfth. Then, why was he such a blazing fool as to leave the body lying about there for MacWilliam to find, instead of clearing it away while it was still dark ? No, I'm not saying this murder idea makes the whole puzzle easier to explain."

" You bet it doesn't. Meanwhile, you've got a long afternoon in front of you trying to get on to the trail—which probably means pub-crawling, if I know your methods. What about a pick of lunch to fortify us in the meanwhile ? Miles, I'm so longing for you to see the old ladies who are staying in this hotel ; they're such fun. I nearly burst yesterday evening, wanting to discuss them and having nobody to discuss them with. The old dears ! "

CHAPTER XI

THE DEVIL'S DIMPLE

THE BLAIRWHINNIE HOTEL—for as the Scots have churches that are dedicated to no saint, but named after the quarter of the town they are built in, so they have hotels named after no sort of cow, lion, or dragon, but simply after the town itself—the Blairwhinnie Hotel, as I was saying, is hydropathic in intention, but in practice exists for the benefit of week-enders from Glasgow, who like to sit in deck-chairs on a drive, watching the scenery. I will not describe the institution here, for it was thoroughly true to type, and its type is (north of the border) sufficiently common. Enough to say that it inspires in every detail a sense of massive comfort, but not of ease ; it appeals, let us say, to the orderly rather than to the

70

imaginative mind; neither its architecture, which is Scots-Baronial of the eighties, nor its furniture, which is Scots-unbreakable of any period, invites the patronage of the Bohemian world. That nameless wit who, adapting Aristotle, said that the moral is a mean between two extremes, the immoral and the Balmoral, might have pointed to the tone of the Blairwhinnie Hotel as erring, in this matter, by excess. True, in these degenerate days, a. few flashy people of the younger set drew up their cars at the door and ordered cocktails at tea-time, but they never stopped the night. There was a clash of atmospheres which made the thing unthinkable. All the same, it was not a Temperance Hotel, as most hydros are. It possessed, not only a licence, but a sort of indecorous excrescence fronting on a side-street, in which you could fill jug or bottle, and satisfy your thirst at a common bar. Needless to say, the two activities of the institution were kept severely apart.

But, if most of its *clientèle* came to the Blairwhinnie for contemplation rather than for health, the word HYDRO still figured on its gigantic signboard, and it was felt, therefore, as an advertisement, not as a criticism, when Dr. Purvis and his black bag were seen entering or leaving it. A thrill of health seemed to run through the veins of the guests when they reflected that, if anything *did* go wrong, there was always a reputation like Dr. Purvis's to fall back on. Not that, if the truth must be told, Dr. Purvis took the hydro part of the hotel quite as seriously as the management would have liked him to. It was his firm conviction that anybody who came to Blairwhinnie in search of health was a *malade imaginaire,* and he always insisted on visiting such patients at the very end of his morning round. So it was that Miles Bredon, after a day spent in fruitless telephone calls and a night spent in restless speculation, ran into the doctor at about half-past eleven the next morning, just when he and Angela were preparing to set out for the Devil's Dimple.

" Hullo, Doctor," he said, " you'll never guess where I'm going."

Dr. Purvis's face, when the information was given him, registered first bewilderment, and then a flicker of amusement. Bredon hastened to explain that he hadn't really been converted to the Major's theory about Bolshevik kidnappers; he only thought there was just the off chance that Colin might have taken refuge in this lonely fastness on his own account, and left traces of his sojourn. The doctor's face suddenly became grave. " You know, Mr. Bredon, I don't really think it's very safe for a couple of people to go and inspect the Devil's Dimple at this time of the year when they're strangers to the district. The climbing up there isn't any too good when there's frost about; though, of course, there's no danger if you know the right path to take. Look here, I'm engaged for the next half-hour with an old woman upstairs who's as healthy as a mule, but thinks there's something the matter with her. If you don't mind putting off your start, and being prepared for a late luncheon, I'll come up with you myself and do the honours. How would that be ? "

Bredon accepted with enthusiasm, more for the sake of cultivating the doctor's acquaintance than from any doubts of his own mountaineering capacities. It was noon when they set out, with Angela at the wheel, first along the populous main road, then into lonelier bypaths, where you had to climb well on to the bank if another car wanted to pass you. Low stone walls separated you from the bleak hillside with its melancholy promise of heather; the rare houses were little better than one-storey cabins ; the deep beds of the mountain streams were spanned by precarious bridges, that looked as if they would hardly survive the next spate. Even here, roads met you and crossed you, and at each turn your direction was carefully mapped out for you by signposts ; for the Scots do not like to admit that some parts of their country are thinly populated, and dig out the names of remote farm-houses to create the illusion of human neighbourhood. At last they left the road altogether, by way of a neglected gate hanging from one hinge, and started bumping over a mere track of cart-ruts, that dipped and rose towards the solitary horizon. The dry heather-branches rattled against their mudguards, and their tyres sputtered over the spongy peat. Old ewes, long unaccus-tomed to such disturbance, shied indignantly this way and that.

There comes a point beyond which you do not drive your car, even in Scotland. When they got out, it looked as if they had an endless moorland walk before them, but in scarcely ten minutes' time they were undeceived. The gradual upward slope ended in a sudden hill-brow, which fell away sharply for the best part of a thousand feet, and showed them an unexpected world of midgets swarming at their feet—midget cars toiling along narrow ribbons of road, midget kirks and school-houses and byres dotting the solitude.

They had to crane their necks over the verge before they could see what they had come to find—a platform of some five feet in width, not far below them, overhung by the entrance of a narrow cave. The climb down to it did not look, and in itself was not, formidable ; you were not at all likely to lose your foothold, but the imagination was daunted by the thought of what would happen if you did. " I'll go down first," announced Dr. Purvis, " because then I can direct you where to set your feet, and maybe lend a hand to ease the climb a bit. Don't start, please, till I shout up to you." Watching him, they could see that he was a practised climber ; and he was standing on the ledge a couple of minutes later, frowning in some surprise at the cave's mouth. " I believe you've struck lucky after all," they heard him cry out. " There's been somebody here not long since, anyway. Now, take the path I came down by, and catch your hands on the heather, not on the stones, for the stones are loose, some of them, but the heather holds."

Bredon insisted on going first, and made Angela promise not to follow till she had seen him land safely, so as to make sure it was fool-proof. She looked over, watching her husband's course, watching the tall, impassive figure of the doctor as he stood waiting underneath. She made a short job of her own climb, too excited at the prospect of discoveries in the cave to imagine the possibility of danger. " You see there ! " said Dr. Purvis, pointing to a couple of matches on the rank grass floor of the ledge, white and clean as if thrown there yesterday. " We shall want matches ourselves," he added ; " I'd have brought a torch with me if I'd thought of it." And he struck a light against the side of the cave, shielding it with his hand against the draught. " My word, though," he added, " you don't need to go inside the cave to see something you came to see. What do you make of that ? " On the rock, just beside him, at a point where it had been worn smooth by the dripping of an old spring, somebody had carved an inscription. It was not alone, to be sure ; for in summer weather the Devil's Dimple was a great place for picnics, and visitors had not been slow to leave their sign-manual. Here were a couple of interlaced hearts ; here was J. Elphinstone, of Glasgow. But a single inscription caught the eye, because it was newly made ; because, too, it was of some length, and a clearing had been made in the moss as if the writer had designed it to be still longer. Its legend ran :

73

" C. R., xiii.ii. (the date of the year followed). HERE HE
LIES." It looked as if space had been left at the end for
completing a quotation. The letters were in capitals, the
figures in straggling Roman script, except those of the year,
which were Arabic. The most interesting point about the
whole thing, at least to those who were now inspecting it,
was the fact that the final " i " of the " xiii " had been
scratched out, with a faint but unmistakable line, perhaps
two inches long, sloping up from left to right.

" Coo ! " said Angela.

Her husband bent down a little, and scanned the inscription
eagerly ; the erasion above all. Yes, you could not delude
yourself into the belief that it was some fault in the rock which
had been there all the time. You could even distinguish—or
was he being too subtle ?—the fact that the cross-wise line
was later in date than the figure " i " ; it seemed to have frayed
the edges of the original inscription. Inevitably a question
suggested itself. " Doctor," he said, " take a good look at this
and tell me one thing about it ; was the hand that scratched
this figure One the same hand that scratched it out ? "

A moment of excitement could not shake Dr. Purvis out
of his judiciousness. " For the hand, I'll not say ; but it's
perfectly plain the erasion was not done with the same instrument. It's a much thicker line, you can see for yourself. I'd
say that the inscription was made with the point of a very
sharp piece of flint ; it wouldn't be hard to find such pieces
round here."

" Not with a knife ? "

" A knife cuts with a very thin line, unless you're working
on wood and can scoop it out. No, this might be something
made of blunt metal, the buckle of a wrist-watch or something
like that ; but it'll hardly be a knife. You could do it with
a flint, though. But if the fellow that wrote that figure
Thirteen remembered afterwards that he'd got the date wrong,
and wanted to take out one stroke of it, he must have mislaid
his instrument by then, or he couldn't take the trouble to use
the same one. He used something with a broader point ; and
something softer, I would say—or it may be he couldn't get
so good a grip on it and couldn't scratch so deep with it."

" And do you really believe it was the same person who
did both ? "

" Eh, it's you that are the detective, Mr. Bredon ; I'm only
an old saw-bones that has to concern himself with flesh and

74

blood, not with flinty tables like this one. I'll only say that this is a lonely sort of a place in the wintertime, and it's not very natural to imagine that folk have been queueing up to see the Devil's Dimple in the sort of weather we've been having. Let's see, Thursday—it's only ten days since those figures were cut; or eleven, if you're going to make out that it was just a slip writing Thirteen in the first instance."

● "I suppose we're not going inside the cave at all," Angela murmured from behind them, in the demure voice of a small girl disappointed of a treat.

The doctor stood aside politely. "Won't you go in first, Mrs. Bredon? If you hadn't reminded us, we might have argued here all day."

Angela hung back, nevertheless. "I suppose it's dashed cowardly of me, but I'm not sure I wouldn't rather you went in front of me, Miles darling. It's just the tiniest bit grooly, isn't it?"

A cave has, for all of us, an atmosphere of inviting yet terrifying mystery. The anthropologists would tell us, no doubt, that it is due to race-memory, carrying us back to times when the question, who or what lived in this particular retreat, was a life and death question to the knocker at the door. The cave of the Cyclops, the cave of Ali Baba, the cave of Cacus, pirates' caves, brigands' caves, smugglers' caves, and the caves where Jacobites or Covenanters lay hid from their pursuers— all our early reading reinfected the imagination with deliberate horror. A cave which somebody has been using lately bids us pause still longer on its threshold; and if evidence that the somebody is dead ought to make us certain that he is no longer there, it does not always have quite that effect . . . especially when it is somebody whose corpse has had, by general testimony, an uncomfortable habit of disappearing and reappearing at intervals.

Miles, however, did not share these scruples. Bending his head a little, to avoid the low arch of the roof, he stumbled forward a step or two, lit a match, and peered at the flickering scene around him. One eminently practical detail his eye took in—a candle-end perched on a shelf of rock about the level of his own arm. He piloted the match towards it, and was rewarded first with a splutter, then with a steady flame. By the side of the upright candle-end was a second, rather longer, which lay on its side; there was also a box of matches, about two-thirds full, of a Scottish brand which remains obtrusively

Scottish in its outward appearance, though it has been bought
up by an English firm long since; you buy it in Scotland
everywhere. The shelf was not all level, but was of a convenient width, so that it had naturally been used by the
occupant as his larder and store-cupboard. There was a tinned
tongue which had been opened, but remained in good preser-
vation—surprisingly, until you remembered that in this sunless
spot, with frosty weather outside, there was no excuse for meat
to go bad. There was a small tin of biscuits, almost empty,
and the paper wrapping, quite empty, which had belonged
to a sizeable slab of milk-chocolate. Nothing else appeared in
the way of nourishment, but there were one or two toilet
accessories; a tooth-brush, such as Bredon had desiderated on
the person of the corpse, and a tube of tooth-powder, sucked
almost dry. It was a common enough brand of tooth-
powder; but Bredon remembered with a certain thrill that
he had seen just such a tube on the washing-stand of Colin
Reiver's room, when he turned up the corner of a dust-
sheet to examine it. A fire had been made with dry twigs in
one corner of the cave, though only for warmth, it seemed,
since there was no kettle or cooking utensil. No clothes were
to be found, no literature, no comforts; the cave-dweller had
confined himself to the barest necessities.

"What about that food, Doctor?" asked Bredon. "How
long would you say it would keep a man going for, just that
much?"

"Well, if you spaced it out properly, I wouldn't say but you
might last three or four days on it, though I wouldn't say it
would be very comfortable in cold weather. He's eaten the
most part of the tongue, you see. But what will last a man
if it's spaced out properly is not at all the same thing as what
will last him if he eats when he feels hungry, and eats as
much as he feels like. There's very few men that wouldn't
get through that amount of food in a day, if you left them to
themselves, or a day and a half anyhow. And the body, you
know, didn't seem to have wanted for nourishment when they
examined it. Of course, he may have had more than what
he's left traces of."

"He'd have left the tins lying about, wouldn't he?"

"He might, but you've to remember that a man looking
down over a height has a great tendency to throw things over,
merely to see them drop."

"Oh yes, that's true enough. But I must say I should

have expected more traces of food to be left about. It fits in, though, in a way. Angela," he added suddenly, " what's the thing you most notice the absence of, in this *ménage* ? "

Angela knew well enough when seriousness was expected of her. She puckered her forehead, took a look round as if visualizing the cave in occupation ; then she said, " Soap."

" M'yes," admitted her husband. " Well, it just shows. Now, Dr. Purvis, I want to take your advice, not as a doctor, but as a resident and as a friend of the family. What are we going to do with these things ? Cart them away and destroy them ? Or give them to the family ? Or leave them here ? "

" I'd leave them here in case you want to show them to somebody else, if I were you. You can always take them away later on, when you're through with the enquiry. And you needn't be afraid of other people coming up and finding them without being meant to ; there won't be a hiker or a picnic party going this way before April ; you may be certain of that."

The advice was adopted, and they passed out of the cave again, giving one more scrutiny as they did so to the pathetic scrawl at the entrance. " Here he lies," read Dr. Purvis, with a pleasant reverence of manner.

" I know that," replied Bredon, with something of bitterness in his voice. " But, confound it all, the question is, Who ? "

CHAPTER XII

ANGELA MEETS THE COUNTY

THE BLAIRWHINNIE HOTEL, after the manner of hotels everywhere, had the kind of garden behind it which nobody—not even the people who stayed there and enjoyed staying there—would have tolerated in the neighbourhood of a private house. There is no reason why hotel gardens should not be beautiful ; it is a mere fact of observation that they are not. The garden we are here concerned with, like all such gardens, had wide paths with very clean scrunchy gravel, and lawns where nobody played croquet, and depressing plantations of ferns in enormous concrete jugs, and long lines of dusty-looking laurels, and summer-houses so uncomfortable that the management had given up the pretence, and kept hoses and mowing-machines in them. There were trees, but among them the monkey-

77

puzzler, aspidistra of the forest, predominated; there were
flowers, but flowers that looked as if they had been stolen from
a public park, staring geraniums and tired, knobby begonias.
The gardener apparently did nothing but mow the lawns and
scuffle the paths with a rake. The beds were edged, for the
most part, with large lumps of stone, painted white. The
whole was pervaded by a heavy smell of petrol.

In these repulsive surroundings, but happily unconscious of
them, Bredon and Dr. Purvis walked up and down after luncheon; for Dr. Purvis had stayed to luncheon, and admitted
that he could afford a quiet half-hour or so with a cigar to
digest it in. Bredon was fascinated by his curious deliberate-
ness of speech; a quality which, in others, might have suggested a furtive habit of mind, or a pedantry of outlook—with
him, you felt it belonged to one who was an epicure in truth.
He showed no disinclination to be " pumped " about the tragedy of Colin Reiver, and proved unexpectedly useful as a
source of information.

" You told me this morning that Colin Reiver's body did
not look as if he had wanted for nourishment," Bredon was
saying. " Did you see it yourself ? "

" I saw it; but not professionally, you'll understand.
They rang me up when it was found, but I was away then
looking after a poor fellow that had had an accident. They
were in a hurry, naturally, so they called in a colleague of
mine, Dr. MacLaughlin from Pensteven. It was he examined
the body, and made the autopsy for the Procurator Fiscal."

" Could he have been mistaken, do you think, about the
time of death ? "

" He said the condition of *rigor mortis* had set in when he
made the examination. That's not a thing it's very easy to be
mistaken about. But if you ask me whether doctors are always
right, Mr. Bredon, well, I could tell you tales out of school
that would surprise you. Whatever way it was, I didn't see
the body myself till it was too late for me to be of any use.
I didn't go up to Dorn till I'd finished my morning round;
and that would be about noon, as you've seen for yourself.
I went there more as a friend of the family."

" Well, then, there are several things you could probably
tell me about it which would interest me enormously, though
I hadn't the heart to ask about them while I was staying up
at Dorn. Here's one—was Colin Reiver naturally pale, so
that his face in death, for example, would not look very much

different from his face in sleep? I suppose it would be noticeably pale when you saw it? "

" He never had any complexion, Mr. Bredon, rather a leaden sort of look about him always. But, of course, in death what colour he had had left him—it's not quite the same thing."

" Of course not—thanks. Now, did you see what he had in his pockets when he was found, or hear any account of it? "

" I asked to see; for I was puzzled about the whole thing, naturally—you'll recollect I was one of the people who were called out by MacWilliam on the Monday. Well, there was very little found in his pockets; scarcely anything at all. Just a few shillings in silver, and a handkerchief, and a penny packet of pipe-cleaners."

" Pipe-cleaners! And no pipe or tobacco. He smoked, I suppose? "

" More than was good for him, but it was a pipe mostly. I was surprised myself that it wasn't found on him, because if a tramp had been by he'd have left the pipe and taken the silver."

" And what were his clothes like? I understand they didn't suggest that he was on tramp—weren't the kind of clothes one would choose, I mean, if one was going to rough it. Did they look as if he'd been out in all sorts of weathers? Were the shoes clean? Had he grown a beard? You'll understand that what we found this morning has made me interested in all that."

" About the shoes, you couldn't tell very easily; there were bits of straw caught in them, as if he'd been walking, but no mud. The collar was soiled, and his other clothes stained rather, very much as they might have been stained by living in a damp cave up there. But he was shaved clean enough."

" Straw in the boots? Yes—anything else obvious in the way of grit or fluff? Occasionally one can get a hint from those tiny things."

" Well, just here and there you could see wisps of straw sticking to his clothes, just small ones."

" Straw, eh? Well, there are lots of places where he might have picked that up. Then, let's see, he had a wrist-watch on, they told me; that had stopped, I suppose? "

" Naturally."

" At . . .? "

" Half-past three."

79

·" Before he died—well before he died—or an hour or two after; that looks as if he hadn't been to bed. I should think even a man going to bed in a cave, on a supper of tongue and milk-chocolate, would wind up his watch; one's so dreadfully a creature of habit. I wish all watches were made to register twenty-four hours instead of twelve. Or, in this case, even seventy-two. But, of course, it may have been out of order."

Dr. Purvis smiled in a rather embarrassed way. " You'll think I'm setting up to be a detective myself, I'm afraid, but I'll tell you what I did ; I just gave a turn or two to the winder of the watch, and it was going fine."

" I wish I could take you into partnership, Doctor. You seem to have all the right instincts. Well, of course it won't help us to choose between Sunday night and Tuesday night as the date of death. But it defeats me rather, why the watch should have stopped just then. He was still alive in the afternoon of Tuesday, and he's almost certain to have looked at his watch once or twice ; every civilized creature does. And every civilized creature who finds his watch has stopped winds it up again, though it's no good really, without the opportunity of setting it. So it looks more as if it had stopped after the death, at three in the morning. That certainly suggests that he was out all night, somewhere. Possibly by the roadside, in a sort of faint. I say, Doctor, wouldn't you have expected some good Samaritan to have come along, and at least noticed him lying there, if he was there four or five hours, perhaps longer ? "

" There's a lot more priests and Levites on the road these days. And small blame to them, for some of the folk you would meet on the road late at night are not people to stop your car for. I would think they'd just pass him by, taking him for a tramp asleep ; it was a cold night, you see, but not absolutely freezing.."

" Still, when there was all that fuss in the papers . . . A motor head-light always shows up a patch of stones so, and a dark figure against it is easily seen. I tell you, Doctor, it's the complete silence of the whole country-side about seeing the young man or hearing of the young man during those four or five days that beats me altogether."

The conversation was in reality longer ; but much of it does not need to be set down here, since it covered ground which we have already traversed. Angela, meanwhile, who had broken away because she knew that a conversation *tête-à-tête* makes men more communicative, was captured by the reigning queen of Blairwhinnie Hotel society, Mrs. Wauchope. This was an old lady whose taste for frequenting hydros could only be ascribed to a passion for noting the oddities of human nature. She belonged, you knew at once, to the governing class, or what used to be the governing class; she was so sure of herself, so outspoken, so careless of all the niceties of good breeding as these are laboriously instilled by books of etiquette. She shone among the Glasgow ladies like a diamond among sham jewels; you knew at once that she was on calling terms with the county, and might have been staying at Dorn if she had taken the trouble to ask herself. She was doing embroidery at a great pace on a large cane chair close to the garden entrance, and shouted to Angela as she left the dining-room.

" Come here, my dear," she said, " and be seen talking to me. When you're my age, you'll know what it is always to want to be seen talking to somebody thirty years younger than yourself; it shows the old bodies that you're not altogether on the shelf yet. You'd better get your knitting first, though; I hate having people looking at my embroidery and saying to themselves how ugly it is. Now, don't go away and not come back." Nor was Angela unwilling; Mrs. Wauchope, for all her domineering manner, was infinitely likeable, and she might even be useful in providing information about the family at Dorn, its life and its history. For I need hardly say that she knew all the ins and outs of every old family in Scotland; who married whom, and who bought which place from whom, and why and when. The Scots have no affectation of despising pedigrees.

" Well, and what are you two doing at the Blairwhinnie ? " Mrs. Wauchope went on (she very seldom stopped), as Angela rejoined her. " As for health, it's quite easy to see *you* never had a day's illness in your life. And neither of you looks the kind of person who would come and settle down among a set of old frumps such as we are here, merely for the love of the thing. Now, I'll tell you what my guess was, just so as to give you time to make up a story if you don't want to tell me the truth. I think one of you, I'm not quite sure which, is writing a novel, and has come down here to study frump-life in its native haunts. I saw you talking us all over and laughing at us at dinner last night. *Who's that old witch over there ?* you were saying as you looked across at my table.

81

Now, come on ; don't tell me neither of you is writing a novel ; I should be dreadfully disappointed."

Angela felt the only thing to do was to make a clean breast of it. Mrs. Wauchope was hugely delighted. " Really, that's a most sensible way of making a living," she said. " I always have such an admiration for people who manage to cheat insurance companies, because the people I go to are complete ogres, and you might as well try to get blood from a stone. So Donald Reiver went to the Indescribable, did he ? He would, of course ; he always wants to get the last ounce out of everything. Such a prootty place, Dorn ; you haven't been up there ? Oh, you must certainly get your husband to take you over there. That poor boy—what an extraordinary story, wasn't it ? Of course, there was always something wrong about that boy ; he was never quite normal. I expect you know that story about when he was small ? "

" No, I don't think I heard anything about that. I never heard the Reivers mentioned in my life till this business cropped up."

" Ah, of course, you're from the South. Well, it's a story I don't like to tell, not because I disapprove of gossip, but because I do hate having to use long words—don't you ?— when I'm not certain whether I'm going to pronounce them right. Well, Colin Reiver, when he was quite small, only five or six, was found to be a pyromaniac. Is that how you pronounce it ? Anyhow, I can't spell it, so you'll have to make the most of it."

" You couldn't have a try ? Because, you see, I shall want to look it up in the dictionary afterwards to find out what it means."

Mrs. Wauchope crowed heartily. " I do like honesty," she said. " I assure you I often used to look up the long words I came across in reading novels ; but nowadays they all seem to mean something so dreadful that I don't bother—I just blush and go on. However, pyromania—I'm nearly certain it is pyromania—isn't that kind of thing at all. It's perfectly respectable, though very uncomfortable for society at large, and, of course, hell for the insurance companies. Means you have an uncontrollable impulse to go round setting light to things, buildings for choice, and the odd thing is that afterwards you don't know you've done it. Like sleep-walking, only different. Well, they caught Colin Reiver at it two or three times when he was quite small, and it was very awkward, because Dorn would burn like match-wood, and some of the stuff there's really rather valuable, you know. However, they all said he would grow out of it, and sent him to school just like any other boy, and I'm bound to say nothing dreadful came of it, though we all said he ought to wear an extinguisher on his back, like the man in the advertisement, don't you know? But it's very hard to know, isn't it, whether one really does grow out of these things? He was certainly a very repressed, unforthcoming sort of boy, and very little comfort to Donald Reiver while he lived. Dr. Purvis always said he ought to be put down; you've met Dr. Purvis? He has a mania for telling the truth; I expect it really is a kind of disease, truthomania, or whatever one would call it. And far more dangerous, often, than setting light to things."

"Isn't there a curse on the family, or something rather distinguished like that?" asked Angela. She did not want Mrs. Wauchope to desert the subject of the Reivers too soon.

"If you call it a curse, never to be succeeded by your eldest son, yes," admitted Mrs. Wauchope. "But really so many eldest sons are nincompoops of one kind or another that I'm not sure it isn't a blessing, really. As a matter of fact, inheriting any estate is a curse in these days. Look at Henry Reiver, now—that's the cousin who'll succeed; let's see, who did he marry? I think it was an artist's model, I'm not sure; anyhow, it was the kind of person one was supposed not to marry in those days, and I know Donald Reiver made a great song and dance about it. She's dead now. He'll have a job to keep the place going at all, by the time he's paid the death duties. If Colin Reiver had succeeded, and only lived a year or two, without marrying, of course, they would have been something frightful. Henry Reiver is something like a curse, I grant you, and I don't suppose the people on the estate look forward to his succeeding much. He's got the temper of the devil; always had. Still, Colin would have ruined the place, there's no doubt of that; unless, of course, he'd married a wife who would have looked after it for him. There was a story at one time that he was in love with Dr. Purvis's daughter—oh yes, didn't you know? He's a widower; always has been—I don't quite mean that, but he was a widower when he came here. Quite a prootty little thing too, the daughter; but I don't suppose there was anything in that really. She'd have made a good wife for him, if she could have kept him away from the bottle. Well now, my dear, it's very kind of you to sit chatting to me like this, but I really must go up and rest. I preserve my complexion, you see, as a kind of ancient monument. I can see you believe it's done on that modern principle of spraying stuff on, which they say is so good for old buildings, but it isn't that, honour bright. I'll see you later on, and don't you and your husband discuss me at dinner any more ; it makes me so nervous that I can hardly remember which hand to put my knife in. Ah, there's your husband coming back. Tell him he positively must take you up to Dorn one day."

Bredon and Purvis were sauntering back from their stroll. " There's just one more thing I'd like to ask," said Bredon, " though it's on a rather different subject, and perhaps you won't be able to tell me, or won't want to.' But have you any idea whether the provisions of Mr. Donald Reiver's will are known publicly ? . . . One has to consider these things."

" I can't tell you for certain, Mr. Bredon. But there's no harm in saying that the old gentleman made a will that night he was taken so bad, the Sunday night ; and he had it witnessed by the butler and myself. So it's not likely he wanted it talked about, you see, or he would have asked Mr. Hemerton. But, after all, what's that but guess-work ? "

CHAPTER XIII

A LECTURE ON NUMERALS

" WELL," SAID BREDON, dropping into the cane chair, " so you've got off with the Empress Eugénie."

" No good, my angel ; we were perfectly wrong about her ; she's not an old dreary in the least. The great detective badly astray for once. She talks nineteen to the dozen, but it's all good, high-class stuff, fresh from Mayfair. Also, she's a dear. Also, she's been rather interesting about the Reiver family, whom she appears to have known in their various cradles ; so you needn't think you're the only one who's been doing any work this afternoon."

" Go ahead. As you know, I'm not easily shocked. What about the Reivers ? "

" Well, for one thing, Colin Reiver was a—oh, bother, I've been and forgotten the word ! Would it be a pilomaniac ? "

" Not pyro, by any chance ? "

84

" That was it. It's repulsive of you to look as if you knew what it means. Well, that's something you didn't find out by staying two nights at Dorn and leaving me to vegetate among the begonias. Miles, don't tell me you're not excited about it, or I shall cry."

" I am excited about it. You mean, of course . . . "

" I mean that I'm going to have the first say this time, because it's my discovery. Colin Reiver was alive on Tuesday night, because it was he who set light to the straw-stack. There ! "

" If that's your idea, it will probably interest you to know that there were bits of straw sticking in his clothes when the body was found. Dr. Purvis has just been telling me about it."

" Oo, that fits in beautifully. Miles, aren't you pleased ? "

" I'm thankful for anything about this business that looks as if it fitted in at all. Not but what you're rather leaping to conclusions, you know. Let's say the burning of the straw-stack round about the time of Colin's death is a circumstance which would naturally be connected with his early tendencies by those acquainted with both sets of facts. Not quite so snappy as your way of putting it, but still. . . . Now, what if I tell you, once more on the authority of Dr. Purvis, that Colin Reiver was a regular smoker, and had indeed a packet of pipe-cleaners in his pocket at the time of his death, but neither pipe nor tobacco was found on him ? Nor even matches—which are useful to light ricks with. As also, that he had no money on him, except a little silver which he carried loose in his pockets—oh, but we knew that before. Well, what about it, anyhow ? "

" It looks as if he had lost his great-coat. That's what you want me to say, isn't it ? "

" Exactly. Only I think we might go further, and say it looks as if he had been parted unexpectedly from his great-coat. A traveller, for example, may put his money and his smokeables into his great-coat pockets—or overcoat pockets ; it may have been no more than an aquascutum—because he knows that he will be wearing it or keeping it close beside him, and he will be wanting to get at his money or his pipe at frequent intervals. For a man tramping along roads, perhaps even living in caves, not so good. Let's see, what else was there ? "

" Oo, you asked me in that cave what I thought was most

missing. And I said soap. I was too well trained to ask you about it at the time, but you might tell me whether I was right or not."

" Not quite. What about a razor, and shaving things ? "

" I never thought of that."

" Precisely. Because you're a woman. A man would have thought of them."

" Miles, I believe you're being cryptic. I say, what about that cave, anyhow ? It was pretty smart of Major Henry to think of the Devil's Dimple, wasn't it ? "

" I don't know. Evidently it's a kind of local side-show, and it wouldn't be very difficult for two people to think of it independently when they asked themselves, What is the best out-of-doors hiding-place round here ? But it bothers me, this idea of Colin Reiver wanting to go and hide up there, in the sort of weather it was. Why hide, anyhow ? And if he was hiding, why come down and hang about the ancestral estate, and die there ? It's all dashed queer, whatever way you look at it."

" Still, you're not going to say that C. R. was somebody else, with the date and all ? And the quotation—wasn't it part of the poem you'd been reading in that Stevenson book ? He must have been cracked, Miles ; and how often am I to tell you that if a person's cracked it's no good starting in to ask *why* he did this and that. I suppose one just behaves like a person in a dream."

" Colin Reiver seems to have behaved like a person in a nightmare, if you ask me. Well then, having written up the date as the thirteenth of February, which was just what we wanted to know, why does he go and spoil it all by scratching out the last One, so as to make it look as if it had been the twelfth ? "

" Hang it all, one often does that. I've got the same kind of muddle-headedness ; I always think the day is one later in the month than it really is, and if you ever read my letters you'd know that I quite often correct it. Or again, it may have been just an accidental scratch in the rock, that crossing out."

" Heaven help the woman, she talks as if it didn't make any difference. *Unless* Colin Reiver was the same kind of mug you say you are, then it was the thirteenth when he wrote that, and it isn't true that his dead body was discovered by the roadside that morning. At least, probably not ; he isn't likely to have scratched that inscription before starting out on his walk."

" Why not ? "

" Because he'd have been working by candle-light. And a man writing by candle-light keeps well inside the cave, so as to avoid draughts. When a man writes just in the mouth of the cave, it means that he is using daylight, and probably fairly full daylight, or the shadows would balk him."

" Yes, I suppose so. It would have saved us all a world of trouble if he had written ordinary English figures instead of Roman ones. Come to think of it, why didn't he ? They're shorter."

" But they've got curves in them. I suppose they never let you scratch your name on a desk at school ; otherwise you'd know that one can go on carving and carving as long as it's all straight ups and downs and sideways. It's when you get to the curve that you have trouble. The Latins, my dear Angela, since you insist on having a lecture in palæography, started by scraping inscriptions on tombs and things, so their figures were mostly straight. The Arabs, using pen and ink, could afford curves, and they did. Colin Reiver was handicapped already by curvy initials ; he wasn't going to waste any labour over the figures—until he came to the year, of course. A year looks so frightfully long when you write it out in Roman figures ; there'd hardly have been room. But notice this—getting the date wrong meant, in this case, having all the sweat of carving an extra figure and then scratching it out. Knowing that, wouldn't he have taken the trouble to remember the date accurately before he started ? "

" Well then, let's say it was the thirteenth. And there was already an accidental scratch on the rock, crossing his final One, but he didn't notice it, perhaps because he was finishing up late in the evening. Or his tool slipped down the rock by mistake after he'd finished. Or—well, any other ' or ' would mean that somebody else has been in the cave since, wouldn't it ? At least, I can't think of any reason why Colin Reiver, having taken all the trouble to write up the date accurately, should then take the trouble to lie about it."

" I know. That's what makes it all so confoundedly interesting. And if there was somebody in the cave after Colin left it, who thought it worth while to fake the date, what sort of person was it ? "

" Donald Reiver for choice. But he'd hardly go gallivant-

87

ing over the moors when he's only just out of bed. Failing him, somebody who is going to benefit by his will."

"When shall I begin to teach you habits of accuracy? Not somebody who is going to benefit by his will, but somebody who *thought* he was going to benefit by the will. And that makes it all much more complicated. It *might* be possible for us to find out who is the heir to that insurance money, if Donald Reiver had died. Though he has inconsiderately gone on living, we might still find out; we might ask him, for example. But we should be no further on, because the intruder we want is an intruder who *thought* there was money coming in; and our identification can only be done by guesswork. Meanwhile, it will hardly have escaped your attention . . ."

"That the faking was done the wrong way round? Yes, I *had* noticed that. So long as the date stood as 'thirteen,' the Company was liable under the terms of the policy. When it was changed to twelve, it was no longer clear whether the Company was liable or not. Inference, that some director of the Indescribable, acting on your instructions, came up here and changed the thirteen into twelve."

"An excellent idea; but any one of them would have to slim for months, you know, before he could climb down that rock. Meanwhile, as you say, it is rather difficult to see why anybody who wanted to *defer* the date of Colin Reiver's death should have scratched out the last One. More useful, one would think, to try and join up the bottoms of the last two Ones, so as to make it look like XIV."

"Miles, this is rather far-fetched, but I suppose it couldn't be a sort of double-bluff? I mean, suppose Colin Reiver really wrote up XII. Then somebody comes along who thinks it's in his interest to make the Company pay up. Shall he just scratch in an extra I? That would be too obvious; probably he would get the spacing wrong, or his toll would be slightly different from Colin's, or somehow his addition, under the expert's microscope, would give itself away. How can he divert suspicion? Why, by adding his I *and then scratching it out*; that will divert suspicion from himself by throwing it on to the other side. How's that?"

"You know, Angela, that's far from being an uninteresting suggestion of yours."

"I am rather clever, aren't I?"

"Exactly, you're rather clever; that's what makes you so

useful to me. Because I can use the way your mind works as a thermometer of the way other people's minds work ; criminals', for example. The sort of criminal one comes up against in insurance work is, as a rule, rather clever. Now, if you had been *very* clever . . ."

" Here ! Come off it. Do you mean to say you think my idea's a dud ? I suppose you'll say things don't really happen like that ; it's what you always do say when you can't think of any other way of crabbing my inspirations."

" In this case, I don't care whether things do really happen like that. All I really care about is whether a rather clever person like you *thinks* that is the sort of way things really happen ; if so, well and good—it is the kind of thing that *might* happen in real life. The only point I'm not quite clear about is why, on your supposition, the erasion was so faint ; you'd have expected a firmer erasion, so that there could be no question of mere accident about it. Meanwhile, keep steadily in view the fact that there was no razor in the cave."

" What you mean is, if Colin Reiver had really been in the cave as early as Sunday the twelfth, his beard would have grown to a noticeable length by Tuesday night. . . . Oh, but then we're not sure it was Tuesday night. Curse the man ! Let's see—you mean that if he had been in the cave as early as the daylight hours of Monday the thirteenth, his beard would have grown more by Tuesday night ; is that it ? "

" Yes, I dare say that's what I mean. Let me try you with another point : Dr. Purvis tells me that the face of the corpse was dead white. Does that convey anything to you ? "

" Without much experience of corpses, I should say that was rather what one would be apt to expect."

" Well, well. No, I'm *not* going to tell you any more about what I suspect, because it's vital to me to be able to see the whole thing through the eyes of somebody who doesn't share my suspicions ; otherwise I shan't see the evidence straight, it will come to me distorted through my own mental lens. Did the Empress tell you anything else of interest ? What's her name, by the way ? "

" Mrs. Wauchope. Oh, she chatted a lot about the family, you know ; said Henry Reiver—that's the cousin, isn't it ?— had the temper of a devil, and it was lucky for him Colin died before his father, because otherwise there would have been double death duties to pay. Then, let's see, she said at one time there was an idea Colin was going to fall in love with

89

Dr. Purvis's daughter. Also that Dr. Purvis has a mania for telling the truth. Oh yes, and that she preserves her complexion by going upstairs to rest in the afternoon."

" The doctor's daughter ? "

" Mrs. Wauchope, you fool. Miles, I shall enjoy introducing you to that woman. You've no idea how she flattens you out and rolls over you, so to speak, in conversation. It will do you all the good in the world. That boy seems to have got a telegram for you ; at least, he's looking to see whether you're the right man. You may open it, if you'll apologize to me first. Any news ? "

" No, just the usual absence of news," replied her husband, frowning. " The Company uses a private agency, you see, for making routine enquiries in a case like this ; saves me no end of trouble. But do they do their work well ? They swear there's no trace of anybody giving the name of Reiver having landed at Southampton during the last fortnight."

" Perhaps he'd forgotten his name, if he lost his memory."

" Yes, but they usually put it on one's passport. Wonderful what a lot of red-tape there is about the passport office. No, don't say he might have landed under an assumed name, either, unless you're prepared to explain how he came to have a borrowed passport. Lord, I suppose we shall have to get the steamship company to wireless the captain of the *Squandermania*. I hate doing it, because it begins to make the whole thing public. I've half a mind to cable the consul at Madeira on my own. By Jove, I believe I will."

" Would he know anything ? "

" He will, if I'm right in what I think's happened.. I suppose I really ought to do it through the enquiry people, but I don't suppose the Company will mind. What a sweat, though. Hullo ! I believe that's the Hemertons' car."

It was, indeed, the powerful Tarquin in which Bredon had been driven to the hotel the day before ; and it was Vincent Hemerton who climbed out of it. He was plainly bursting with news, and as soon as the introductions were over he launched out on it : " You know, it's the most extraordinary thing ; you remember Major Henry, that day he came to tea and let loose his preposterous theories, saying as he went away that he was going to investigate this business of poor Colin's death on his own ? Well, we've just had a letter from him by this afternoon's post to say he's made a find which will, he thinks, be of the utmost importance. One never quite knows what Henry Reiver will or won't think important. But as he asked me to go over I felt it would be only decent to look in. He didn't say anything about you; but I'm sure he wouldn't mind your coming along, as you're so much interested in this tangle of ours. Perhaps Mrs. Bredon would like to come along too? You ought to meet the Major, Mrs. Bredon; he's quite a character."

But Angela, as she explained, had letters to write before the post went, and it was Bredon alone who joined Hemerton in his mission. "I wonder what the Major can possibly have come across," he said. "It looks to me as if I should have to take a back seat, with such an energetic amateur making rival investigations. I hope he's got proof of his kidnapping conspiracy, all complete."

Hemerton gave a short laugh. "I should think it's probably a mare's nest whatever it is."

They took the turn towards Pensteven when they reached the bottom of the drive, and in a few minutes were hooting their way through the leisurely population of the old town. "They want automatic signals here," said Vincent Hemerton.

CHAPTER XIV

WHAT THE MAJOR FOUND

HENRY REIVER'S WAS a house that did not seem to have quite made up its mind whether it was the last house in Pensteven or the first house outside it; whether it was a rather isolated villa or a rather attenuated manor-house. It was trim and tidy, but definitely not attractive; built of stone which was ruined by being pointed, ruined still further by being pointed to look as if it was natural; rough surfaces bulged unpleasantly from unpleasantly straight lines of mortar. The window-frames and staircases gloried in the nakedness of a pitch-pine which, in any other country, would have been decently veiled with paint. The front door faced you down a wide flight of steps, for the house was carved out of the side of a hill; on a small square of grass opposite to it rose a huge white flagstaff, with which the Major indulged his patriotism when national events or anniversaries gave him the opportunity. He was an enthusiastic gardener, of the kind that loves to make rare exotics flourish on a soil which Nature seems to have designed for heather, bracken, thistles, and " Stinking Willie." He dug, pruned, and weeded, not to delight the eye with colour and symmetry, but to beat records and inform the *Rhododendron-lover's Monthly* that he had done so. You felt that the terraces at Dorn would be transmuted into the semblance of a Himalayan ravine when he succeeded.

He met them in a hall overgrown with barometers and antelopes' heads. " Come in and sit down," he said. " I want to tell you about it first, before I show you the things. The doctor will be here in a moment; I wanted him—tell you why when he comes. Dr. Purvis, yes; can't stand that ass MacLaughlin. Now, Hemerton, you thought me a fool when I said I was going to search the hedgerows; saw it in your face."

" Well, I don't deny I'd have betted against your finding anything, Major. Especially, of course, if you're right in thinking there's been foul play—I'm still waiting to be convinced of that. If there has been, why couldn't the people concerned make a neater job of it ? Now, if I committed a crime, I flatter myself that anybody would have a job digging out the traces. Thank you, just a spot. Well, tell us about it, do ; I thought you wouldn't mind my bringing Bredon, because naturally he's interested."

" Perfectly right. I'd have asked you myself if I'd known you were still in the district. They didn't tell me. Ah, here's Purvis ; one moment while I go out and fetch him in. Don't spill that on the carpet, Mr. Bredon ; pre-war." He shuffled out and back again, full of self-importance ; the doctor came in with a twinkle in his eye, as if he, for one, were convinced that the great discovery would prove a delusion. " I'm pressed for time, Major," he said. " Let's know the worst at once. No, thanks, not between meals."

" Well, this was my point," the Major explained. " One thing's clear, the poor boy's body was carted about like a sack of coals. Now, you can do that two ways : you can go quicker in a car, but you can move more secretly without one, because you can leave the road and trek across country. Now, my gentlemen weren't the kind of people, if I'm right about 'em, to commandeer a car easily ; couldn't be seen driving it, either, without suspicion. *And*, mark you, there's no trace of a car having been about on the Monday morning ; 'cept yours, Doctor, and yours, Hemerton, when you went to look for the body. How did I find that out ? Asked the police. They made special enquiries, both ends ; nothing on the main road. Took the side-roads one after another, asked at all the villages ; nothing doing. Very well then, they didn't take him in a car ; carried him across country ; that's plain, huh ? "

" Yes, all right so far, if you grant that there was any *they*," Hemerton admitted.

" Very well ; now, they didn't cart him off down the road— stands to reason ; they'd have been seen. They went through the hedge ; must have. Which hedge ? Not the one into the park—too dangerous ; anybody might have found them. You'd have seen 'em, Purvis, if they'd been lugging him off that way. That means they went through the hedge on the further side. Which is the nearest track ? The one that goes off over the moors, towards the Devil's Dimple. Going to have a look at the Devil's Dimple myself to-morrow."

" I've been over there this morning," Bredon put in. " Dr. Purvis came with me. We'll tell you about that later, Major."

" There you are, then. Now, on the night between Sunday and Monday, there was a bit of a thaw, plenty of slush on the ground. If the police had known their job, and searched the other side of the hedge, they'd have found tracks, bound to. Instead, they went fooling about looking for tyre-marks on the road. I didn't know anything about it ; nobody called me in. On the night between Tuesday and Wednesday, it was a lot warmer ; round about fifty. So there was no reason why they should have left tracks ; in any case, they'd have been obliterated before I came round looking for 'em. No use, then, unless you could find some permanent traces—if they'd made a fire, for example. Or, just possibly, they might have left something behind. Sounded unlikely ; you thought so, Hemerton. But, I said to myself, you start lugging a corpse about, you want to go carefully or you'll drop something out of the pockets. Very little in poor Colin's pockets when he was found ; no pipe, no matches. Very well then, I said, I'll just make sure they didn't drop anything. And, about half-way between the place where he was found and the track to the Devil's Dimple, I found—what d'you think I found ? "

" The pipe," suggested Bredon. " That would slip about easiest."

" Boy's overcoat. Whole bag of tricks—pipe, tobacco, all sorts of things."

" Ah ! That's what I was expecting," said Bredon.

93

Dr. Purvis made no attempt to imitate the detective's *sang-froid*. " His overcoat ! On the other side of the road ! What makes you know it's his ? "

" His ! Whose else is it likely to be, huh ? What do people want to go about leaving perfectly good overcoats under hedges for, huh ? What kind of tobacco did he smoke ? "

" It would be Worker's Army Cut. I persuaded him to take to that, for the stuff he had before was too strong for him."

" Well, you'll see that was the stuff in the pouch. And I for one will be very much surprised if his sister, or one of the servants up at Dorn, doesn't recognize the pipe. Pouch is a new one ; comes from Dirtcheap's ; so's the electric torch."

" He had a torch with him ? " asked Bredon, with more of animation.

" Course he'd have a torch with him ; can't sleep out in caves without having a torch on you. Then there's a cigarette-case with money in it."

" Was that new, too ? "

" No, old gunmetal thing. Pity he didn't leave a visiting card in it, for chaps like you, Doctor."

" And that was all ? " pursued Bredon. " There was no passport ? "

" Don't need a passport for travelling in Great Britain, thank God," said the Major. " Haven't got Home Rule in Scotland yet, huh ? "

" The right thing to do with your passport," said Hemerton with decision, " is to pop it into your hand-bag before you shut it up at the Customs ; then you don't lose it, see ? That's what I always do."

" To be sure," said Bredon, with the ghost of a smile. " But then, your brother-in-law was not, I should imagine, a person of very careful habits. I'd have expected him to put it back in his overcoat pocket as soon as he'd produced it at Southampton. But, of course, he may have lost it since."

" May have lost it," agreed the Major. " Or, tell you what, these chaps who got hold of him, they may have pinched it, huh ? Help 'em to get out of the country if they had to run for it, huh ? "

" It isn't awfully easy to get out of the country on somebody else's passport," Bredon objected. " I should have put it rather beyond the compass of your local Communists. Besides, it doesn't look to me as if anybody had been through the pockets. They missed the money, anyhow. How much was it ? "

" One pound ten ; not much to get excited about. Still, as you say, they'd probably have taken it if they'd come across it. Stick at nothing, these fellows."

The doctor was still drumming on his knee, as if dissatisfied. " You'd have some difficulty in getting past a jury with that opinion of yours, Major," he said. " Here's an old cigarette-case, such as is made by the thousand, and a pinch of tobacco such as half the world smokes, in a bran-new pouch, with a bran-new electric torch, and a box of matches, and that's all. Or rather, there's a pipe, and I grant you pipes are easily recognized by their owners ; but who's going to swear to it that this pipe was smoked by Colin Reiver and no other ? There's the coat itself, to be sure ; where does that come from ? "

" Coat ? Bought in Oxford. Not many Oxford men round here."

" And there was nothing else ? "

" Look here, you answer me a question first. You vetted Colin Reiver while he was alive ; did he ever take pills ? Liver pills ? "

" So that's why you asked me to bring a box of Drayman's Tablets over with me ? Why, Major, you made me hope you were going to turn into an invalid at last. He had some of those on him, then ? "

" He had a tube—you know, one of those talc things—with white tablets in it, and the name on the outside was Drayman's. Bought them at a London chemist, somewhere in Piccadilly. Point is, *were* they Drayman's Tablets'? Thought it'd be a good thing to make sure they looked all right, anyhow. Then you could take 'em away with you ; analyse 'em."

" I say, though, what's the idea, Major ? " asked Hemerton, as mystified as the others.

" Drugged him," explained Major Henry. " Drugged him ; that's what they did. Suspected it all along ; that's what was wrong with him when MacWilliam found him that first time ; drugged. Stands to reason a feller like that wouldn't make the mistake of thinking—— "

" But surely, Major Reiver," Bredon broke in, " I thought your idea was that MacWilliam was one of the conspirators, and that they really did think he was dead when they prepared to leave him by the roadside on Monday morning ? "

95

"Oh, as to that," said the Major, hastily readjusting his theories, "MacWilliam may have been. Nothing likelier. But, look here, how's this? They dope poor Colin, and leave him lying about in all that cold till they think he's dead. He wakes up, see, just at the wrong moment? Anyhow, that's what you'll find the stuff is; dope. Here, I'll get it; get the whole bag of tricks."

He went out, and returned with an aquascutum of a very ordinary pattern, its pockets bulging with souvenirs of the tragedy. "Put 'em back just as I found them," he explained proudly; "here's the pipe, here's the pouch, here's the matches. See you're a pipe-smoker, Mr. Bredon; you have a look at 'em. What d'you make of those?" He talked as if he expected Bredon to provide him with the names and addresses of the murderers out of hand.

"May I borrow a pipe-cleaner from your mantelpiece?" Bredon asked. He rammed one down the barrel of the pipe, and drew it out quite clean. Then he felt the tobacco in the pouch, and gave a puzzled frown. "Do you smoke a pipe, Mr. Hemerton?" he asked.

"No. Only cigarettes. I don't like overdoing my smoking, and you pipe-lovers never seem to know when you've had enough."

"Ah, then you wouldn't realize the oddity of the position; the Major will. The pipe's clean, as if it hadn't been smoked for some time. But this tobacco's fresh, or next door to it. You know, Major, how tobacco goes dry and dusty if you leave it for a few days in a pouch. How do we account for that, if the overcoat was Colin Reiver's?"

The Major felt inside the pouch with a troubled face. "You may be right; but this stuff keeps pretty well, not like your mixtures. Tell you what, I don't believe it's been more than a week in the pouch. Looks to me as if Colin hadn't put it in long before he died; that's true enough."

"I'm no use over tobacco, either," observed the doctor. "May I have a look at those tablets, Major? I'll be more in my element there." As he spoke, he took out a tube from his pocket, removed the cap, and shook out a few white tablets into his hand. The tube which the Major produced from the pocket of the aquascutum, with all a conjurer's pride, was of the same brand evidently, though the label on it proclaimed that it had been bought from a London chemist and, unlike the doctor's, it was not quite full. A few of these tablets

96

were shaken out on the window-sill, side by side with the others, and the doctor scrutinized them minutely.

" I wouldn't say that I can see any difference," he announced. " And, mind you, you can generally tell the difference between a machine-made article such as these tablets are, and the things a chemist makes up. If this was any unusual drug, you see, it's not likely that the tablets would be made up by the thousand. But, of course, as you say, it would be well to analyse one of them ; unless I can have your leave, Major, to try it on the dog. Victor there doesn't look as if he needed any drugs to keep him quiet, though, as long as he can lie by your fire-side." They turned, to see the Major's spaniel looking up and blinking at them with that uncanny air dogs have of knowing when they are being talked about.

" See you take one yourself first," retorted the Major, who knew the doctor's reputation as a champion of the Research Defence Society. " May be poison, for all we know."

" Well, I'll soon be able to tell you," replied the doctor, as he scraped together his own tablets and shot them back carelessly into the tube. " I'll analyse two or three, in case they're not uniform."

" How many are there left, by the way ? " asked Hemerton. " If there is anything wrong with these tablets, it'll be as well to know what dose the poor boy took."

" That's true," assented Bredon. " And, by the mercy of heaven, they're the kind that leaves little rings of white dust where they lie, so that we can easily tell how many there were to start with. One, two, three missing."

" I thought there were more than that," said Hemerton. " No," he added, counting the rings in his turn. " I must have been mistaken."

" Well, if they're the genuine article, he won't have done himself much harm with that," commented the doctor. " Once daily before meals, the label says ; and they'd always be on the safe side. He did worry about his digestion sometimes ; do you know, Hemerton, if he ever took those things ? "

" Eh ? Yes, I believe he did. Mary would know."

" Mr. Bredon," the Major broke in, " you told us that you had been up to the Devil's Dimple, and were going to give us news of it. What was it you found ? Somebody been camping there ? "

Bredon described fully the state of the cave, and the odd

puzzle which the inscription at the mouth of it had set them. It would be hard to say whether Hemerton or the Major seemed more excited by his account. The Major was triumphant ; " What did I tell you ? Just the sort of place those scoundrels would choose. Have a man up at the top with a revolver, or big stick, even, and they'd prevent him climbing up. Simply meant waiting till the weather was cold enough to kill their man off. Monday night must have done it ; Tuesday night, as I was saying, no frost at all. That would be it."

" I must be off," announced the doctor, consulting his watch. " Can I give you a lift back, Mr. Bredon ? It will save Hemerton having to go round by Blairwhinnie on his way home."

" I wonder," said Bredon, " if I might take the torch off with me ? It looks as if it came from Dirtcheap's, but there's a chance that he got it at some smaller shop ; and if it was in Pensteven there's just the possibility that they'd remember him. Thanks very much. I don't want to miss any chances."

His doubt about its origin did not prevent him from stopping at the Pensteven branch of Messrs. Dirtcheap, and buying a torch exactly similar. He was not going to leave all the experimenting to Dr. Purvis.

CHAPTER XV

THE SUSPECTS

" Now THEN," SAID Bredon to his wife, " tell me all about it." They were sitting in their private room after having tea downstairs. Dr. Purvis had refused tea and would only delay his journey to see a patient at the hotel. As if the illumination of the room had been otherwise insufficient, Miles Bredon had an electric torch on either arm of his chair, switched on deliberately.

" I'm sorry, my angel, but I've got to hear about those torches first. I don't know if you're expecting a bonus on this case, but I don't see that we can afford burning away sixpences like that."

" There are two reserve batteries in the box, in case you hear a mouse to-night. It's not really very complicated. I told you about all the fun the Major's been having yesterday

98

afternoon. This little chap on my left—we will call him Charles for short—was the torch found in the pocket of that aquascutum, on the left-hand side of the road to Pensteven, behind the hedge. The other, Horace, is one I bought myself this afternoon at Dirtcheap's. It has not escaped your observation that they are doubles. So I am having a burning match, to see which lasts longest."

" Meaning that if Horace outlives Charles by, say, twenty minutes, you'll be able to say with certainty that that was the exact amount of juice poor Colin Reiver had got out of his torch before he died ? A fat lot of good that's going to do."

" No doubt. But supposing Charles lasts exactly as long as Horace, won't that be rather interesting ? It would suggest, I mean, that a young man who had been living in a darkish cave, and travelling mostly at night, apparently, had this torch in his pocket at least part of the time, but never used it. That, surely, would be interesting. Now tell me all about whom you suspect and why. Giving your working in full, please. Let us have no womanly intuitions."

" Under protest, then. You see, Miles, you haven't introduced me to any of these people, except Mr. Hemerton just for a moment, and the doctor, of course. What is the use of having suspicions about people one hasn't met ? You must make some allowance for atmospheres. Well, let's start at the beginning. Mr. Leyland told me once you should always start by suspecting the man who brings the first news that the corpse is dead. That would be MacWilliam in this case. I don't think I suspect MacWilliam."

" Why not ? "

" Well, of course, there would be advantages about suspecting him. You could get out of all that frightful difficulty about the two appearances of the corpse by supposing that MacWilliam was lying ; we've nobody else's word for it. That's where Major Henry's theory scores. But it's too fantastic, surely, to suppose that a rather negative, colourless person like Colin Reiver should be generally hated on the estate, even if he did drive carelessly. Most of us would have very few friends left if every fatal car accident led to a murder. And it's fantastic, I think, to imagine that Mac-William would rush up to the house with a story of murder without making sure that his man was dead ; after all, he was in no hurry."

" To which you may add, that there was no reason, assuming

99

a conspiracy, or even assuming MacWilliam's guilt, why the body should not have been left by the roadside until it was found by a passing stranger. No need to associate yourself wantonly with the murder by admitting that you were on the spot soon after it happened."

"Very well, we'll clear MacWilliam, for the time being. We'll take Mr. Donald Reiver next, because he's easy to clear. He was in bed all the time, and bed (with nurses running in and out) is a very useful sort of alibi. There's no evidence that Colin was ever up at the house, after he left for his tour, and no evidence that his father knew where he was. It's conceivable, of course, that his father might have had accomplices who would do the job for him; but in that case we've got to find the accomplices first. That's sound, isn't it? "

"Good enough. And, of course, if Colin really died on the Sunday night, it lets his father out on the mere ground of motive. Nobody could be such a fool as to murder a highly-insured relative on the very night on which he sent off the latest instalment of the premium."

"Which is also worth considering when you come to think of the other people at Dorn; the Hemertons, I mean. They knew that the premium hadn't been paid up yet, because the old man was getting all hot and bothered about it. So, why kill Colin just that night? Of course, when you come to think of it, it might be a specially good opportunity for them, for some reason we don't know of."

"That's perfectly true. They were the people most likely to know whether Colin was coming back from abroad, and when; though they deny all information about it. It might have been a plot to murder Colin in such a way as to let it appear that he had died on his way back from the cruise. Well, what do you make of the Hemertons, then? "

"I don't know her; I've nothing to go on except your account of her. And you're not terribly good at understanding women, Miles; I suppose because I've trained you so well. She'd got plenty of reason, of course, for supposing that she would count in on her father's will, though there's no evidence that she and her husband were hard up. If, for private reasons of her own, she did kill her brother on the Sunday night, she had the best possible reasons for concealing the fact till the Wednesday morning, after the Indescribable had pocketed its cheque. And I gather she is all for Tuesday night as the date of death."

" Of course she is ; you needn't make a murderess of her
merely on the strength of that. She wants her money, same
as everybody else does, that I ever met. And I think you can
count her out, considering her as a sole agent—I mean, apart
from her husband. I know you have the lowest possible
opinion of your own sex, but I don't see how she could have
managed to arrange that her brother should die of exposure.
You can only do that, as far as I can see, by some threat of
violence ; and threats of violence aren't a woman's weapon."

" Very well, then ; let us consider Mr. Hemerton instead.
I don't know that I like him frightfully, just from the glance
I got of him ; he strikes me as rather a hard type—the sort
of person who stands no nonsense. He seems to be one of
the hush-hush brigade ; the two of them, I mean, seem to
have been quite happy about burying Colin Reiver and taking
it for granted that he'd met with some kind of nasty accident,
instead of pressing for an enquiry. He was at Dorn when
the thing happened, and it wasn't difficult for him to be up
to games just when the old gentleman was so ill, and everybody except himself had their hands full. He posted off
pretty quick this afternoon, to hear what Major Henry had got
to tell him, as if he was a bit uneasy in his mind."

" On the other hand, he called here and picked me up
quite gratuitously. That doesn't suggest that he has a very
guilty conscience."

" May have been trying to lead you up the garden, my
angel. It's been done before. Still, it's difficult to imagine.
that he knew beforehand what Cousin Henry had been up to.
Let us also remember that he was the person who suggested,
on Monday morning, that the police should be sent for.
That beats me rather. I mean, if he was a murderer, I should
have thought he would have left it to somebody else to
suggest that."

" Precisely. And if he had managed so skilfully—God
knows how—to engineer a murder which was going to look
exactly like death from natural causes, why suggest a guilty
conscience about it by lugging in the police ? No use to
say he was leading *them* up the garden, because the results of
their investigations were nil."

" It's odd, you know, Miles, that he should have sent for
the police, even if he wasn't a murderer. Because, as we
agreed, he was one of the people who knew Colin Reiver
wasn't covered by the insurance policy on Sunday night ; and

he was one of the people who might obviously expect to be benefited by the will. Who was with him ? The doctor, a family friend, and his lawyer. There was just a chance of hushing the thing up, if he limited the information to them and the night-nurse and. the gamekeeper. But to fetch the police in was asking for trouble, if only the corpse had been found."

" Yes, but if he knew there was no corpse there to find ? That might be a reason for fetching in the police, to guarantee the absence of the body."

" Oh yes, there's something in that. If the body was really there on the Monday morning, when MacWilliam thought he saw it, it can't have been the doctor who spirited it away very well, because the doctor was in the house when Mac-William got there. And they found Hemerton pretty soon, didn't they ? He must have made a quick get-away to his bedroom, if he'd just been meddling with the corpse. By the way, did he seem keen on our expedition to the Devil's Dimple ? "

" I didn't ask him. I asked Mrs., and she was fairly keen on it. Indeed, she offered to take me there ; but she didn't seem worried at my going without her. And Hemerton, now I come to think of it, never once asked me if I'd been there. It was only in conversation with the Major that I mentioned our expedition ; and it was the Major who reminded me that I hadn't told them about it. It doesn't look as if Hemerton. had been very anxious about that part of the show."

" Looks as if we'd got to put down Hemerton with a query. He *may* have had a motive, mayn't he ? I mean if he supposed that the old gentleman had drawn out a will in favour of the daughter, there was something to be said for getting rid of Colin, while he was away from home and nobody had any track of his movements. Only I can't see, even at that rate, why he didn't wait till the cheque had been paid in."

" We don't know ; perhaps he did, and MacWilliam made a mistake of some kind. Still, as you say, we can only put him down with a very big query."

" Who else was in the house, did you say, on the Sunday night ? "

" Well, there were the servants, of course. We've no reason to suspect any of them, and I didn't feel I could go round chatting to them while I was in the house. It's the devil and all, this not being a police business. Apart from the servants, there were only three people, the night-nurse, the doctor, and the lawyer. Henry Reiver came and went, of course."

" Well, let's wash out the night-nurse ; she'd probably never heard of Colin Reiver till she was told he was dead. I think we may as well wash out the lawyer too, don't you ? Because it was only by an accident that he was in the neighbourhood, and he'd been fetched in at the last moment. Probably he didn't know his way about the house or the grounds—by your account that needs some doing. And he'd no car, so I don't see him getting up to much mischief on a February night. The doctor remains on trial. Miles, I like that man, don't you ? "

" Do I ? Yes. And yet, you know, there is something rather cold-blooded about him. I've a sort of unpleasant feeling that if he wanted a corpse rather badly for some reason or other, I'd do. Tell us about the doctor, anyhow."

" Well, he doesn't come into the money side of the picture, does he ? I mean, even if there's anything in Mrs. Wauchope's story about Colin being struck on the daughter, and even if that had been stop-press news, which Mrs. Wauchope evidently didn't think it was, neither he nor the daughter would stand to gain by Colin's dying. He was insured, but it was his father who held the policy and paid the premiums. Very unlikely that she would expect to figure in the old man's will, even if they'd been married. All that seems to let the doctor out, don't it ? "

" On the question of motive, yes. I don't see how we can fix anything on him. But let's consider whether.he had the opportunity, just in case."

" Opportunity ? Well, that rather depends on when and how the death occurred, doesn't it ? Specially *when*. Why did he sleep in the house that night ? Did they ask him to ? "

" I asked Mrs. Hemerton about that ; and she told me that the doctor seemed very keen to get back home ; only she forced him to stay. Which is perhaps important."

" Well, I suppose it clears him of having been up to any dirty work *late* that night, because he'd had to change his plans unexpectedly. On the other hand, if he'd been up to some game *before* Mrs. Hemerton asked him to stop—on his way from Blairwhinnie, for example—one might explain his keenness to get home as keenness to get away from the scene of

103

trouble. But all that assumes the death took place on Sunday night; whereas we don't know that it did, and can't see how it can have. If Colin died on Tuesday night, let's see, where was Dr. Purvis? Oh yes, he went out to look after a workman who'd had an accident. That's an alibi which might be investigated."

" It will be, before we fix anything on the doctor. Meanwhile, you've left out the chief ground of suspicion against this candidate."

" Such as what? "

" Why, the mere fact that he *is* a doctor. If murder was done here, it was concealed superhumanly well as death from natural causes. And a doctor's much more likely to be able to fake that sort of thing than even an experienced criminal."

" M'yes; he seems to have bungled it, though. Anyhow, I'm against running in Dr. Purvis; I think he's rather sweet. Who've we got left? Oh yes, Major Henry. I want to see him, Miles; I can't picture him properly. So far as motive goes, we can't let him out, can we? Because Mrs. Wauchope tells me that it would have broken him if the estate had had to pay double death duties, first on Donald Reiver, then on Colin. So Colin's dying first was all jam for Henry."

" He was a little sudden about it, wasn't he? Death duties, if I remember right, are not paid if the late owner was less than two years in the saddle. So he might have given Colin a few more months' run for his money."

" Might have. All the same, Mrs. Wauchope says Dorn would have gone to pieces if Colin had taken it over, so perhaps Henry wanted him out of the way as soon as possible. I gather it was touch and go whether Donald Reiver would live through that Sunday night. And perhaps Henry thought it would look less obvious what was in the wind if Colin died first."

" Yes, it's possible. And the opportunity? "

" Henry's weak there, too. He was careering about in a car late at night, with no check on his movements, except that he must have posted that envelope some time. And, look here, if Cousin Donald told him *he* wasn't going to touch a penny of the insurance money, mightn't he, in a sort of spirit of revenge, hurry the unfortunate Colin out of the world simply so that he would die uninsured, and the relations would look fools? They weren't at all on good terms, I gather."

" Yes, that's really the nub of the whole problem. Who,

104

if anybody, was anxious that Colin should die uninsured?
Major Henry may have had a sort of motive, as you say,
though it makes him out a bit on the caddish side. But then,
what about Henry's goings on since the body was found?"
    " He must be devilish deep, if he's really guilty. Because
he wanted to bring in the police, just when everything was
nicely hushed up; that's almost too good to be double bluff.
On the other hand, if he was concerned somehow in Colin's
death, it would explain why he makes such good shots now
and then. It was he mentioned the Devil's Dimple, wasn't it?
And he who found the overcoat. On the other hand, why
should he want you to trace Colin's last movements like that?
Unless—oo! you don't think he's trying to convince you about
Colin having died uninsured, do you? 'Cos then it might be
he who scratched out that last figure in the inscription, and
made it look as if Colin had been in the cave on Sunday, but
not on Monday?"
    " I know, but it makes him out devilish constructive. To
me, the Major seems a pure fool. The question is, Can he
be acting the fool as well as all that? I think I shall have to
introduce you to him, Angela. Meanwhile, we lunch at
Dorn to-morrow; I accepted for you, because I know you like
eating a lot at other people's expense. Confound these torches
—still at it. I'd no idea there was so much blood in them."

CHAPTER XVI

MR. CARSTAIRS WRIGHT

    " I THINK," SAID Miles, as they drove up towards the lodge
next day, " that I shall get more inspiration out of this visit if
I can separate the old gentleman from the other two. If he
wants to chat to me privately after luncheon, well and good.
But if it seems that we are going to sit about, or walk about,
all five of us together, the party will want breaking. Could
you manage that, with your well-known skill? I mean, look
soulful at Mr. Donald Reiver and suggest that you want to
have a heart-to-heart talk with him?"
    " I'm out of practice with my vamping rather, but I'll do
my best. As a matter of fact, I'd set my heart on getting
hold of Mrs. Hemerton and seeing if I couldn't turn her inside
out a little. But it's quite unlikely she'd respond to treatment;

whereas the aged male needs very little encouragement, as a rule, to become communicative. Miles, what a queer house ! " Their arrangements were upset by an unforeseen development—the presence of a stranger when they were ushered into the library. Donald Reiver, promoted to coming downstairs, but still wedded to the chimney corner, introduced them ; it was now placed beyond doubt that the stranger's name was Carstairs Wright ; but who or what he might be, how he fitted into the household, whether he was staying in the house or not, whether he was friend, relative, or business agent, was left to the imagination. We are always secretly hostile towards the unexpected fellow-guest ; was the party, after all, invented in his honour, and were we only hauled in at the last moment to amuse him, or to fill up the table ? Is he an old friend, and do our hosts wish we hadn't come, so that they might enjoy his society uninterrupted ? How is it that he seems so much more at home than we do ? Mr. Carstairs Wright was young, and had a look of freshness and innocence about him such as you expect of a school-boy home on a visit ; but his manner was assured, his speech ready, his hand-grip formidable ; he seemed to make himself intimate with you at once, and to have discerned in you another fellow who, like himself, did not bother about the formalities. Perhaps the most sudden feature about him was the fact that he addressed Mr. Reiver as " Donald," although he looked a full thirty years his junior. Nor did he appear to be a member of the family ; the Hemertons (although he treated them as old friends) seemed cold in their manner towards him, and perhaps even faintly hostile.

Angela, while she cooed sympathy to the laird on her left over the discomforts of illness and convalescence, listened hard with the other ear to pick up scraps of the conversation between Mary Hemerton and Mr. Wright. He was not staying in the house, not a member of the family ; yet he had been to the house before, and seemed to know both it and the grounds intimately. He was staying in Blairwhinnie, at an hotel, not theirs ; he was, or had recently been, at Oxford— perhaps a friend of the dead Colin ? Yet there was no allusion to any such friendship ; no consciousness, even, in his manner, that he was in a house of mourning. Moreover, it was fairly clear that he had invited himself to luncheon ; Mary Hemerton was so glad he had thought of ringing them up, so glad that her father was well enough to be down that day, did hope that he hadn't minded the long walk, but of course she didn't

realize that he had no car—of course he must go back in theirs.
It was no trouble, it would have to be going down, anyhow, to
pick up some things in Blairwhinnie about three.

The effort of making one conversation and listening to
another so occupied Angela's thoughts that she quite forgot her
husband's directions, quite failed to wonder how she should
adapt her conduct to the new situation. She awoke to hear
her host saying that he was now allowed to be wheeled out
in a chair when the afternoon was fine ; to hear Mr. Carstairs
Wright picking him up immediately with, " I say, Donald,
do let me wheel you round the garden. I'm well known for
my gentleness as a chair-pusher ; I've pushed for my College
before now." You recognized, as soon as he had said it, a
false note. It produced what was called, nearly a generation
ago, in the original and highly esoteric sense of that term,
" a floater." Everybody looked embarrassed simultaneously, so
that in the general dropping of jaws it was not easy even for
a close observer to notice whose jaw had dropped how. It
was not merely the flat jocosity of the remark ; not merely
the *gaucherie* of this evident attempt to exchange his present
company for a *tête-à-tête* ; there was something in what the
young man had said which created a disconcerting atmosphere
all round. Angela was only conscious of her husband's feelings—if Mr. Wright was going to monopolize their host, it
meant that she would be left among the rest of the company,
a non-conductor so far as discussion of the mystery was concerned. She rose to the occasion automatically. " One to push,
and one to pull ; may I be donkey, Mr. Reiver ? My husband
has told me such a lot about the garden, I should awfully like
to see it while I'm here." The situation was saved.

The effect was to postpone old Mr. Reiver's outing ; and Mr.
Carstairs Wright had been shepherded off the premises by the
announcement that the car would be ready for him any time,
before the party disintegrated itself. The Bredons were not
allowed to go yet ; Mr. Reiver was wheeled to a stone
recess in the garden, where Angela could talk to him at leisure,
in the sun and out of the wind, while the Hemertons took
possession of her husband. This last move was evidently part
of their programme, no less than of his ; they had been talking
over the discovery of the rain-coat, and of the relics up at the
Devil's Dimple, and Mary Hemerton, especially, was anxious
to get full details about both. " It's awful," she said, " to
think that he was alive and so near us for so long ; that if

107

one had only happened to go up that way one might have come across him. It's wonderful how right you've been, Mr. Bredon, first of all in guessing that he must have been up at the cave, and then in prophesying that we should find his rain-coat."

"You feel certain, then, that it is his rain-coat? I only ask because the doctor seemed rather scornful of the idea; and, thinking it over, I saw his point. It's not, after all, a very new coat; and though tramps don't usually discard clothes as good as that in the hedgerow, or leave money and other useful things on them, I suppose you could imagine, without much difficulty, other explanations of how it got there. By the way, I was meaning to ask, Mrs. Hemerton—I suppose that was not the coat your brother was actually wearing when he went off for the cruise? I mean, it seems rather light for that sort of thing; the first day or two at sea must have been pretty cold, I imagine."

Mrs. Hemerton paused for a moment, as if trying to get an eye-picture of her brother's departure. "No, of course you're right," she said; "Colin was wearing his heavy tweed coat when he went; but I remember advising him to take a rain-coat with him as well. It looks rather as if he had lost his heavy coat on the cruise; or possibly he wanted to travel light, just in those last few days, and took something which would make walking easy."

"Yes, it looks like it. Of course, it means one still wonders where the great-coat is; and whether conceivably his passport would be found in that, although his other things seem to have been carried in the rain-coat. The torch interested me, you know."

"Yes, why did you carry that off?" asked Hemerton. "I wondered at the time; I should have thought the pipe would have been more interesting to you, especially as a smoker."

"I'd like to carry that off to-day, if I may, and the tobacco. As for the torch, I wanted to see how much it had been used; and, do you know, it hadn't been used at all—or only just for a minute. I tried it out side by side with another torch of the same kind, you see."

"It looks as if he must have bought it quite soon before he died."

"Yes, but where? I don't think they sell those things except at Dirtcheap's. I went into their branch at Pensteven, when I bought the other one, and took the opportunity to ask whether they had sold one lately, and if so, who to. Well, they had sold one or two in the last fortnight, naturally; but they couldn't remember the young man in the rain-coat. I didn't mention to them, of course, that it was your brother I was asking after. It looks to me as if he had bought it in London, where he certainly bought the tablets—in that case, there was the name of the shop to tell us. Now, if that's so, you'd have expected that it would have been more used, by a man living in a cave for several nights."

" You mean . . ." began Mary.

" I only mean that I'm still wondering whether it was your brother's rain-coat after all. An Oxford man, or an Oxford resident, who has lately been in London—that doesn't really tell us much about the owner. Did you try to identify the things at all yourself, Mrs. Hemerton ? "

" Oh yes ; Vincent brought them back with him. But one's so stupid about these things. I don't know how often I must have sat opposite Colin when he was smoking a pipe, but it never occurred to me to look at it closely, so that I could distinguish it from a hundred other pipes. The coat was certainly the shade of a coat he had, but it's a very common kind. I asked Sanders here—that's the butler, you know—whether he remembered it hanging in the hall, and he said he couldn't be sure either. No, it's only the difficulty of accounting for its being found just there that makes one wonder."

" That was the Major's point," said her husband.

" It's all so inconclusive, though, even if you accept the identification. That was a good idea of yours, of course, about the number of tablets in the tube. I mean, if there had been many gone, we should have been able to say with some probability that the owner of the coat had been alive, and in possession of the coat, so many days since he left London. There's the chance of his taking a double dose, but it's unlikely. As it is, there were just three gone ; that might mean one on Friday, one on Saturday, one on Sunday. Or it might mean one on Saturday, one on Sunday, one on Monday. Or he might have only taken them when he felt rather run down ; one can't say."

" Shouldn't have thought he'd have taken one on Friday, if it was Colin," observed Hemerton. " Though, of course, we're prejudiced parties," he added with a grin. " Much best to take those things first thing in the morning."

" I know ; and yet a person who's just landed, after a

109

roughish passage, might buy them on his way through London, and think it wouldn't do any harm breaking into them at once; I don't know. It's so exasperating—you'll understand that my interest in the whole question is to be able to make some report to my Company about the probable date on which the actual death took place. All I can say is that Mr. Colin Reiver may have written up his name in a cave on Sunday, or again it may have been Monday; may have taken a pill on Monday, or again he may not—and whether he was alive early on Monday morning is precisely what my Company wants to know! I've every hope that they'll give your father the benefit of the doubt, of course, but they won't give me the benefit of the doubt—they'll want to know why they employ an agent at all, when he leaves the doubtful point exactly where it was."

"You couldn't guess anything from the amount of food that was left in the cave?" Mary asked.

"I put that to Dr. Purvis; and he said the food that had apparently been eaten would have kept a man going for three or four days. But, as he pointed out, you don't know what a hungry man may do at a sitting."

"And what's your explanation of the crossed-out figure?" asked Hemerton. "That seems to me the rummest part of the business."

"Well, one can only go on the probabilities, can't one? What I have been supposing is that your brother-in-law made a mistake about the date in the first instance, writing on the Sunday, and then, noticing the mistake, proceeded to correct it, but without taking much trouble over the correction, since he'd no reason to think that it was important. Of course, that doesn't in the least preclude the possibility that he was there on Monday too; it's only a question of when he actually happened to scribble on the wall."

"I'd been wondering," said Mrs. Hemerton, "whether this might not be an explanation—that he wrote on Monday, and naturally put down the right date, the thirteenth, and then it occurred to him that thirteen was an unlucky number, so he altered it to twelfth—the day when he first went to the cave, or the day when the inscription was actually begun? I know it sounds silly; but if poor Colin had some presentiment of his end, I can imagine him just fighting shy of a bad omen like that. We're all inclined to be a little superstitious, you see, Mr. Bredon."

110

" Very difficult to know how thirteen came to be thought an unlucky number," her husband moralized. " There's no evidence of it, they say, before the Reformation. Still, it's wonderful what a hold it has. All sorts of hotels you'll find which don't keep a room number thirteen, for fear of putting off their clients. I should like to have a look round on the spot myself, and see whether there isn't any chance of the thing having been accidental—a slip of the tool, or what not."

" I was thinking of trying some of the shops in Pensteven," said Bredon, " in case they could remember selling that tongue, for example. They might possibly remember it."

" Oh, I don't think you'll get much good out of that," objected Mary. " It's hard enough to get the Pensteven shops to keep their books accurately, let alone remembering what they sell over the counter. And it's extraordinary how the habit of buying stuff in tins and boxes is growing up in these days. Very few of the women on the estate ever take the trouble to bake a scone."

" No, I suppose it would only be an off chance. I think the best thing I can do, really, is to go off to Glasgow myself —I suppose that would be the likeliest place, and see the men in the Cloak Room and Lost Luggage Office there. When one writes to these people, they always answer in a perfectly red-tape, mechanical sort of way. If you go round and make a fuss in person, they occasionally wake up a bit. What is Major Henry doing next, by the way ? Or hasn't he told you anything ? I can hardly imagine him giving up the search, somehow."

" He's had rather a set-back," explained Hemerton. " We had a message from Dr. Purvis this morning ; he'd got a man to analyse several of the tablets, and they were perfectly honest-to-God liver pills. The Major had set his heart on their being some kind of drug. But when I left him last night he announced his intention of going carefully all over the ground between the Devil's Dimple and the place where he found the rain-coat. It's really given him a new interest in life."

" I hope it's not frightfully inquisitive of me," Bredon said as he rose to his feet, " but I couldn't help wondering who Mr. Wright is ? He seemed to know your father so well, Mrs. Hemerton, and yet I couldn't quite understand what they had in common."

" Mr. Wright ? Oh, he belongs to the Circles, you know ;

this religious movement Dad is so interested in. I was terri-
fied of his going out to join Dad in the garden, because I'm
sure it's bad for him to be worrying about that kind of thing
while he's still in weak health. We were really very grateful
to Mrs. Bredon for heading him off. I expect he's a very well-
meaning young man, but I think one ought to be at the top
of one's form if one's going to worry about religion, don't
you ? He's been here, apparently, for one or two of these
week-end parties Dad allows them to have here ; that's why
he knows the place so well. But we'd never met him before ;
and it really wasn't very considerate of him to turn up. Oh,
here you are, Mrs. Bredon ; I'm so glad you were both able
to come. I hope, now you've found your way here, we shall
see more of you."

CHAPTER XVII

THE SECOND RAIN-COAT

It is a profound difference of national character that the
Scot takes pleasure in his job, the Englishman only in his
relaxations. This it is that makes' shopping, for example, such
a wearisome business in England. The old-fashioned English
shopkeeper has only two remarks to make : " Nice day again,"
followed by, " And the next article ? " His more modern
successor has been taught the foul art of " salesmanship "—
that is, he reels off a string of lies taught him by a commercial
traveller, intended to conceal the shoddiness of the machine-
made horror he lays in front of you. They do these things
differently north of the border. The shopkeeper throws himself into the transaction, not from any love of his percentages,
but from sheer delight in fulfilling a mission—that of introducing the purchaser to the thing he wants. He will not
try to make you buy substitutes " nearly as good " ; he will
even refuse to sell you, for example, a particular kind of
tobacco because the tins he has in stock are too old, and will
have become dry. He applauds your good taste in demanding
this or that particular brand, adducing the testimony of other
customers in its favour ; he is desolated that he should be out
of stock ; he directs you meticulously to the nearest shop where
they might just have some left. He, and still more she ; nor

will any maidenly reserve prevent her from discussing the merits of rival shaving-soaps.

This instinct for introducing the human touch into commercial transactions has infected even the railway system. Nowhere will you get such loving care from the guard as in Scotland; nowhere will you receive such minute directions, often quite wrong, from the porters. And Mr. James Macpherson, whose duty and pleasure it was to superintend, for a certain period of the afternoon, the Lost Luggage Department at St. Buchan's Station in Glasgow, did not exercise his office in that spirit of melancholy detachment which reigns, in England, behind every glass door marked " Enquiries." He moved like a priest in his temple of absent-mindedness; or you would suppose that this promiscuous harvest of the rack and the luggage-van was, to him, a connoisseur's collection; to be handled lovingly, to be yielded up not without full use of his conversational powers—and these were considerable.

Accordingly, when an apologetic knock at the glass partition ushered in a pleasant-looking youngish man who already claimed acquaintance by correspondence, " about some luggage, you know, with the name Reiver on the label, which might possibly have got here," Mr. Macpherson did not repel him with suspicious defensiveness, or put him off with the curt, red-tape answers which are the stock-in-trade of the bull-dog breed farther south. The visitor was well dressed; he carried over his arm a heavy great-coat of undeniably prosperous appearance, but it would have been all the same if he had been a street loafer, provided that he came on business. Mr. Macpherson did the honours of the establishment with all the hospitality of a Highland chieftain, lifting up the wooden counter which served as portcullis to his stronghold. " I remember your letters well; come in, Mr. Bredon, come inside. I'm afraid it's beginning to look as if the articles had gone astray altogether; I've still no record of them. But you shall have a look-round for yourself," he added, his eye lighting up with the prospect of showing off his treasures to a connoisseur.

And indeed it was a harbour for philosophy, this limbo of inanimate foundlings. Limbo, not Purgatory, like the Cloak Room opposite, a place of transitory detention; all but a few, you felt, of these exhibits would moulder on in disuse, until they met, at last, an inglorious fate on the bargain counter. And what took the imagination was the variety, the unexpectedness of the exhibits. Not umbrellas merely, and gloves, and walking-sticks, votive offerings such as are commonly exposed at the shrines of Lethe, but gramophones, tool-bags, motor-signs, bird-cages, wall-maps, tennis-rackets, paint-pots, and even, in one corner, a wash-basin complete with waste-pipe that found no contact with its parent earth. Mr. Macpherson did not fail to underline the moral of the establishment; he would throw open a locked drawer with, " What do you think of that now ? Here's a fellow left his false teeth behind in a first-class compartment; would you have thought it possible ? " But of course the commonest objects of his care were pieces of actual luggage, suit-cases mainly and dispatch-boxes, in the arrangement of which the custodian took special pride. " You wouldn't believe, Mr. Bredon, what a lot of these things there are, fully packed, whose owners you can't make shift to trace when you've been through the contents. Those that have initials on them are put here, you see, arranged in alphabetical disposition. You're sure, now, that there was C. R. on the ones you were looking for ? Here's a C. L. and a C. H. W., but no C. R.s. Where there's no initials, we just grade them according to the shade of colour; it's an idea of my own. But it's no use your looking there for what you've come about; there's no initialled ones there. And the coats, you see, I've graded them according to their colour too; with just a wee slip of a ticket on each, to facilitate reference to the files. And with all that, you'd be surprised to see how few of them ever get back to their owners. By my way of it, a traveller who's feckless enough to leave a thing behind him in the train is too feckless to apply for it in the right quarter, with the proper formalities."

His visitor paid little attention to the bags, and devoted himself more, as was natural, to the great-coats. " I wonder you don't get a good few of these identified in error," he said. " These things are turned out by the thousand, and there's not much to distinguish them. Take this grey tweed, for example; there's no name in it, and it doesn't feel as if there was anything in the pockets. What's to prevent me saying I lost just such an overcoat on the boat-train to Ardrossan ? "

" Nothing at all to prevent your saying it, but you see, that's just where the tickets come in. Now, where's my file-book ? " Mr. Macpherson buried himself, chuckling, in an enormous volume of files, and emerged triumphant from his researches. " There's the unfortunate fact, Mr. Bredon, that the coat you're looking at was left in a local train and taken out at Motherwell. So you wouldn't do business that way. You see here? Motherwell. And the next Kilmarnock. Now, if your young friend had left his coat, it would be in a Glasgow train, you'd think, or else on the Pensteven line somewhere. Here's one now, labelled 586, that was taken out at Perth; I'll just go and have a look at that one." He returned in a few moments with a formidable garment, faced prosperously with astrakhan. " That's no use, you see; there's a name in it—H. Clowes—and who's to trace him among all the Cloweses in the directory?"

" It's the wrong date, too. Young Mr. Reiver—you'll remember seeing about it in the paper—was certainly dead by the fifteenth, and this wasn't lost, apparently, till the seventeenth. From the date, I'd be more interested to see Number 579; that goes back to the fourteenth—Tuesday, wasn't it? But it's an aquascutum, the file says, and it was a heavy coat I was expecting to find. Could I just have a look at it?"

The request was hardly necessary; for the rain-coats, in their hierarchy of fawns and greys, hung just behind him as he spoke. Number 579 had no owner's name in it, and the maker's label was from London. But there was a promising sort of bulge in one of the pockets, which suggested possible disclosures. " You don't take the things out of the pockets, then?"

" Only the valuables, Mr. Bredon, and now and again something that would help to identification. There's a letter here," added Mr. Macpherson, drawing it out and unfolding it as he spoke, " but you'll see the address at the top is torn off, as folk do when they want to make a note of an address; there's no envelope, and the signature is just a Christian name, Denis. There's a parcel, too; I don't just remember to have looked at that. But it's from a shop, you'll observe, and hasn't been through the post, so there's not much chance of an address there. But we'll open it on the chance, Mr. Bredon, since you're interested."

The parcel was of thick brown paper, with the ends raggedly torn off; the string was coarse and rather dirty. You would have said at once that it came from an ironmonger's, and the event would have applauded your guess. There was only one object inside, a perfectly new chisel. The other pocket contained a briar pipe; nothing else. Mr. Macpherson and his subordinates were clearly within their rights when they classed this coat among the articles that could not be identified.

" About that letter," suggested Bredon ; " what's the other name ? I mean, if it's signed with a Christian name, it will hardly start *Dear Sir.*"

" That's true, but the luck's still against us, you see ; it's just given under an initial letter, *Dear C.*—and that's not much to go by. I forget now what young Mr. Reiver's name was ? "

" Colin ; that fits all right. And the curious thing is, he had a great friend called Denis. Might I just have a look ? "

" Certainly, Mr. Bredon, certainly ; it's very short, but you're welcome to what there is of it." Mr. Macpherson was fully justified in his estimate. There was no date, and the communication simply ran :

Dear C.,—Just to wish you the best of everything and no end of a blind to-morrow night. Fish-slice follows. Yours, Denis.

" It's an odd business, this," observed the visitor. " The name fits, and the initial fits, and the message is very much what one undergraduate would write to another who was just keeping his twenty-first birthday. Young Mr. Reiver was twenty-one, I understand, last year. But to make the identification certain we'd have to find the writer of that letter, wouldn't we, or at least get a specimen of his handwriting. I think the best thing I can do in the meantime is to get hold of Mrs. Hemerton—that's young Mr. Reiver's sister—and bring her over here to see if she can identify the coat. It's odd, too, because there was a rain-coat found not far from the house, and we'd all been thinking that that was the one the dead man had been wearing."

" Eh, there's no necessity at all for you to bring the relicts of the deceased along here. If you'll just let me have your address, where you're staying, and sign a certificate to say that you've got the coat with you and the articles contained in the pockets, it'll be all right to take it along with you. The Company's only got a limited responsibility, so they're not strict with us except about articles of value. Or I could wrap it up and send it, if that's more convenient to you."

" Oh, no need to do that. I'll take it, if I may, and let you know in a day or two what they make of it up at Dorn.

By the way, where was that coat taken out ? It wasn't on the Pensteven line, was it ? "

" We had it from Aberfoyle. He'll have taken his place in the wrong train, by the look of it. Though it's just possible that he took the Aberfoyle train, and changed half-way for Pensteven. But it would be a daft way of getting to Blair-whinnie."

" Well," asked Mrs. Wauchope, " how did you get on with Donald Reiver ? Did he try and convert you ? "

" I thought he was sweet," said Angela, hunting a truant stitch. " But, you know, I felt rather sorry for him."

" You should never pity a man for the religious delusions he gets in his old age. I've got none ; but then I don't accept old age, you see ; I fight against it. There's nothing gives these people more solid satisfaction, I believe, people who've led quite respectable lives really, than bothering about their sins. Unless, of course, you mean you were sorry for Donald Reiver about losing his son like that, but really——"

" Oh, but I didn't mean either," interrupted Angela, seizing a favourable moment. " What I meant was I was sorry for him just then, because he was told off to talk to me, while my husband was having a crack with the Hemertons, and I think he really wanted to be talking to a friend of his, one of these ' Circles ' people, a Mr. Wright."

" Ah, now you're being modest. Of course an old fool like Donald would always rather be talking to a young woman like you ; anybody knows that. Lots of time to talk to his religious friends whenever he likes. Though why anybody should want to—really I think if I ever took to religion I should have to be an R.C., because they're the only people who ever let you alone. What's the good of talking to other religious people ? They've all eternity to do it in, by their way of it ; it seems only polite to waste a few words on us sinners while they have the chance. Though I don't know why I should include you in the list, my dear—let's see, what was I saying ?

" Oh yes ; Donald Reiver likes that sort of thing because he's naturally religious. All the Reivers are, I think ; Henry is always saying unkind things about the ministers, but he's very superstitious, and that's the next best thing, isn't it ?

I mean, it shows you know you've missed something."

" Is Major Henry superstitious ? I should never have guessed it."

" You know him, then ? "

" No, only heard of him. But he didn't sound to me the kind of man who would be."

" The kind of man who would be superstitious is never the kind of man who is. Henry ? Good gracious, he nearly murdered one of the housemaids when she brought some peacock's feathers into the house one day. That's why he's got so hot and bothered about this business of poor Colin. Thinks MacWilliam will be seeing *him* lying about next. If MacWilliam did, I believe Henry would curl up and die, same as the blacks do ; they say so, anyhow."

" You don't think he really suspects the men on the estate, then ? All this cry of Bolshevism is just a blind, you mean ? "

" Oh, not merely a blind ; people's minds don't work in tidy compartments like that. He believes in his Bolshevik plot because he wants to believe in it ; he wants to believe in it because he'd sooner think the Reds were after him than the bogy man. You see, all this business of the family curse is pretty uncertain. The story you're told, as I was saying yesterday, is that the estate never goes from father to son. What's really true is that a lot of heirs have died before they came to inherit. Same with any county family really ; the squire's a rich man, and can afford to dodder on in cotton-wool till he's the wrong side of eighty ; and the wretched heir, for want of anything better to do, goes off shooting in East Africa and gets into difficulties with a hippopotamus, or he fights, or he drinks himself to death—always happening, naturally. But Henry means to have Dorn, and he's terribly afraid the bogy man will get him first ; that's my reading of it."

" You don't think it's possible that he's out to prevent his cousins touching the insurance money ? It sounds rather mean, I know, but——"

" Oh, whether it's mean or not doesn't come into it ; when you get to my age you'll know that everybody has a streak of meanness in them, and it mostly comes out when they're dealing with their own relations. But Henry knows which side his bread's buttered, don't he ? And he knows that if Donald Reiver touches the insurance money he may spend some of it on the estate, repair a few of the fences and all

that ; if he don't, Henry will have no fun when he inherits ;
the estate has gone back shockingly. Mark you, I think it's
quite probable Donald will give the whole lot away, now he's
all wrapped up in these Circles. . . . Good gracious, my dear,
what are you being athletic about ? You quite startled me."

" A mouse, over in that corner ; didn't you see it ? " lied
Angela, as she retrieved her ball of wool. " I'm so sorry.
Oh, hullo, Mr. Wright, are you looking for somebody ? "

Not even Mrs. Wauchope could produce embarrassment in
Carstairs Wright. He addressed himself in an apparently
confidential tone to the whole lounge in which they were
sitting. " Yes, I was wanting a word with you, Mrs. Bredon.
It's about Donald, you know ; I rang up a little while ago
to ask if I could come up and see him ; and they said he was
worse again, and not seeing anybody. Well, you know, the
doctor's not been sent for ; I met him and asked. It looks
to me as if they were trying to bottle Donald up somehow.
Did you notice anything wrong with him at lunch ? He
seemed to me rather braced to see us."

" I expect he was just tired," suggested Angela soothingly.
She had her own ideas on the subject.

" Well, what I came to say is, I'm going up to reconnoitre.
I've climbed into most of the Oxford colleges when I went
in for that sort of thing, and I'm not going to be put off by
those synthetic battlements up at Dorn. I hear your husband's
away ; would you mind telling him when he gets back ?
Then, if I don't come back to report, he'll know where I am.
I'm with you in this, Mrs. Bredon. It won't do, bottling a
man up like this ; it's not good enough. See you again,
later." And he left, with swinging steps, leaving a kind of
moral draught to match the physical draught of his going.

" No," said Mrs. Wauchope decidedly. " I don't think
you need have wasted your sympathy on Donald Reiver."

CHAPTER XVIII

THE OPEN GRAVE

THE RAILWAY, FOR all its discomforts—and the train by
which Miles Bredon travelled back from Glasgow illustrated
most of them—does at least shield us from first-hand contact
with the weather. He cursed himself, as he emerged from

the shelter of Pensteven station into a night of bitter cold,
for having told Angela that it didn't matter about the car, he
would manage by bus. The next moment he had run into
the little Major; a bluff "Hullo! You there?" followed,
and the offer of a lift. The Major had business, it appeared,
at Blairwhinnie.

"It's awfully good of you, Major; the only thing is, I was
rather wanting to go up to Dorn. They don't dine till eight,
I think. You see, I've made another discovery."

"Take you up to Dorn, of course. No, not out of the
way really. What you been finding? Luggage?"

"N-no, not exactly," Bredon admitted, as he climbed in.
"Curiously, you know, it's another aquascutum; and it looks
to me as if it must have been your cousin's."

"More rain-coats? Must be a coincidence. What did
he want with two, huh? Anything in it?"

"Very little. Look here, Major, if you don't mind, I think
I'd sooner wait till we're up at Dorn before I tell you about it.
It saves telling a story twice over; and, after all, the things
aren't mine—they belong, if I'm right, to the family."

"Expect you're right. Must be a mistake, though." And
the Major relapsed into silence, except for an intermittent
crooning noise with which, like many other car-drivers, he
loved to keep up his spirits in the dark. In a few minutes,
it seemed, the eldest of the Misses MacWilliam was tugging
at the heavy gates of the Pensteven lodge, and they dived
into a long tunnel of trees, accentuating the glare of the
head-lights that played, with cinematographic radiance, on the
rabbits scuttling before and across their path.

Donald Reiver, it appeared, had gone back to bed an hour
since; and, though he was still awake, the Hemertons
naturally pleaded that he should be left undisturbed; he
should be told next morning. Meanwhile, Major Henry was
invited to be present at the examination of the new find.
Evidently he was in no mood to be convinced; he peered
suspiciously at the offending garment as if he suspected it of
deliberate impersonation, and read scrupulously through
Mr. Macpherson's inventory of the contents as if Mr. Macpherson, too, might have given in his name to a conspiracy
against the house of Dorn. Vincent Hemerton was more
open-minded. "The only thing is," he pointed out, "why
did Colin want to take a train like that, which leads to a dead
end at the best of times, and would be an insane way of

trying to get at Pensteven ? I suppose that would square out, though, with the idea that there was a loss of memory."

"Well, I'm not sure that it does," Bredon objected. " I mean, that line wasn't familiar to him in any way, was it ? He hadn't used it for going to school, or anything of that sort ? I should have thought it probable that, if conscious memory left him, he would automatically go through familiar actions—the mere fact of entering St. Buchan's Station would instinctively take him to the Pensteven platform."

"Then you think it may not be the right coat after all ? " said Mary Hemerton, with a shade of disappointment in her tone.

"Oh no, not necessarily. But it looks, doesn't it, as if we might have to take a different view of his movements ? ' This journey on the Aberfoyle line doesn't look to me the act of a man who has lost his memory. Rather, mightn't it be the act of a man who had all his wits about him, but was determined to come home by a circuitous and unfamiliar route, because for some reason he didn't want to meet people—porters and so on—who would recognize him ? "

" By Jove, that's an idea," put in the Major. " But, y'know, you people will have it that he was a free man in control of his actions. What if he was a prisoner, huh, or practically a prisoner ? Just what those fellows would do—cart him about by a twopenny-halfpenny line like that. What you say, avoid notice."

" Assuming they hadn't a car at their disposal," suggested Bredon. " Honestly, I don't think it would be a very practicable idea, taking a prisoner about in a railway-carriage. And why make the mistake of leaving the rain-coat behind, if there were several of them looking after him ? "

" False clue," said the Major, game to the last, though the assurance had ebbed from his voice.

" Anyhow," suggested Hemerton, with a little impatience, " we may as well make certain of the identification first. There's a letter, you say, which looks as if it might have been sent to Colin ; is it still here, in the pocket ? "

" No, I have it on me ; here it is. I must apologize for reading it, Mrs. Hemerton ; but in the circumstances I had to, and fortunately there was nothing private about it. Would you recognize that letter as having been sent, or likely to have been sent, to your brother ? "

Mary Hemerton knitted her brows over it. " He had a

121

great friend, of course, who stayed here once, whose Christian name is Denis. But I shouldn't know his handwriting, and the name isn't so uncommon as all that. Was there nothing besides the letter ? "

" There was this," said Bredon, producing the ironmonger's parcel and opening it. " That's an odd thing to carry, isn't it ? I wonder what you'll make of that ? "

" But, my dear fellow, it's as plain as a pike-staff," cried Hemerton, his face lighting up. " He wanted the chisel because he meant to finish off his inscription in the cave'; wanted to dig the whole thing deeper, probably, as well. As a· matter of fact, of course, this would have been no use to him ; it's only meant for carving on wood ; still, he wouldn't know that. But that makes the whole thing clear ! It was only a sort of rough copy he was scratching up in the first instance ; so, of course, he didn't mind a casual scratch which looked, to us, like an erasion. As it is, we know he was alive—let's see, when was it ? "

" The fourteenth—Tuesday. Yes, if only Mrs. Hemerton could identify the writing ; or if only the correspondent had been accurate enough to give us a date, even . . . "

" I know," burst in Mary Hemerton, " the Visitors' Book ! Run and get it, Vincent ; it's on the round table in the library."

The Visitors' Book left no kind of doubt that Denis Strutt was the correspondent. The writing was rather affected ; the Ts, with strong crosses to them, especially characteristic. The book showed, too, that Strutt had been staying in the house just before Colin's twenty-first birthday, which accounted for his remembering the date.

" Well, Mr. Bredon," asked Mary Hemerton, with a rather forced smile, " are you satisfied at last ? "

" Who, I ? Oh, but, you see, it's not a question of satisfying me, Mrs. Hemerton. I'm only here to report to my employers. Of course, I shall have to report this find, and the inferences I draw from it, which are the same as yours. And I should hope that they would rest content with the evidence we've collected ; though, of course, it's not evidence one could take to a jury very well, if it was a matter for legal decision."

" Should think not," broke in the Major, whose silence for the last few minutes had been one of obvious dissent. " All you know is, a letter sent to Colin was in that pocket.

122

You don't know it was he put it there, huh ? And if he did, what d'you know about the coat, huh ? You know it was left in one particular damn train ; you don't know it was Colin left it. May have been dead by then ; *was* dead, I say ; anybody may have taken his coat, left it about by accident, left it in that train for a blind, anything ! A jury—good God ! "

" That's just what I was saying, Major. But the jury's out to expect fraud ; my company isn't, in these particular circumstances. I mean, it only wants to make sure that there's been no fraud practised by . . . well, by interested parties. And whatever you make of this last find, it doesn't suggest that."

" The chisel and the letter were the only things in the pockets ? " asked Hemerton.

" And a pipe. Very much like the one we found in the other coat. Here it is—but, as Mrs. Hemerton says, it's not the sort of thing one recognizes, even if one's seen it again and again."

" Oh, but I do recognize this one," said Mary, taking it from him. " Now I see it, of course I recognize it. As you say, it's very like the one we found the other day. But how well I remember that thinning of the bowl on the left-hand side, where Colin always would knock it out against the fender. Do you remember, Vincent, how you used to tell him he was ruining the bowl by knocking it out like that ? And the mouthpiece, nearly bitten through—poor Colin had very strong teeth. Yes, that's Colin's pipe all right ; there's no mistaking it."

The Major shrugged his shoulders, and walked twice up and down the room, as if seeking to imprison his feelings. At last he said, " Well, you know what I think. Can't stop here ; you'll be wanting to get your dinner. Coming, Mr. Bredon ? I'll put you down at the Blairwhinnie— trouble ? No trouble at all. Trust me, Hemerton, you'll hear more of these chaps yet." And he stalked out, still unappeased.

He returned to the subject as soon as they had passed under the arch which carried the enclosed garden over the drive. " Cock-and-bull story, young Colin touring all round the country-side like that. D'you believe it, huh ? Believe he was still alive that Tuesday ? "

Bredon was just about to reply, when a singular interruption prevented him. A figure was seen limping eagerly towards them across the grass, a voice hailed them, and in the full glare of the head-lights the features of Carstairs Wright became recognizable. " Hi ! " he shouted, " can you give me a lift ? I've hurt my foot. Oh, it's you, is it, Bredon ? Excuse me, but . . . this gentleman, is he a friend of yours ? "

Bredon effected the introduction rather awkwardly. Mr. Wright's chumminess always had the effect of making it look, to a stranger, as if you were one of his oldest friends. Still, he was obviously in need of a lift. " This is Major Reiver," he said, " of Langbrae. We've just been up at the house, and we've going to Blairwhinnie."

Carstairs Wright did not seem so anxious, after all, to get in. " Excuse me, Major," he said, " but are you in with that lot—the Hemertons, I mean ? They told me—somebody told me the family relations were a bit strained. Yes, I will ; I'm going to show you something. Turn off that engine for a moment, Major, and come this way." People who leave no opening for a refusal do not, as a rule, meet with it ; and Mr. Wright's mixture of sincerity and energy had this kind of irresistible quality. The Major turned off his engine and followed, with Bredon at his heels, to the wall of the enclosed garden ; nor did he even demur when he found that he was expected to climb the wall, by means of a brittle-looking hurdle up-ended to serve the purposes of a ladder.

" It's like this," Carstairs Wright went on, apparently un-conscious of achieving the sensational. " They wouldn't let me see Donald ; told me over the telephone that he was worse. Well, I wasn't going to be put off like that, so I thought I'd climb ; it isn't much of a wall, anyhow. This looked the best place to me, and so it is, for climbing. But take care when you get over—stay there, Major, till I come and direct you. I've got a torch." A wavering circle of light showed them the ground on which they stood, covered with dead leaves which crackled in the frost. At one point, the leaves had been roughly cleared away, and the corner of a glazed wooden frame had been disclosed—a frame of the kind used in vegetable gardens. A star-shaped hole in the glass bore witness that Mr. Carstairs Wright had put his foot in it.

" That's a nice sort of thing to run up against in the dark," he commented.

" Man-traps ! " cried the Major. " Illegal, of course. I told you there was nothing that fellow MacWilliam wasn't up

to. Place rotten with poachers, to be sure; still, man-traps
—it isn't done."

Bredon hesitated for a moment; then, " They'll be at
dinner now," he said; " what about clearing away these
leaves a bit ? I've got to look into this. I want to see how
deep a hole there is underneath, for instance. Come on."

The leaves, which were thinly scattered, did not take long
to clear, and the frame, though it was of formidable size, some
six feet by four, was easily lifted off. It disclosed a hole,
about a foot and a half wide, perhaps a little under six feet
in length. The depth had been left uneven ; it was nowhere
greater than a foot.

" Good God ! " ejaculated the Major. " A grave ! "

" Looks like it," admitted Bredon, flashing Wright's torch
round the shadows. And you might almost say, a family
grave. Look there ! " And he pointed to something at one
of the two ends which glittered dully in the light. It was a
horse-shoe, the family emblem of the Reivers. Bredon risked
one glance at the Major, and read his inches. He was short,
as the Reivers were generally ; not more, by the look of him,
than five foot seven.

The Major's arm trembled as it touched his. " A horse-
shoe ! The villains ! And now, Mr. Bredon, perhaps before
you make a report to those directors of yours you'll try and
find out who it was that grave was dug for."

" Personally, I should be even more interested to know who
dug it. But, as you say, the horse-shoe can hardly be a coincidence. Your idea is, then . . ."

" No two ways about it ; the thing's as plain as if it were
written there in print. They made away with poor Colin ;
who comes next ? No need to worry about poor old Donald ;
he won't last long anyhow, huh ? It's me they're after, Mr.
Bredon ; remember that threatening letter ? I'll take them
to law over it, sir, that's what I'll do. This ain't Ireland,
thank God ; there's still justice to be got here."

Carstairs Wright stood looking at the Major in gentle
amazement during this outburst. Then he said, as if to himself : " Donald ! They've dug it for Donald ! "

Bredon forced back an access of purely hysterical laughter.
" I say, you know," he protested, " we mustn't lose our heads
over this. There's nothing in the world to show how long
ago this pit was dug ; depend upon it, it was meant for young
Colin. Confound it all, we've known all along there's been

some hanky-panky about the way his corpse was treated. Oh, I don't say this fits in ; God knows how anything fits in to a story like this ! But it's ten to one this grave here is part of the old mystery, not a fresh one. What's become of the earth, by the way ? "

" It's thrown just under the wall there," explained Carstairs Wright. " I came across it when I was looking about for a place to climb up by. It's cleverly hidden, though, in the middle of a great whopping clump of nettles. I say, this is awful ; poor Donald ! I must go up to the house."

" Oh, don't be a fool," said Bredon. " Excuse me ; I'm a fool myself to lose my temper. But, don't you see, if you're right, they haven't finished digging the grave yet. And it's common sense to dig your grave first and kill your man when it's ready for him. Nothing's going to happen to-night. I say, we can't mend this glass. We must just pile up the leaves again and make it look as natural as possible. Then you'll dashed well come back with us and let the doctor have a look at that leg of yours. I'll go up first thing to-morrow and have it out with the Hemertons ; I've got one or two things to say to them in any case. Come on, Major ; ease it over this way."

They said hardly a word as they drove back to Blairwhinnie. The Major refused to come in and dine ; nor did Bredon press him, for the little man's nerves were so obviously rattled that a drive home late at night would have been an unkind ordeal for him. Carstairs Wright was put down at Dr. Purvis's surgery. It amazed Bredon, as he passed through the hotel lounge, to find that the clock registered only five minutes to eight ; so much of incident had been packed into a short hour.

" Well," he said to Angela, as he dressed hastily for dinner, " you'll be glad to hear that your husband has been behaving like a real spy to-day, a real, low-down, sneaking police-spy. Leyland would have thought no end of my performance. By the way, Angela, speaking as one spy to another, d'you think it's likely a woman would recognize a pipe belonging to a male relation ; so as to be certain, I mean, coming across it suddenly, that it was his ? If you saw a pipe lying in the lounge here, for example, would you know whether it was mine or not ? "

" I might, but only by the smell. You seem to have quite an individual knack—oh, all right, don't get worked up about it. Who's been recognizing pipes ? The Hemerton, I suppose ? But I thought you told me she was quite uncertain about the pipe that was found in the aquascutum ? "

" She was, about that pipe, found in that aquascutum. Blast this tie. But, you see, there's been another aquascutum found since I last saw you ; and this one had a pipe in the pocket too. And Mrs. Hemerton, that very level-headed woman, pounced upon it and said at once it was her brother's. Is that quite natural—or am I fancying things ? "

" M'm, I don't think it's a bit impossible, Miles. When you see the wrong pipe, the one you haven't seen before, it has no message for you at all, positive or negative. But when you see the real one, you suddenly find that you can recognize it, by a hundred little marks you aren't conscious of ; it shrieks to you somehow, *Yes, that's the one*. Like forgetting the name of an acquaintance, don't you know, until somebody mentions it by accident in another connexion—then it comes back to you."

" Your psychology, Mrs. Bredon, is most penetrating, and might, in other circumstances, be helpful. But there's one crab about it in this case which seems to me to be quite fatal."

" Such as what ? "

" Oh, only that it was the same pipe, both times."

CHAPTER XIX

BREDON EXPLAINS

Mrs. Wauchope dined at their table that night : Angela had made the arrangement with enthusiasm, but it proved scarcely fortunate. The Bredons were both longing to discuss the latest developments up at Dorn ; and, even if it had been discreet to take Mrs. Wauchope into their confidence over such matters, it could not have been done over the dinner-table ; for she had, in a crowded room, a voice like a fog-horn. Miles toyed abstractedly with his bread and his napkin-ring, Angela registered a feverish and overdone interest in the conversation ; Mrs. Wauchope went on placidly, unconscious of any constraint in the attitude of either. Nor, as it proved, was her monologue without practical interest.

For at one point *à propos* the Reiver finances, she let slip

127

a phrase about " poor Mary Hemerton, living continually on the edge of a financial volcano."

" But I thought," said Bredon, pricking up his ears for the first time during the meal, " the Hemertons were supposed to be very comfortably off ? "

" That's just what they ain't, of course. Well off, if you like, but it's silly to talk about being comfortably off, with people like that. I'm *comfortably* off, because my income's all in trust securities, and I have the sense to realize it beforehand when tight times are coming. But Vincent Hemerton, now, he's regular gambler. Don't you get taken in by all that old-maidishness of his about wearing overshoes at night and keeping his razor-blades facing north. He's the sort of man who'd haggle for twenty minutes about a cheap return ticket and then sink fifty thousand in a Czecho-Slovakian gold-mine. Oh, I grant you they're all prootty much alike, these business men, nowadays. That's money— that was ! "—and Mrs. Wauchope turned her head smartly from left to right with a gesture familiar to those who study newspaper advertisements. " I think we're fools to trust our money to other people the way we do ; and really I've some-times thought of keeping all my little worldly wealth in a stocking, only these stockings they make nowadays—ah, I see, you're feeling uncomfortable, Mr. Bredon. My dear, how wonderful it must be to have a husband who still wrinkles the middle of his forehead ever so little when one talks about stockings. But what was I saying ? Oh yes, about Vincent Hemerton. He's not one of your safe men ; he's what they call a wizard of finance. Call it conjurer instead of wizard, and you get a clearer idea of the truth. Though indeed a conjurer plays about with two packets of soap and pretends it's only one, whereas your financier plays about with one packet of money and pretends it's two. But Vincent Hemerton's juggling with money all the time ; and depend upon it he wants that insurance money your directors are so interested in to play about with ; perhaps for the fun of the thing, perhaps to save his skin—you can't tell till you've been through his private accounts, and you won't get leave to do that in a hurry."

" He's an infernally slow chess-player, all the same," suggested Bredon.

" Ah, that he may be ; but, you see, one plays chess under artificial conditions ; you can take your time thinking about the next move. Ever seen him playing poker? No, and I don't suppose anybody else has either; he's not a card man, Vincent Hemerton. I suppose that's because he plays his games for relaxation, and doesn't want to go on gambling all night when he's been gambling all day. Put him by the fire-side, and he'll spend ten minutes scratching the cat with the top of the King's rook. But put him up against a sudden crisis, and he can't help himself; he'll plunge."

From this Mrs. Wauchope branched off on to other topics. Her views, though stimulating in themselves, have no relevance for our present story. There was something providential about her announcement, when dinner was over, that she must be off now to a concert which was being held in aid of a local charity; " not that it matters, because if I'm at all up to my usual form I'll be asleep by the time they get to Annie Laurie, and that's all that really matters; so good night, my dears, and you can tell all the other old women that you only asked me to sit at your table because I insisted on it, and then we'll have no jealousies about it." As a matter of fact, the Bredons took no risks of further interruption; they retired to their room at once, with the evening before them to discuss possibilities.

" The same pipe, you were saying," Angela began, when Miles had described the interview at Dorn. " From which I assume that the later aquascutum, exhibit B, was your own contribution to the mystery.[1] Marvellous what intuition I have."

" It's much more marvellous what intuition other people haven't. I can never really believe I'm taking people in; one's own fakes always seem so unconvincing. Yes, I admit I thought it was my turn to start finding things."

" You seem to have got round the authorities at St. Buchan's all right."

" Oh, there I had luck. I was prepared to do something thoroughly clumsy; I had an aquascutum over my arm, underneath my own great-coat, and I had the things I wanted in the pockets.[2] I expected that I should have to leave it unlabelled on one of the shelves, and persuade the man that his assistant had forgotten to register it. Or possibly detach a label from one of the other parcels and stick it on; I wasn't quite sure how they managed things. But, as it proved, an aquascutum had been left in a train about the date I wanted.

[1] p. 114. [2] p. 119.

I suppose in Glasgow, where it's always raining, you always take one to the station with you, and leave it in the rack when you get out into the country, because it's cleared up. It hadn't, of course, been left on the right line ; that was too much to expect. Nor, actually, was it anything like the same shade as the one the Major produced, which Mrs. Hemerton had been prepared to identify as her brother's. But it was just good enough, my story; and of course all I had to do was to shift my stage properties into the pockets of the strange aquascutum while the superintendent's back was turned.[1] His little chit, with an inventory of the things found in the pockets, did wonders."

" Well, I suppose you won't be happy till I admit that I still don't quite know what you did it for. Was your idea just to see how much the Hemertons would swallow ? "

" Oh no, it was much more definite than that. You see, so far everything that we've found—the traces at the Devil's Dimple, and the first rain-coat, and the things in the pocket of the first rain-coat, have either suggested that Colin Reiver was dead by Monday, or they've left the question open. Now, what have been the reactions of the parties concerned ? "

" So far, the Major has been rather enthusiastic about the finds. But then, the date of Colin's death doesn't, as far as we know, make the slightest difference to him. Also, it was he who thought of the Devil's Dimple as a probable hiding-place, and it was he who found the first rain-coat. We all like proving that we were in the right of it. Whereas the Hemertons, as you were about to remark, haven't shown any signs of going up to the Devil's Dimple, for example, to look round for themselves, and they were quite doubtful about the identification of the first rain-coat. All which suggests . . . "

" Yes, what ? "

" Why, in the first place, that they aren't keen on an early date for Colin's death; though, indeed, that goes without saying. And in the second place, that, if anybody besides yourself has been leaving faked clues about, it's not the Hemertons, or they would have had the sense to leave the kind of clues which would have made out that Colin was still alive on Monday and Tuesday."

" Yes, you're coming on. That is exactly the point. Only, to make sure of my facts by what is known, my dear Angela, as the Method of Agreement and Difference, I thought it

[1] p. 121.

130

would be a good thing to see what happened if we had a fresh find, and this time it was one which favoured the late date for Colin's death. I didn't want to make the evidence absolutely clinching, as it would have been if, say, there had been a copy of the Tuesday's paper in one of the pockets. I wanted evidence which would *point* to Colin's being alive after Sunday, but leave it open to resist the conclusion if one wanted to. The chisel was meant to suggest what it suggested to Hemerton, that Colin's amateur efforts in rock-carving had given him a taste for doing the thing in more style ; that he had gone into Glasgow on the Monday for other purposes, and had bought a chisel, on the inspiration of the moment, when he found himself there. The Hemertons lapped up my story ; therefore they don't want to prove an early date for the death, but a late one ; therefore if there has been any faking of clues, it must be somebody else who did it. That's sound, isn't it ? "

" Yes, I don't quite see the hole in that. How did you get hold of that letter, by the way ? "

" Oh, I pinched that when they let me look round Colin Reiver's room up at Dorn ; it obviously came from Mr. Denis Strutt, and I had the idea that it might be useful to know that young gentleman's address, in case I should want to get in touch with him.[1] I tore off the address, though, before I made use of it this afternoon—otherwise, people would have been wondering why the Lost Luggage Office hadn't communicated with him. Yes, it all worked out pretty well. What I'm asking myself is, whether the Hemertons were really taken in by my story—in which case it looks as if they must be in good faith all through ; or whether they pretended to be taken in, because the evidence it suggested was all on their side ? In that case, they must have done some quick thinking. Which is why Mrs. Wauchope's conversation interested me rather more than I let on."

" And the Major—how does he come out of it ? "

" Oh, he may be all right ; it may be just pig-headedness. You see, he was all against my aquascutum being genuine *before I let him know* that it helped to fix the date of death. He objected to it from the start, merely because it wasn't *his* aquascutum."

" And what were you saying about excitements on the way home ? "

[1] p. 69.

131

" Oh yes, Carstairs Wright's grave."

" But, good heavens, what's happened to . . . "

" I'm sorry, the expression was misleading. I meant his by right of discovery, not by right of tenancy—as in the case of the Major's aquascutum. Well, it was like this." And Bredon told the story, with a certain flippancy of tone which marked his reaction from the grim experience of two hours back.

" Oh Lord ! " said Angela, when he had finished. " Is this going to be another blind ? More false clues, I mean ? "

" Not really, if you come to think of it. People who leave faked clues about leave them about where they are likely to be found by the right people, and not by anybody else. It would take Carstairs Wright to go climbing over garden walls and putting his feet through cucumber frames ; it is his *métier*. You and I wouldn't do it. No, the bother about that grave is that it's something quite genuine, confound it, and for the life of me I can't see what."

" Well, the Major's got a theory, and Carstairs Wright's got a theory ; we aren't so badly off."

" Confound it all, that's just the trouble. They've bagged the only two possible theories, and both are impossible, if you see what I mean. It's very difficult for a total stranger to go digging graves in another man's garden without evoking comment. And even if he could, why should he want to ? Whereas Vincent Hemerton is at liberty to dig as many graves as he wants to up at Dorn, which is Wright's idea. And the men on the estate might easily do it on the sly, or find some excuse for doing it, which is the Major's idea. But who else could or would do it ? And yet both those theories are impossible."

" Would you say more than very improbable ? "

" I say impossible, woman. A couple of people living under the roof of a highly respected landowner can't suddenly make away with him, park his body in the garden, and put up a stone to say, ' Sacred to the memory of Ponto. ' Questions are going to be asked about what happened to the old gentleman ; more especially as he was in bad health and they were supposed to be looking after him. On the other hand, granted that the men on an estate have got a grouch against the next heir, why should they go and dig a grave for him within a stone's throw of the big house, where people are passing all day, when they've got the whole estate to dig graves in without anybody noticing what they're up to ? No, don't you see, this buried-him-darkly-at-dead-of-night business only comes in useful when you've got a corpse left unexpectedly on your hands, and nobody knows that it's there, because everybody imagines the dead man was miles away at the time. That's verified all right, you see, in Colin's case; and yet that idea is as impossible as the others. Why dig a grave with considerable labour, and then leave your man planted out by the side of a high road?"

" Oo! I don't know about that. It only means they had to change their plans for some reason; or the corpus was discovered accidentally when they hadn't meant it to be discovered. One could surely think up ways in which that might have happened."

" Yes, but get back to the beginning of things. What did they want to murder Colin for, or, if you prefer it, why did they want to play about with his corpse when found? Only because his life was heavily insured, and there was something wrong about the payments. Now, what on earth's the use, in that state of affairs, of burying your man secretly in a place where nobody will find him? Can you seriously imagine that my directors would pay up the insurance when his friends and relations came round and pointed out that he had disappeared? Why, he might have disappeared to South America and be living there under another name! No, you've jolly well got to produce your corpus if you do business with the Indescribable. And don't say that they meant to bury the body for a day or two and produce it afterwards. Because, you see—well, it's an unsavoury topic; but, in cold weather like this, the less you bury your man, the better he keeps."

" Yes; there's no need to be disgusting over it. What are you going to do about it all, then?"

" Well, I've already cabled to the consul at Madeira. If I get nothing out of that, the only thing is to get in touch somehow with Mr. Denis Strutt. But that means a journey south, and I don't want to leave the scene of action just yet. By the way, are you familiar with that haunting poem of de Musset's in which every verse ends with the refrain :

> Qu'est ce que c'est que le tong
> Maintenong ?

Because I told Carstairs Wright I'd be in the lounge at half-past nine, to hold his hand a bit. Twenty to ten ? I must fly, or he'll be off to Dorn again. That man has no intervals of repose."

CHAPTER XX

THE FLIGHT OF THE REIVERS

" My tobacco," said Miles, after filling his first pipe next morning, " is lasting out, you will be glad to hear, well. All the same, it would have rather a good effect if you would remind me to-morrow about getting some more. Do they, I ask myself, keep the right kind of tobacco in these parts ? Not even a Scottish saleswoman will reconcile me to a strange brand."

" Added to which," suggested Angela, " you will only be able to get it from one of those beastly little shops that stay open on Sunday to sell newspapers. Do they, I wonder, even have those in Scotland ? "

" Good Lord ! D'you mean to say it's really Sunday to-morrow ? Do you realize we've been nearly a week on this stinker of a job ? "

" Things have been moving, all the same," Angela pointed out. " Let's see, it was only a fortnight ago to-morrow, wasn't it, that Mr. Reiver was supposed to be dying, and . . ."

" Yes, that was on the Sunday.[1] . . . Great suffering Jerusalem ! Angela, would you mind doing a little memory-work and informing me when it was that the cheque in payment of the premium reached the Company ? "

" Monday morning, Sholto said—at least, it reached the Perth office then.[2] I don't think he told us when it reached London. Why particularly ? "

" Oh, nothing ; it was only just an idea I had."

" Miles, don't be tiresome. I know perfectly well what you look like when you've thought of something rather important. Your face gets all long, and your mouth quite round, and you look as if you were wishing you'd been taught to whistle. Come on, let's all have it, as the schoolmasters say."

" Not a word, till I've verified something ; and probably not even then. Let's see, who'd be the right man to ask ?

[1] p. 21.   [2] p. 38.

Hullo, there's Dr. Purvis ; he'd do. He's coming into the hotel too. Lord, I must hop down and ask him ; there might be something in this."

The doctor, it proved, was himself bursting with news, and must needs have his say first. " Excuse me, Mr. Bredon," he said, after the merest shadow of a good morning, " but could you tell me where the Hemertons have gone ? I had no idea . . ."

" Gone ! Why, I saw them both yesterday evening, and they said nothing about going away. Surely there must be a mistake."

" I had it from your friend Carstairs Wright. I was attending him professionally this morning, and it seems he had just been ringing up Dorn. It was the butler who answered, and he said they had all just left for the station."

" All ? Not Mr. Reiver too ? "

" Mr. Reiver too. That's what's worrying me, of course. He's not fit to travel. Your friend Mr. Wright has got hold of a curious idea that the Hemertons are wanting to murder him. I wasn't very clear about his reasoning ; but I will say if that's what they want, they're going the best way about it. I don't know what can have possessed them. Though, fortunately, there's less people die of open air than we doctors ever let on."

" But this beats me," Bredon said, half to himself. " They can't be doing a bolt altogether—they must have left an address. By the way, did Carstairs Wright talk to you about his reasons for suspecting the Hemertons ? "

" He did—he's a communicative sort of a young man." You could guess that Dr. Purvis had already learned to associate Mr. Wright with the " Circles " and disliked him accordingly. " But I'm not concerned with graves, you see ; that comes after I've finished with my patients, and so I told him. I was wondering, Mr. Bredon, whether perhaps you and I mightn't go up to Dorn, and find some excuse for being just the least little bit inquisitive about what's happened ? Sanders is a good fellow."

" Right ; we'll do that. Have you your car ? No, now I come to think of it, I'd better get mine out ; I might want to go on elsewhere afterwards—I'll put you down first, though. Just one minute, while I talk to my wife about it."

So far as the formalities are concerned, a great house deserted by its owners collapses like a flat tyre. Dorn stood there to-day exactly as it had stood yesterday, but its atmosphere was subtly changed. The chauffeur was cleaning the car within sight, singing heartily within earshot, of the front door. House-maids were seen through the glass panes sweeping vigorously, as if they had been only waiting for this opportunity to have a real field-day with duster and broom. A gardener's coat lay prominent on a window-sill. Even Sanders himself was in a kind of morning *négligé*, not ordinarily to be seen by front-door visitors. His attitude was that of the good man who feels sure that there must be some explanation, but has no idea what it is. Regretful concern strove with polite reassurance in his manner.

" No, sir, they left no message at all. I'm sure they would have done, if they had thought there would be any uneasiness. I had the impression, sir, that you had concluded your enquiries last night, and would not be needing any further information." (Butlers, after all, stand behind chairs, and are not deaf.) " Would you be wishing to go round the house at all ? I am certain Mr. Reiver would be glad to let you come and go exactly as you wish."

" Well, no, I don't think so, thanks," replied Bredon, rather lamely. " But I'd no idea they were going so soon, and there were one or two points I still wanted to ask Mrs. Hemerton about. I suppose you have an address for forwarding letters, if I sent them here ? "

" Their luggage was labelled for London, sir, but I don't think Mr. and Mrs. Hemerton would be going to their London address ; the house is almost shut up. I expect you would know their country address, sir—Crossways, near Devizes ? That would certainly find them at present ; though I think in a day or two they will be taking Mr. Reiver to the seaside to recuperate."

" Oh, thanks very much ; Crossways, near Devizes ? I suppose Mr. Reiver didn't say when he'd be back ? No, of course he wouldn't be certain ; it would depend on his health."

" I hope," the doctor broke in, " that you saw Mr. Reiver was well wrapped up ? It's an awful kind of risk to take, travelling in this weather, so ill as he's been. You shouldn't have let him go without seeing me, Sanders."

The butler's expression indicated that he was gratified by this testimony to his influence, but that, professionally, he was unable to accept such compliments. " I did venture to ask him whether it was wise, sir ; but it wasn't my place to interfere with his plans. He was feeling very well in himself, he said, and he wanted to get away from the place. But I saw him into his fur coat, and put in a couple of hot-water bottles with him for the journey. And they were travelling first-class, White tells me. I think it will do him good, sir, after all he's been through."

" Oh, there's one thing you could tell me," put in Bredon, as if struck by a sudden idea. " I might have some news to send to Mrs. Hemerton to-morrow evening. Can you tell me what's the last post out from here, or from Pensteven ? "

" Five o'clock from here, sir, and eight from Pensteven—on Sundays, that is. They collect up to midnight on week-days. Should I write down Mrs. Hemerton's address ?. "

" No, thanks, I'll remember it. Well, Doctor, I'll have to take you back, or your patients will be getting anxious about you. Good day, Sanders, and thank you very much. You know," he added, when they were out of earshot, " I believe Sanders really would have kept Mr. Reiver back, if he hadn't thought he was fit to travel. I suppose it was touch and go with him, that night when he had his crisis ? "

" I won't deny but I was worried about him. The heart's not strong, you see. I was here for the night, and I didn't get much sleep either."

" Yes, it must have been a trying time for everybody. Did the Major sleep the night, too ? "

" No, he just saw the laird for a little, and then he saw Mr. Gilchrist—that's the lawyer—and went back home to Langbrae."

" Quite early, I suppose ? I was wondering, I mean, whether he would have seen . . . seen anything that was lying by the roadside earlier than, say, nine o'clock. Oh, but of course, he would drive down by the other lodge ; I was forgetting."

It was quite impossible to tell whether the doctor knew he was being drawn. " He wouldn't be away," he said, " till ten or half-past. And, as you say, he'd have no occasion to pass along that piece of road, between the two lodges. But it's my belief he would have seen nothing, even if he'd come along that road, going from Blairwhinnie to Pensteven. The body, you see, was behind that big heap of stones when it was found—that is, if MacWilliam's telling the truth when he says it was found the same way on Monday as on Wednesday."

" Yes, that's interesting. Only a car coming from Pensteven

137

would have seen anything; and there weren't likely to be many coming that way, because Pensteven is an obvious place to put up for the night. Well, Doctor, I hope you'll keep Carstairs Wright in bed for the day; we don't want him rushing round too much. I suppose . . . I suppose if I wanted to come and see you—unprofessionally, I mean—to-morrow would be as good a day as any ? "

" It would suit me perfectly, if it was in the afternoon, at least. You see, we're Sabbatarian folk round here, and we don't even send for the doctor on Sundays unless it's exceptionally urgent. You'll be welcome round at my place."

" Jump in, Angela," said her husband, when the doctor had disappeared from view. " You said you wanted to meet the Major, and it seems to me this morning's news is a good excuse for going and having a crack with him. You see, he's not on the telephone."

It was, perhaps, from an unconscious reminiscence of his visit to Dorn that Langbrae, too, smote Bredon with a premonition of desertedness. His ring seemed to echo in the house; there was no answer to it at first, and the melancholy barking of a dog suggested desolation. The door was opened at last by a bewildered parlour-maid.

" He's away, sir," she said. " Would you be the gentleman he left a note for ? I'll just get it."

" Will he be back to-night ? " asked Bredon, fingering the note.

" I don't think he will. He took his luggage with him in the car, and he said he'd let us know when he'd be coming back."

" Oh, I see. He didn't say where he was going, did he ? "

" I couldn't say. His letters was to be kept till he came back."

" Ah, then it's not for long. You don't know if he went by train, I suppose ? "

" I couldn't say. He might have left the car at the garage, perhaps, and gone south. Or he might be driving himself all the way. "

" Do you know which garage he uses ? "

" I couldn't say."

" Thanks very much. No, there's no answer to the note needed. Good morning." And indeed Angela, to whom the note was handed as they went down the drive, was within her rights in knitting her brows over the contents. A plain card, with the address of Langbrae at the head of it, was inscribed only as follows : ." . . . sang out with joy and . . ."

" What exactly," asked Miles, " are we meant to understand by that ? "

" I couldn't say," returned Angela, with a tolerable imitation of the parlour-maid. " Of course, it's jolly of him to have left any message at all, but he might have made it a tiny bit more explicit."

" That's rum, too, if you come to think of it. He seems to have expected me to call, but I didn't tell him I would. I wonder whether the Hemertons let him know by post that they were flitting ? Oh, confound and blast it all, what are they all up to ? Total absence of Reivers—you know, it looks dashed fishy."

" Said the great detective. You are a one for noticing things. Perhaps they were just getting sick of aquascutums ; you can't press people beyond a certain point. Or do you think the Major's gone to Harrogate, perhaps ? You can read the word ' gout ' into the message, you know."

" I wish you wouldn't always rag at the wrong times. Well, I suppose the only thing is to read that dashed cipher somehow. It must be a cipher of sorts ; I told you, didn't I, that the man tries to solve Topcliffe every week ?[1] And he knows I'm a fan too, so I suppose he thought it would be all in my line. ' Sang out with joy and . . .'—must be a quotation of sorts. Sure you don't know it ? "

" I'd give my eyes to know it ; it'd be such a score. Also, before I told you I'd make you explain what it was you were so stuffy about this morning ; you know, about the posts from Pensteven. I bet you don't work this out before lunch."

It was a *dea ex machina*, however, who solved the knot for them. Mrs. Wauchope sailed in upon them as they sat in a little writing-room, with an uncomfortable gas fire, which was the only retreat, as a rule, that promised solitude at the Blairwhinnie. " Paper-games ? " she inquired. " I've a passion for paper-games. So restful to see you modern people at it ; I always say the young people nowadays have given up playing them because they're all too stoopid to use their brains. Now, tell me, what's this one ? Oh, but I can recognize that ! "

" Don't tell him, Mrs. Wauchope," cried Angela. " He'll be quite unbearable if you don't bargain with him over it.

You see, he was keeping secrets from me this morning, and that's very wrong in a husband, isn't it ? " '

" Certainly you shall have the secret," said Mrs. Wauchope, sitting down with the air of one who means to make a morning of it. " And so will I ; I love secrets. Otherwise, Mr. Bredon, you shall never get a word out of me, even by torture. And I give you a fair warning that you'll never work it out for yourself, if you haven't got it already."

Miles shifted uneasily as he answered. " I don't mind telling you in the least," he explained, " only there's really nothing to tell. It was just an idea that might have had something to say to clearing up all this mystery about Colin Reiver's death. But you aren't interested in all that, Mrs. Wauchope."

" Indeed I am. The Reivers are some of my oldest friends, and I should be delighted to hear they'd been murdering anybody. Now, are we to have it ? "

" It's only," said Miles, " that the Major, that Sunday night, didn't leave till ten or half-past. And he left promising to send a letter off by the late post.[1] On a day of coming and going like that, people forget that it is Sunday ; and of course he couldn't really have posted it that night to any good purpose, because the last post goes out at eight. But it reached Perth first thing next morning."

" Are we expected to guess what happened ? " asked Mrs. Wauchope. " How exciting ! I'll tell you what ; I believe Henry Reiver must have taken it in to Perth by car."

" I know ; it's the only way he can possibly have done it. But, don't you see, at that rate he must have passed the very place where MacWilliam said he had found the body next morning. Passed it twice, one would think, because he must have been well down the drive before he remembered it was Sunday ; likely enough not till he reached Pensteven. So he would go from Pensteven to Perth through Blairwhinnie, and back again ; and he'd be likely to see, with head-lights, if there was anything lying by the side of the road."

" And you mean there wasn't ? " suggested Angela in a rather disappointed tone.

" If there wasn't, why hasn't he said so ? He must have read about the inquest ; he must have realized that the police were looking out for any car that had been near the place late that night. And instead of coming forward, he's left it to

[1] p. 23.

140

be assumed that he knows nothing. I see you're not much impressed. Now, the message, Mrs. Wauchope ! "

Mrs. Wauchope sat down at a derelict piano in the corner of the room, and accompanied herself in a short exercise of carol-singing :

" When Christ was born of Mary free
In Bethlehem, that fair city,
Angels sang out with joy and glee :
   In excelsis gloria.

How's that ? " she went on. " I can see you don't have waits in your part of the world. That's what it is, though it beats me where Henry got hold of it ; probably off a Christmas card, I should think."

" Yes," agreed Angela, " that's what it is. Angels—glee : sounds useful. Miles, what are you jumping up and down about ? You don't see what it means, do you ? "

" You don't suggest, surely, that you *don't* see what it means ? Well, well, I score up after all. It's an anagram— you've got that much ? And it must be the name of the place where Major Reiver is, for there is no other communication he could make which would be likely to interest me. It's got to be a complete address, in ten letters ; you can't get in Cadwallader Mansions or anything. One word, that tells you at once the name of the country and the place and the building."

" Shut up, Miles, can't you ? How am I to work the beastly thing out if you will go on talking ? "

" I want to start, confound it, instead of hanging about here. Did I mention that the Major has taken his golf clubs ? "

" Oh, you cad ! And I was just getting it ; I swear I was."

CHAPTER XXI

A FACE IN THE MIRROR

BY THE TIME they reached Gleneagles, luncheon was a need more imperative than the Major's society. Actually, they found him in the dining-room, sharing his table with a stranger. Not a sinister figure, this, by any means ; his rosy cheeks and twinkling eye, and his evident enjoyment of all

141

that Providence sent him to drink, proclaimed a mellow old age. In the dining-room, the two parties only exchanged bows; afterwards, over coffee, they came together, and the stranger was introduced as Mr. Gilchrist.

"The Major heard I was staying here," he explained, "and, you see, I've done all the family's legal business these years past. So he thought if you and he was to have a talk, it would do no harm for me to be present; wasn't that so, Major? It's wonderful what a lot of confusions and mix-ups would be avoided in the world, Mr. Bredon, if people never talked business without a lawyer present."

"There's one thing beats me, Major," said Bredon; "and that is, why you expected me to want a talk with you? I *do*, you see, but only because you left Langbrae so suddenly. And if you only left Langbrae because you preferred not to have an interview without the presence of your legal adviser . . .".

"No, that's not it," the Major broke in. His air was that of a man who has been fencing with a situation too long, and is determined at last to have it out openly. "I came here because the place was getting on my nerves—Dorn and all that. I know what you think it is, cold feet. So it is, I dare say; but it frets away a man's nerves, waiting for something to happen when he doesn't know what. Something's going on there, don't tell me it isn't; that grave was the last straw. Same time, you've been suspicious of me all along; don't pretend you haven't."

"Suspicious? How exactly?"

"Why, that rain-coat; you know it was never in that train, huh? You put it there, huh? God knows why, but it was a try-on; anyone can see that."

Angela crowed slightly, and got up as if to go. "I think you'll be better without me," she said. "A lawyer's one thing; but it's not fair to expose a man in the presence of his wife. So bad for the family discipline."

"Nonsense," said the little Major decisively. "You stay here; we'll have it all out; have the whole dashed thing out. What's worrying you, eh, Mr. Bredon?"

"Well . . . all sorts of things are worrying me. But there's only one question I'd like to ask you, and Mr. Gilchrist shall decide whether it's a fair question or not. Which drive did you leave Dorn by, that night—a week ago last Sunday?"

"Which drive? The Pensteven drive, of course. Who'd

want to go round by Blairwhinnie ? Miles out of the way."

" Of course. You didn't, then, in the course of that night drive past the place where your cousin's body was afterwards found ? "

" I don't see what you're getting at. What on earth could have possessed me, to want to drive from Dorn to Pensteven through Blairwhinnie ? "

" Oh, let's talk plain sense. A letter was entrusted to you on the Sunday night, which you undertook to post—the letter by which the insurance premium on your cousin's life was paid up. The Pensteven post had gone. It was in the letter-box of the Indescribable office at Perth the first thing on Monday morning. Therefore you or somebody else delivered it by hand. My point is, was it you ? "

Major Reiver's eyes consulted his lawyer for a moment. Mr. Gilchrist nodded, very slowly, and knocked the ash off his cigar.

" Yes," the Major said at last, after appearing to seek inspiration in the grounds of his coffee, " I did drive from Pensteven to Perth that night, passing through Blairwhinnie. Anything about it ? "

" Excuse me—what time would that be ? "

" Is it any business of mine to answer that question, Mr. Gilchrist ? "

" You're under no compulsion, Major ; I told you that. But if I were you, I would tell Mr. Bredon just exactly what he wants to know. If the thing ever came into court, you'd be bound to."

" All right ; make what you can of it. They gave me that letter to post, and I undertook to post it—we'd all forgotten it was Sunday and no late post. Suppose it comes of a fellow being ill, and doctors and nurses coming and going all day ; didn't seem like Sunday, anyhow. When I got to Pensteven, the date on the pillar-box reminded me ; I took the letter home with me—no need for hurry. Then, you know, I couldn't sleep. Don't know how it is with you, Mr. Bredon, but once I've said a thing I hate not doing it. There was Donald believing his cheque would reach the Company first thing on Monday. Only one way to do that—take it to Perth ; I knew there was a branch office there. That night, it seemed silly to take all the trouble. But I slept badly ; kept waking up. Next thing I knew, there was I on the road at five o'clock on the Monday morning, going all out for Perth to get the

143

dashed letter posted. Wish I hadn't, now—makes a fellow look such a fool; that's what I did, though."

" Ah ! And on the way there you saw nothing unusual ? "

" No, That's easily answered."

" I never supposed you did—you'd have turned back, I dare say, if you had. But on the way back—did you see anything on the way back, Major ? "

There was a fresh pause, a fresh consultation of the oracular dregs. Then, " I did, confound you. Thought I did, anyhow. Not the same thing, curse it all, seeing a thing in front of your own eyes, and seeing it in a looking-glass."

" You mean the one opposite the driving-seat of your car ? "

" That's it. What do you and I know about it all ? Camera plays tricks ; why shouldn't looking-glass play tricks ? Anyhow, there the picture was, as plain as life—poor Colin's body lying there, up against a great heap of stones. Just for a moment ; then the angle of the car shifted, and I saw nothing. Of course—well, I don't know if you'd have felt as I did."

" You drove on ? "

" I did ; no use denying it. Trod on the accelerator, too. Mark you, if I'd thought, then, that it was really Colin, dead or alive, I'd have stopped to see if I could do anything ; anybody would. But—I dare say, Mr. Bredon, you'd have heard that story about the next of kin in our family getting a warning when the heir dies ? [1] Well, that's what I thought it was— just a reflection in a mirror of something that wasn't there. If they'd only told me there was some chance of his being at home ! Thought he was in Madeira."

It was strange, Bredon reflected, what poor justice a monosyllabic conversationalist like the Major could do to a horrifying experience. You saw it all—the white ribbon of the road under the moonlight, the hurrying car, and the dark, huddled form against the stone-heap reflected, for a moment or two, in the looking-glass, receding at first, then jerked out of sight by a tiny alteration in the angle of travel. Donald Reiver lying as good as dead up at the house, and this eerie silhouette of the vagrant heir, supposedly cruising in the Tropics, quite still by the roadside. One did not blame the Major for putting his foot on the accelerator ; but it was abundantly evident that he blamed himself. But for that moment of panic, perhaps a life might have been saved. . . .

[1] p. 8.

"I see," said Bredon, after a pause. "And you told us nothing about it?"

Here the lawyer interposed. "Now I'm not sure, Mr. Bredon, that that isn't a leading question in the circumstances. You see, the implication of it is that the Major constituted himself in some way an accessory after the fact, if not worse, by failing to report that he had seen his cousin lying there dead. But I put it to you, Mr. Bredon, that he was not certain of what he saw, and not certain whether it was natural or preternatural; that the subsequent appearance and disappearance of the body gave him *prima facie* reason for believing that what he had seen was preternatural; and that a man might reasonably shrink from the ridicule that would be aroused if he associated himself publicly with a story that all the country-side was treating as an old wives' tale.[1] Mind, I'm not saying the Major was right; I'm only suggesting that would be a reasonable interpretation to put upon his actions."

Bredon sat making rings with his pipe on the table, in profound embarrassment. He couldn't deny that the lawyer's plea was good as far as it went. And yet, was he really to believe that the Major's part in the story was confined to seeing an apparition in a mirror, and keeping quiet about it? Was it really a coincidence that the Major had drawn his attention to the existence of the Devil's Dimple, where all those traces of the missing man had been found? That the Major had known where to look for the abandoned rain-coat? Was there no guilt, only terror, in his flight of this morning? Well, there was nothing to be done about it; he could only proceed for the moment on the assumption that the Major was telling the truth. "I confess I wish you'd mentioned it earlier, Major," he said, looking up at last. "Of course, you've a right to your own opinion; but I don't believe in these warnings and apparitions which seem so common in these parts. And you'll see at once, Mr. Gilchrist, how important this new piece of information is from my point of view. Did you happen to notice the time, Major, when you started back from Perth? Or when you reached home, for that matter?"

"Not exactly. But, see here, I can fix it more or less from the time I started. It was half-past four when I started, I know that. You'll think me a fool not to have waited till later on; but when I can't sleep, I go for a spin in the car. Couldn't sleep that night; not a wink. Started at half-past

[1] p. 49.

four, and there was no hurry, of course. Still, with the roads empty like that, I must have made a moderate pace. Should think it took me three-quarters of an hour to get into Perth, and if you reckon the same time going back—what would that be ? A little before six, wouldn't it ? "

" Ah ! " said Bredon. " That ought to help us to date things a bit. Do you remember passing any cars, on either journey ? "

" Few lorries, of course. Cars ? No, I don't remember passing any cars. Still, plenty of time for dirty work while I didn't happen to be passing, huh ? "

" Yes, but look here, Major—assume for the moment that some person or persons unknown dumped the body down by the road there, say about half-past five, and removed it again, God knows why, soon after half-past six. Probably they came and went the same way both times. Now, we know that when they took away the body they didn't make for Pensteven, or the watchman would have seen them on their second expedition. If they'd made for Perth, you'd have been almost certain to pass them on their first expedition. So it begins to look as if whatever was done was done from near home."

" That's what I said all along—men on the estate. You see, you're coming round to it."

" Mr. Gilchrist, I think you slept in the house that night ? And went out to look for the body on the Monday morning ? "

" You're right ; I did. There was no train back to Edinburgh, you see, so late as that."

" I wonder if you can remember this—did Mr. Hemerton have to unlock the garage when you went out in the morning ? "

" I remember him doing it. He had to fetch the key from the butler's pantry."

" It's not likely, then, that anybody could have got at his car, or the doctor's for that matter, without attracting attention. That narrows it down a bit."

" Carts at the farm," the Major pointed out triumphantly. " There's a garden-car, too ; not certain where they keep it, though."

" I suppose you yourself weren't awake at all, Mr. Gilchrist, until Hemerton woke you ? You didn't hear anything out of the ordinary before that ? "

" Well, I was awake for perhaps a quarter of an hour, in the dark, but I've no notion at all what time it would be.

146

And I did hear a bit of a crash, as if somebody had run against the umbrella-stand in the hall, I thought to myself. But you see, I couldn't be certain of the direction ; and when there's a sick man in the house, there's so much coming and going and carrying of coals, that one doesn't attach any importance to a bit of noise like that."

" Well, Major, I won't pretend that I didn't hope to get something more definite out of this interview. But it's something to have your corroboration of MacWilliam's story; there've been times this week when I was tempted to think it was all nonsense. I suppose I could get at you on the telephone if I wanted you to-morrow ? Or you, Mr. Gilchrist ? There are one or two lines of enquiry I have on hand which might produce something ; and it would be only fair to let you know at once if anything of importance does turn up."

" I'll be here for the week-end, anyhow," admitted the Major. " Gilchrist too. Well, if you're going off now, we'll have time for nine holes. See you to the door."

" Well, and what do you make of the Major ? " asked Bredon, when they were nearly home. " Don't, for God's sake, say he's rather a pet. A bad habit of yours."

" I wasn't going to say anything of the kind. But I don't find him sinister or anything, if that's what you mean."

" What I want to know is, whether the man's lying."

" I should say almost certainly not. You see, I think he's too stupid to have got his own psychology so right."

" As how ? "

" Oo, I mean about why he ran away from what he saw in the looking-glass, and has been running away ever since."

" Frightened of spooks, eh ? "

" Well, I think that's why he trod on the accelerator. Anybody might do that. And, of course, with all his muddle-headed ideas about Bolshevism he may easily think there's a frightful conspiracy about. But that's not the point—the point is what he doesn't mention, not what he does. He knows perfectly well, don't you see, deep down inside, that it was the real Colin who was lying by the roadside when he passed ; and the question which is really bothering him, if he only knew it, is whether he couldn't have saved Colin's life if he had pulled up and rallied round with first aid. So, you see, he doesn't want it to have been the real Colin ; and for that reason he has almost succeeded in persuading himself that it *was* just a spook. That's why he's so anxious, too, for something to be done, something to be found out—in the hope that it will be something which shows he wasn't to blame. That's why he doesn't want Colin to have been still alive on Tuesday; because that would have meant that he was alive, and wanting help, on the Monday morning. Oh yes, I get the Major placed all right, after what he's told us."

" Sounds to me as if somebody had been feeding you Freud."

" 'Tisn't Freud; it's common sense. There's one thing, anyhow—I've given up believing that the Major's all out to do the Hemertons out of their insurance money. Because if he was it would have been so easy for him to say he'd seen Colin lying dead on Monday morning."

" He'd have had to explain, though, why he left him lying dead. And you seem to be rather neglecting the possibility that the Major had some hand in it after all."

" Don't you believe it. If he had, it would have been far easier for him to pretend he saw nothing when he passed by in his car. It was a mere fluke, after all, that he did. No, the Major's too stupid to be acting a part; much too stupid to be acting the part of a stupid man."

" How do you know that he is stupid, in that case ? "

" Mrs. Wauchope. I say, Miles, it looks to me as if that old gentleman with the Mantegna face was on the look-out for you. Is he a friend of yours ? "

" That's the great MacWilliam himself. And he looks suspiciously as if he'd got a note for me. Put the chest-protector on, like a dear, while I go and chat to him."

CHAPTER XXII

THE READER LEARNS
MUCH THAT HE HAS GUESSED

MacWilliam came forward with a more than usually hangdog face, as if he carried secret information which no torture would wrest from him. " There's a letter here," he said, " which is addressed to you; and I'm sorry it's got mud on it the way it has, but it was dropped, you see, just outside the door of my house. It's no stamp on it, so I thought I would just bring it round by hand."

" It's very good of you ; I hope you haven't waited long for me ? "

" Oh no, it's nothing at all ; but I. thought I'd bring it myself and wait to see if there would be any answer to it." Bredon found afterwards, by questioning the hotel servants, that the Highlander had waited an hour and a half, without a glimmer of impatience.

" Well, look here, I won't keep you. It's—why, this is the laird's handwriting, isn't it ? "

" I don't know that I'd recognize the laird's handwriting very well, just scribbled in pencil like that. I wouldn't say but it might be his."

" And you found it this morning—that looks as if he must have dropped it on his way to the station."

" He came past the lodge, of course. And perhaps when he opened the door of the car to ask my Jamie how his bad foot was, the note may have slipped down by accident like. It was my Jamie found it afterwards and brought it to me."

Bredon looked the keeper full in the face, and would have winked if he had dared. MacWilliam, he felt, must realize as well as he did that the old gentleman, with his daughter and son-in-law mounting guard over him, had chosen this means to run the blockade of their vigilance. But not a muscle of the keeper's face betrayed any such speculation ; bred in a perfect school of loyalty, he would not even hint that he knew how things stood with his employers. You could not offer to tip such a man ; Bredon thanked him again and let him go.

" It's no good pretending you don't want to open it," said Angela, as her husband sat at tea with the note propped in front of him against the sugar-basin. " You're just as inquisitive as I am about it ; I suppose it means we shall have a short lecture about something or other. Do get it off your chest, and open the beastly thing."

" You don't seem to me to have any sporting instinct," complained her husband. " When one gets an important letter—and this obviously is an important letter, or the old gentleman would hardly have been at such pains to go dropping it about the drive—one should always sit over it for a little and have a bet with oneself about what one will find inside it. Now, this letter might solve the whole beastly problem. I confess I don't see how, but it might. On the other hand, it might just clear up a bit of the mystery ; and,

149

what's worse, a bit that I've already, guessed for myself. That
would be singularly tiresome. I hate a mystery which comes
away in bits, so that one explanation doesn't lead on to another,
if you see what I mean. It's like making a boss shot with
a corkscrew, and having to take out your cork piecemeal."

"I can imagine that such an exercise of patience would be
difficult for you, my angel."

"Don't be cheap. I think we are now going to hear how
it was that the unfortunate young man's body came to do the
disappearing trick. If so, I'm not very much interested,
because I've guessed. You evidently haven't, so if you like
you may open the letter and read it out to me. With a jam
so liquid and a scone so porous, I find my hands fully occupied.
But you must read it out fairly, not looking on ahead or anything."

Angela took the letter with a poor pretence of incuriosity.
"It's in ink," she announced, "and portentously long; the
old gentleman must have sat up most of last night writing it.
It's a bit shaky, too. Here goes—*Dear Mr. Bredon, I have
hesitated long before writing this, and am not sure even now
that I have been rightly guided to address you. But I hope
you will deal generously with me and mouse*—no, dash it all,
that can't be it—*with me and mine, as far as the situation
allows. I find myself charged with the secrets of others, and
yet compelled by my own conscience*—I suppose that word
is—*to divulge them. A trying situation, Mr. Bredon, and
you will forgive me if I express myself haltingly*—or it might
just be faultily—*and ill. I am not even sure that this letter
will reach you;* I must do my best to post it unobserved.
*Perhaps you will be kind enough to acknowledge its receipt,
typewriting the envelope of your reply and having it posted in
London? My address will be Crossways, Devizes.*"

"Nice people, the Hemertons," commented Miles dreamily.
"I only wonder they let the poor old gentleman get at pen and
ink. Ah, but that would be before they decided to flit.
Hence, possibly, the pencilled address on the envelope. Read
on, Mrs. Bredon—it sounds like the beginning of a music-hall
song."

"I wish he'd come to the point sooner; I'm rather excited.
*Mr. Bredon, I did not telle you all I knew when you came to see
me. You must pardon me; I did not see my way very clearly
then. Let me go back to the night of Sunday the 12th; or
rather the Monday morning that followed. You will under-*

stand that I had had a poor night, very restless and tossing this way and that. It's queer how the senses take in impressions and register them in the memory, when a man's sick, but the brain just can't take hold to puzzle over them. I awoke while it was still dark from a bit of a sleep I had, feeling better in myself. I could see the chink of light where the door of the night-nurse's room stood ajar—it communicated with mine. And I heard something which puzzled me afterwards when I thought about it—a very faint shuffling outside my other door, and a little squeak, as it might be of a wheel that wanted oiling a little. It sounded as if somebody had stumbled against the invalid's chair, that had stood outside the door since I was brought in from one room to another. I thought it was early for folks to be moving; there was no light in the passage.

"I slept after that for a bit, but I think it was only for half an hour or so; then I heard the noise of the front door being unlocked, and there were footsteps coming and going, and hushed voices everywhere; I didn't know what it was at the time, but of course it must have been MacWilliam coming up with the news. Then the night-nurse came in softly, to see whether I was asleep yet; and she brought something in in her hand, and said it belonged to me; it had been dropped in the passage outside. So she put it down by my bed, and I had a look at it while she went over to make up the fire. Mr. Bredon, it was my gold pencil-case, that I had given to my boy and seen him stuff it in his pocket, the night he went off for his cruise.[1]

"I lay there staring at it, and puzzling over it with difficulty, as a sick man will. If I'd been in good health, perhaps I'd have put two and two together in the ordinary way, and said to myself that Colin had come back from abroad, and was in the house. But, with me between waking and dreaming, the effect was different. You will have been told that, in our family, there's a superstition about a warning being given to the family when the heir dies.[2] And I thought at once that Colin was dead, and he had sent me this gift of mine for a warning. I don't think that now, though no one knows how it came where it did. But I still think it was a guidance, to prepare me for the shock that was coming, and maybe to prevent a wrong being done, as you'll see presently.

"Well, the nurse went out before long; and, trying to shut

[1] p. 20.   [2] p. 8.

*the door quietly, she left it not quite snibbed properly, so
that it came a bit ajar. And then I heard footsteps in the
passage again, and a door opening, that I knew was my
daughter's. She must have stood at her door talking to her
husband, and I could hear a word or two now and again,
as you do when people think they're talking quietly, but can't
always control their voices. I heard something about the
doctor being still down on the roadside, and something about
insurance money, and something about what was to be done
with a thing they never named, but I knew it would be the
body of poor Colin. And then I heard something about the
ice-house, but I didn't know what that meant at the time.*

" *It will have been some time after that when my daughter
came in to know how I did; and the first thing I said to her
was, So poor Colin's gone; what have you done with him?
Well, at that she made an awful to-do; and I'm afraid she
lied to me, meaning only to spare me trouble; it's a sad thing
what a lot of lying goes on round a sick-bed. But I wasn't
to be put down; and in the end I told her that if she didn't
come out with the whole story I'd send the doctor, as soon as
he came in, to go and look in the ice-house and tell me what
he found there. That was too much for her and Hemerton;
God forgive me if I pressed them too hard. Anyway, you'll
guess what they said; that they were only hiding the body
just for a day or two, to get the best of the insurance people.
The money, they said, was ours; we'd paid up in good faith;
but if we made the death known now it would be terribly hard
to prove we'd heard nothing of it when I signed the cheque.
And they said I could make a clean breast of it if I liked, but
it would mean prison for both of them.*

" *I think now that I did wrong, but I consented to say
nothing just then, to humour them; I'll wait and see, I
thought, whether the Insurance Company makes any difficulty
about it. And when you came, Mr. Bredon, I hadn't the
heart to tell you just what I knew. I've been going through
a bad time this last week, and you so kind with it all. But,
you see, I've had nobody whose opinion I could ask about it,
nobody whose opinion I'd trust.*—I say, that's rather one for
me, Miles, I had quite a long chat with the old gentleman
yesterday."

" Don't interrupt, just when he's in the middle of his
explanations."

" He's not; he's at the end.—*I hope, under Providence,*

that I may find a way of conveying this letter to you ; you must take what action you think fit, but I hope you will be able to spare our family the embarrassment of an exposure. Please remember me to your charming wife . . ."

" Hey, what's that ? Let me see the letter."

" Well, I put that last part in, as a matter of fact. But obviously he meant to say it ; they must have interrupted him at the last moment. Well, Miles, I should call that a pretty big chunk of cork."

" I rather think I want to retract that comparison. For one thing, when you take out a cork bit by bit, the last piece never comes out ; it always gets pushed back into the bottle. You can hardly have failed to notice that, with your experience. Whereas I am not quite sure that this mystery isn't going to come out by the time we've finished with it. And again, when you're pulling out a cork you can never find one bit coming out in such a way as to give you a purchase on the next bit. Whereas this last piece of information may give us a lead for finding out some more ; you never know. Let us say this case is like an onion ; you peel away coat after coat, but you never seem to get right down to the explanation—so far, anyway. Now, that they put him in the ice-house, that's interesting."

" Simplest place, surely. Didn't you say it was in that wood just close to the Blairwhinnie drive ? "[1]

" Oh yes, that's clear enough. But incidentally, you see, it was a good place to hide their man. Because the body . . ."

" I seem to remember you being crude about this once before. Must you ? "

" I'm only facing the facts. If they stored it in the ice-house, the body would be as good as new when they produced it again ; that's all I'm trying to point out. At least, I suppose it would. Happy thought ; ask the doctor. And then there's all that business about noises in the night : Mr. Reiver heard something ; Gilchrist heard something. And that was *before* MacWilliam found the body ; therefore it looks as if it might have something to do with how the body got there. For the rest, of course, Mr. Reiver's disclosures are hardly disclosures at all."

" Miles, don't be odious ! D'you mean to say you knew it was Hemerton who spirited the body away ? "

" Of course I did. Hang it all, you didn't really think

[1] p. 23.

153

MacWilliam was lying, did you ? I doubt if he knows how. Very well then, the body was there at half-past six on Monday, and had been spirited away by seven. Who did it ? The chances are enormously against anybody happening to come by just then who happened to have an interest in concealing the body. Therefore the probability was, enormously, that the body had been spirited away by somebody who had already heard MacWilliam's story. MacWilliam himself, Purvis, and Gilchrist all went down in a bunch ; they corroborate each other's movements. The wildest imagination could not invent a reason why MacWilliam should have hidden away the body and then announced that he had found it. Only one man is left in the running—Hemerton. He had an interest, as we know, in hiding the body. He spotted that Purvis's engine had got cold, and wasn't likely to start for a minute or two.[1] As Mrs. Wauchope says, he is a plunger ; and he plunged. He drove down the Pensteven drive, doubled back along the Blairwhinnie road, and popped the body into his car, covering it up with that big rug of his.[2] That was the really amazing thing he did—he took a policeman in the front of his car to help find the body, and all the time the body was there in the back. He waited till the coast was more or less clear ; then he and his charming wife went and parked her brother in the ice-house. "[3]

" Smooth work, I must say. Wonder the police didn't find the track of his car. You'd have thought, in turning round, he'd almost certainly leave a mark on the soft grass by the edge of the road."

" I imagine he did. And that's why, when he left the police to their search, he turned round again, and went home by the Pensteven lodge. He wanted to superimpose fresh tracks on the old ones, where his car had turned. "[4]

" And then, you mean, two days later he fired a rick on purpose to distract attention, and left the body lying about again ? "

" Exactly. Firing the rick was the safest way of making sure that MacWilliam came past the identical spot at the identical time.[5] And the public, of course, at once started talking about second sight. Also, Mary Hemerton knew that her brother had been a bit of a pyromaniac in his young days— the burned rick would look as if he had been at work again, just before he passed out.[6] Wrong in his head, people would

[1] p. 30. [2] p. 30. [3] p. 33. [4] p. 33. [5] p. 36. [6] p. 88.

say; and, by Jove, we all did. It was well thought out, you know."

"It was all that. Miles, what on earth are you doing with those electric torches? You're not going to have another staying-power competition?"

"It was just an idea of mine," said Bredon, as he took out the two exhausted batteries, and replaced them by the two which were lying in the box from which his own torch came.

"But, dash it all, those two batteries are both new ones."

"One would think so, but you never know. New ones and spent ones *look* just the same, after all. I was wondering whether it was possible we had got them mixed up, when we tried that first experiment. Anyhow, the whim takes me to light them. Now, what were we saying? Oh, yes, there's not much doubt now how the body came to be where it was on Wednesday morning. But we've still got to find out how it got there on Monday morning."

"And, incidentally, although we needn't bother any longer about what Colin was doing between Monday and Wednesday, we've still got to find out what he was doing between Friday and Monday."

"Is it possible you don't realize that we have to account for his whereabouts for much longer than that?"

"Meaning what exactly?"

"Oh, I forgot I hadn't explained that part. Merely that Colin Reiver never went abroad at all, you know."

CHAPTER XXIII

THE MAN WHO TOLD THE TRUTH

"I'M RATHER SURPRISED at your being taken in by that letter," Bredon went on. "Of course, he didn't make any bloomers in it; he'd got his stuff all right. It was what *wasn't* there that made it fishy; I mean, he didn't seem to have met anybody on the cruise who knew the family, and he doesn't even mention anybody by name who was on it. He is extremely vague about the weather; he doesn't refer to any bits of news he has read in the papers. There's nothing in it that he *might* not have taken out of a guide-book; and I had a good look round in the library, before I left Dorn, to make sure that the books he would have needed for the purpose were actually there—a couple of Baedekers and an old book of travels.[1] The letter wasn't proof positive that he went on the cruise ; only proof negative, if you see what I mean—there was nothing in it which made it impossible that he should really have been abroad."

" But, dash it all, it was postmarked all right. Who sent it from Madeira ? "

" That part was rather ingenious. ' He sent it out in a covering envelope, addressed to the British Consul at Madeira. I dare say he put in one of those international stamps, to pay for the postage. In his covering letter, he must have asked the consul to hand the enclosure to Mr. Donald Reiver, a passenger on the *Squandermania*. In the event of Mr. Donald Reiver not being on board, the consul was simply to stamp it and post it back to Scotland. Colin's own first name, you remember, was Donald too.[2] There was nothing to make the consul suspect that there was anything fishy about the whole proceeding, until he got my cable yesterday. By the way, if Colin had really been enjoying hot weather at sea, his face would almost certainly have been tanned, and the tan would have shown on his corpse. As I pointed out to you, there was no such symptom. "[3]

" But why on earth should he *pretend* to have gone abroad ? "

" Oh, well, if we knew that, the whole beastly puzzle might come out. I'm not sure it would, though. The only thing that occurred to me was to write to that friend of Colin's, Strutt, and ask him if he knew anything about the business ; most men have a confidant of some kind when they start bamboozling their relations. I did that yesterday, and enclosed a telegraph form ; so with luck I ought to hear to-day. Meanwhile, let me call your attention to the curious behaviour of the electric batteries."

" Miles, one of them's gone out ! Already ! Why, it's only been burning five minutes or so—I thought it was a new one."

" That's what we were meant to think."

" But, Miles, what does it mean ? "

" It means that I've got to go and have a talk with Dr. Purvis. I said I'd come round to-morrow, when he's more likely to be free ; but this trail is too good not to follow up ; I must chance it."

[1] p. 54.   [2] p. 9.   [3] pp. 84, 95.

The doctor was out ; but his daughter encouraged Bredon to wait—her father would be back any moment. Mrs. Wauchope had been a trifle over-charitable to her looks, as is the way of good-tempered old ladies ; she belonged to that class for which the Scottish mind, with its instincts of accuracy, has invented the non-committal word " bonny." Still, you felt she might have had attractions for the lonely boy up at Dorn House ; the possibility was worth remembering. They only talked for five minutes or so ; the doctor came in, and explained that he must soon be at the disposal of his patients in the surgery. Bredon, resolved on having his interview, saw that no time must be wasted in beating about the bush.

" You'll remember that aquascutum, Doctor, that the Major found on the path leading to the Devil's Dimple ? And the electric torch that was in the pocket of it ? As you know, I got leave to take it home with me. And, as you probably guessed, when you were kind enough to drive me home and to drop me for a moment at a shop in Pensteven, I bought another torch just like it, to try out how much juice it had left in it. Obviously, if the torch had been much used, it would look as if Colin Reiver might have survived several days after his return from the cruise. If it had been very little used, the inference would be, if anything, that he had died soon after he bought it. That would make Sunday night a likelier date for the death than Tuesday night."

" It all seems rather speculative, Mr. Bredon."

. " Oh, it's that all right. And when I lit the two torches simultaneously, and left them to burn down side by side, I didn't really expect to get any very conclusive proofs out of the test. Actually, they lasted almost exactly the same time. As if Colin Reiver hadn't used his torch at all, you see."

" That must have surprised you."

" It did. So much so that I began to wonder whether there hadn't been some—er—confusion, and whether Colin Reiver's torch might not have been charged with a fresh battery without my knowing of it ; one of the reserve batteries, for example, which I had just bought with my new torch. So I tried out the two batteries that remained in my box, and one of them proved to be practically burnt out. Which suggested very strongly that there had been a substitution ; somebody had taken the used battery out of Colin Reiver's torch, and put one of my new batteries into it instead."

" It would be an action that called for some explanation."
" That's what I felt. And the curious thing is, Doctor,
that the substitution of the one battery for the other must
have taken place in my hotel, and indeed in my room, while
I was having tea downstairs, the day they came into my
possession. Which seemed to narrow the range of investigation." [1]

The doctor still gave no sign of comprehension ; at least,
there was a kind of twinkle in his eye, but wasn't that always
there ? " Go on, Mr. Bredon," was all he said.

" You'll know Mrs. Wauchope, Doctor ; but I don't know if
you will have guessed that she is an admirer of yours. She
told my wife that you had a mania for telling the truth."

" She's very kind."

" To be quite plain, then, I was wondering whether a person
who has a mania for telling the truth could (consistently with
that reputation) substitute a new battery for the spent battery
in Colin Reiver's torch, just when I was on the point of
testing it ? And give me the impression, for what it was worth,
that Colin Reiver must have died soon after he bought the
torch ? "

" I would say this, Mr. Bredon—that such an action would
be the action of a truthful man, if he saw that finding a spent
battery in the torch was likely to mislead you, and make you
think Colin Reiver had used that torch a good deal, when in
fact he hadn't. It wouldn't be deceiving you ; it would be
preventing you deceiving yourself."

" Thank you, Dr. Purvis ; I am sure you meant well. It's
not much good, is it, pretending that we don't understand one
another ? You were the only person who knew what I was
going to do with the torch, and who had the opportunity of
tampering with it while I was out of my room.[2] You tampered
with it, you say, to prevent me deceiving myself. Well, that
means that you knew more than I did about the time, and
perhaps the manner, of Colin Reiver's death. You are
convicted of concealment ; if I had reason to suspect you of
worse than concealment, I would hardly be talking to you like
this. You will hardly wonder at my asking whether you are
not at liberty to tell me a little more."

" Come now, Mr. Bredon, this is interesting. We must
have this out, even if it means keeping my patients waiting
a few minutes. I'd be awfully interested to know why it is

[1] p. 105.　　　　　　[2] p. 105.

you suspect me of nothing worse, you say, than concealment."

" Well, there's that grave up at Dorn ; Carstairs Wright told you about it. I don't believe you ever dug that. But somebody did, and that's the man whose tracks I'm trying to get on to. But—there's such a thing as being an accessory after the fact."

" It's good of you to remind me of it. Now, look here, Mr. Bredon—I'm not fond of meddling with things that are none of my business. I won't pretend that I haven't been led to take a hand in what's been happening this last fortnight ; I felt that it was my duty, you see. And, since you've caught me out in one of my nefarious actions, I don't mind telling you the rest of them, here and now. But, if you'll excuse me, I'm not going to tell you about them in any way that could possibly cast suspicion on anybody besides myself. You'll just have to draw your own conclusions; will that satisfy you ? "

" It'll have to, Doctor ; I'm not the police. My job is to find out when Colin died, not how. You say you changed those batteries because you were afraid I should deceive myself if you didn't. To be more accurate, you thought that . . . well, that somebody else was trying to deceive me ; and you determined to spoil their game by double-crossing them ? "

" I'd sooner impute no motives at all. Let's just say that I didn't want you to deceive yourself. And there's another point I didn't want you to deceive yourself over—those liver-tablets that were found in the pocket of the same rain-coat."

" Ah ! " said Bredon.

" It's this way, you see ; I don't mind telling you that when the Major showed me those tablets there were five missing. Now, a layman doesn't take more than one of those things in a day, when it says on the bottle that one's the dose. Precious little difference it would make, really. Therefore five tablets gone meant Friday, Saturday, Sunday, Monday, Tuesday ; and that would have led you to the conclusion that Colin Reiver was still alive on Tuesday. Since I knew that he was not alive on Tuesday, I thought it would best serve the interests of truth if I just slipped into the tube two of the tablets I brought with me.[1] I did that while you were all looking at the dog.[2] And that meant three tablets gone—Friday, Saturday, Sunday. And Monday morning early was the date of the death."

" Yes, I see. You mean that, whether by accident or by

[1] pp. 101, 102.　　　　[2] p. 103.

design, the contents of the aquascutum carried with them the suggestion that Colin lived till Tuesday night; it was only after you had tampered with them that they suggested the earlier date ? "

" That is so. Only, you will observe, I said nothing about design."

" To be sure you didn't. But you know as well as I do, Doctor—no, by Jove, you don't, because you're not a pipe-smoker. But to anybody who is a pipe-smoker, that whole business of the aquascutum the Major found was a perfectly obvious frame-up. We were asked to believe that the pipe we found in the pockets had been smoked about ten days before, by a man who smoked heavily. I drew a pipe-cleaner through it, and it came out quite clean; which is impossible.[1] The pipe hadn't been smoked for a month at least. Therefore I knew that the aquascutum was a frame-up; and also I was pretty certain that it had been engineered by somebody who wasn't a pipe-smoker—which let the Major out, of course. The tobacco, on the other hand, wasn't nearly as dry as it would have been if it had been lying about in a pouch for ten days or so.[2] Therefore the aquascutum had been deliberately dropped by the side of the path only a day or two before, the pockets containing a pipe that had remained long unsmoked, and some tobacco that had come fresh from a tin. Oh yes, somebody had been trying to lead me up the garden—I knew that—and it wasn't you. Let's see, did you do anything else in the way of . . . undeceiving me ? "

" That's a good phrase of yours, Mr. Bredon. Yes, I took the liberty of undeceiving you up at the Devil's Dimple. It was a piece of luck I was able to accompany you; and, to be sure, it wasn't till I saw what I saw up at the Devil's Dimple that it came into my mind it would be a good thing to practise a little undeception."

" What was it worried you up at the Devil's Dimple ? "

" Why, just the same thing. The moment I had clambered down to the ledge, what should I see but a verse scrawled up on the rock, with a date fixed to it ? The date of February the thirteenth, that was Monday; as if Colin had been still alive in broad daylight of Monday. Well, you see, I knew he was dead before day broke; so the inscription could only be misleading."

" And you scratched out the final One, you mean ? Yes,

<hr/>

[1] p. 102.   [2] p. 102.

but look here, I don't see how you managed that. You were in full view of my wife, if not of myself, all the time you stood on that ledge.[1] How the devil did you manage it ? "

" It didn't look easy, just at first. But it came to me that there was a way of scratching out the final One under Mrs. Bredon's eyes, and she not noticing. I just struck a match, Mr. Bredon, to show you the way into the cave ; and if it so happened that I struck the match at an angle across the final figure One, would you call that deceptive of me ? "[2]

" Oh no, not at all ; it was just an ordinary piece of undeception. Gad, Doctor, I knew you were a chess-player, but I didn't know your brain worked as quick as that. So you mean the whole business of the cave and the inscription was just another attempt to lead me up the garden ? "

" You will do me the justice to observe that I never said anything of the kind."

" Confound it, there's no catching you out. All the same, it *was* an attempt to lead me up the garden. The body was clean-shaven when it was found, and there was no trace in all that cave of a razor or a shaving-brush. Which showed me at once that the traces left in the cave were a frame-up ; and, what is more, that the person who was guilty of the frame-up was not a person who shaved every morning. It was either a bearded man or a woman, Dr. Purvis. "[3]

" About that you must suit yourself. All I know is that if the figure XIII was scratched up by poor Colin, he made an error about the date. So I thought it would be well to put that straight the best way I could. Because I knew, you see, that he died before daybreak on the thirteenth itself. "

" Which reminds me—how did you *know* that Colin Reiver was dead by daybreak on the Monday ? Of course, I know you were one of the party that went down in the first instance to make sure that MacWilliam was telling the truth. But, as I've been given to understand, when you got there there was no body lying against the stone-heap, and no trace to suggest that there ever had been. Was I wrongly informed ? "

" Oh no ; your information was accurate enough. Only, you see, I happened to know that the body was lying there when MacWilliam came along, just because it was I that put it there."

[1] p. 79.   [2] p. 79.   [3] p. 95.

" You . . . really, Doctor, I don't want you to say anything that might lead to awkward questions afterwards. I mean . . ."

" Oh, you mustn't think I laid hands on the lad, Mr. Bredon. Mark you, I don't think he was doing any good by being alive ; but if you and I once started censoring the muster-roll of humanity according to our own ideas on the subject, where would it stop ? No, he was dead as mutton when I found him, and all I did was to move the body a little, just so as to make it more conspicuous. A little more undeception, if I may borrow your own phrase."

" But then—then you've got the key to the whole problem. Where was he when you found him ? "

" You must excuse me, Mr. Bredon, but that's outside the scope of our little arrangement. If I started talking about where I found him, it might mean getting other people into trouble, and that's not a thing I'm just very anxious to do. No, you must take it from me that he was dead all right, and all I did was to move the body, with the best intentions in the world. Surely you must have seen that he was put there by the roadside just to make certain that nobody could possibly miss him."

" Well, Doctor, I suppose I mustn't quarrel with your decision. But it's hard, isn't it, to have the discussion closured just where it begins to point to the solution of all my diffi-culties. However, I mustn't keep your patients waiting any longer. Oh, by the way, though, there's one thing I wanted to ask you about—if a dead body were put in an ice-house, what would be the effect ? Would it arrest the ordinary pro-cesses of . . . decomposition and so on ? "

For the first time in their interview, the doctor's face changed colour. For an instant a startled look passed over it. Then, " What's that got to do with me ? " he asked, almost angrily.

" I was only consulting you as a doctor. You see, I have good reason to think that Colin Reiver's body lay in an ice-house between the morning of Monday and the morning of Wednesday."

" Oh, as to that . . . Why, yes, Mr. Bredon, if the young man just died of exposure, as it seems likely he did, there would be no question of decomposition setting in, with the ice-house a very little below freezing-point. And I'll tell you another thing, *rigor mortis* doesn't set in either in a case like

162

that, until the body is exposed to changes of temperature. So, you see, it looks as if Dr. MacLaughlin might have been right after all."

CHAPTER XXIV

THE POOL AT EVENING

" Well," said Bredon, " that's another coat stripped off the onion. The bother is, it puts us in a worse position than ever. All the clues that might have been of some use to us were bogus clues from the start, except that confounded grave in the garden at Dorn. Colin was never up at the Devil's Dimple ; never wore that rain-coat, or anyhow wasn't wearing it at the end of his life ; never went on that cruise. He may have been anywhere between the day he left home and the day MacWilliam found him—that means about five weeks during which we have lost all trace of his movements. The rest is just Hemerton with a dash of Purvis."

" I've been wondering, rather, how much Mary Hemerton managed to take you in, my angel."

" Not for a minute. You see, it was I and the doctor between us, that night we dined there, who suggested to her it was very odd nobody had seen or heard anything of Colin since his return. She started talking about how lonely Scotland was, and how fond her brother was of tramping about the hills.[1] It occurred to her that she could bear out that impression by taking me up to see his room, and, leaving a book of Stevenson's *Poems* lying about, looking as if he'd been reading it. That was what she did when she went upstairs after dinner—she went into her brother's room and arranged the lay-out for me.[2] Then she suggested my having a look round, as if it was a sudden idea. Having only just come away from it, she over-played her part, as people so often do. She blew into the key, as if it was dusty and hadn't been used for a long time. But really, of course, a key doesn't get dusty like that in the course of a month or two. I saw she was bluffing, and knew that what I found in the room would be what she wanted me to find."[3]

" And then she thought she could bear out that impression

[1] p. 65.　　　[2] p. 65.　　　[3] p. 67.

still further by introducing you to a fresh frame-up at the Devil's Dimple ? "

" No, that was my idea ; I put it into her head. I said I was too busy to go up to the Devil's Dimple on Wednesday, but I would have a look round on the Thursday. That gave her time, you see, to make her arrangements, and she did. But it didn't give her time to consult her husband, because he went up to London on the morning when I came here.[1] He would have told her that if you wanted to make a cave look as if a clean-shaven man had been living in it, you must put a razor there, and a shaving-brush. Also, as you pointed out, soap ; but you, being a woman, didn't think about the shaving part. Which makes me certain that it was Mary, and not the Major (for example), who faked things at the Devil's Dimple."

" It must have been a nasty jar for her when she heard about the last stroke of the XIII being crossed out. I wonder if she suspected the doctor ? "

" I fancy she did. But meanwhile, she had a second line of defence to fall back upon. Her husband had been up in London, buying properties. On the Thursday, they took Colin's old aquascutum—it was really his, I expect—and his old pipe and a cigarette-case to hold the money, and left the whole thing lying about for the Major to find. They also included a torch, nearly burnt out, and a tube of liver tablets, with exactly five missing. Inference—that Colin had spent some time at the cave, and that he had taken his little daily dose on Monday and Tuesday, as well as the three days before. The doctor managed to double-cross them on both points. He must have enjoyed himself, playing chess against Hemerton for such stakes."

" Why was he so keen to butt in, anyhow ? "

" Partly because Mrs. Wauchope is right—he has a mania for the truth. Partly because he knew that Donald Reiver's will was drawn in favour of the ' Circles,' and he hates those people.[2] Oh, he was quite in earnest, but somehow I see him enjoying himself."

" You know, Miles, that aquascutum was rather ingeniously arranged."

" Hemerton's good at details, but he neglects his broad outlines. As I was telling the doctor just now, he should have put in a pipe that was still foul from use, and tobacco which

[1] p. 70.   [2] pp. 23, 25.

had been allowed to go dry. Those points convinced me that
it was a fake, and a fake arranged by somebody who didn't
smoke a pipe—the Hemertons, therefore, not the Major." [1]
" It might have been the doctor."
" Yes, but there you have the lack of motive. Anyhow,
we know now it was the Hemertons. It occurred to me, at
this point, that two could play at the aquascutum game as
well as one. So I went and produced mine from the Lost
Luggage Office, and watched the Hemertons carefully to see
how they would react. The new situation puzzled them
badly ; you could see that. They hedged at first, and would
be certain of nothing ; didn't even think of the Visitors' Book
as a means of identifying Denis Strutt's signature. But when
I produced the chisel, that was too much for Hemerton, and he
plunged.[2] It was such a seductive way of proving that Colin
was, after all, still alive on Tuesday. Then it was all plain
sailing. Mary followed suit, and suggested the Visitors'
Book ; when I produced the pipe, she was ready to swear to
it, though she was quite vague about it when it was found.
earlier on, in the other rain-coat. So I congratulated them,
and left them to think it over."
" Thinking it over seems to have put the wind up them
rather."
" You bet it did. They knew jolly well that Colin didn't
carve that inscription. They knew that Colin hadn't really
been travelling on the Tuesday, because he was dead. Yet
it couldn't be the coat of a total stranger, with Denis Strutt's
letter in the pocket. So they spotted that I'd been pulling
their legs, and they hopped it for Wiltshire, to avoid an
awkward interview. At least, that was partly their reason."
" Partly ? "
" Yes ; don't you see that there was one thing even more
important—to get Donald Reiver out of the neighbourhood the
very first moment he was fit to travel ? He belonged to the
' Circles,' Carstairs Wright belonged to the ' Circles,' and if
they got together there would be a comparing of notes, and
Donald Reiver would come clean.[3] As a matter of fact, he'd
already been writing out his confession, but they didn't know
that. They legged it for Wiltshire ; and I'm inclined to think
they must have had a slight twinge of conscience when they
passed the monument of the perjured old woman in Devizes
market-place. At least, I hope they did."

[1] p. 102.　　　[2] p. 128.　　　[3] pp. 113, 118.

165

" Meanwhile, 'as you say, my precious, you aren't much further on. At least, unless you can get the doctor to come forward with an affidavit that he saw what MacWilliam saw on the Monday morning. But he seems rather coy about the whole subject ; why's that, Miles ? "

" Oh, I imagine he thinks it was the Hemertons who did Colin in somehow ; and, for the sake of the family, he doesn't want to make a smell about it. As a matter of fact, there's only one thing he's holding back which could be of the slightest use to us—namely, where he found the body."

" Any ideas ? "

" Well, it looks to me as if he found it somewhere quite close to where he put it ; possibly just the other side of the hedge. You see, a dead body is a beastly weight to carry about. He can't have got at his car, because Gilchrist says it was in the garage, and the garage was locked. But it would have been dashed risky to pinch, say, a wheel-barrow . . ."

" Miles, Miles, I believe I've got it ! The invalid's chair ! " [1]

" Well, I'm . . . Angela, never let me forget that for once you justified your existence. Of course, he pinched the invalid's chair, and that was what Donald Reiver heard outside his door. He used the chair for carting the corpse about, and—oh, don't you see ? ' The gold pencil dropped out of some pocket on to the floor of the chair, dropped from the floor of the chair when the chair was restored to its old position, and¿ that was why the night-nurse found it ! [2] Steady on, we're really getting on to the track of things. He had to lug the corpse some distance, or a bath-chair wouldn't have been worth the bother. He hadn't to lug it an enormous distance, or a bath-chair would have been too clumsy. Angela, I am just beginning to see daylight. Why didn't you let me bring those patience-cards here ? Well, I shall go a long walk all by myself to-morrow morning, and see if I can't work the thing out. To-night we will go to the pictures. Filthy things, and I should imagine in Blairwhinnie quite despicable. But I must take my mind off the whole business if I'm to come fresh to it to-morrow."

．　　　．　　　．　　　．　　　．

It was a bad habit of Miles Bredon's—his wife had often had occasion to point it out to him—that when he was excited he was apt to sing tunes. They were not new tunes ;

[1] pp. 45, 157.　　　[2] p. 157.

generally they came from pre-war musical comedies, and he
sang them atrociously. He returned from his walk, a little
before luncheon on the Sunday, briskly chanting to himself
the forgotten refrain :

> Ours is a nice house, ours is ;
> What a nice little house ours is !

and the rest of the doggerel. Angela, however, forgave him.
She knew it meant that he was hot on the trail. " You've
spotted something ? " she cried.

" Worked the whole bally thing out ; and, more by a fluke
than anything else, verified it. I've rung up Gleneagles, and
got the Major to come over, and Gilchrist. The doctor will
be hère, too ; tea-time is zero-hour. Now, shall I tell you all
about it ? Or shall I give you till tea-time to guess ? "

" Mmm—have I much chance of guessing ? I mean, you've
been finding something this morning—would it be possible to
guess without knowing about that ? "

" Oh yes ; I'd guessed myself, or I'd never have found what
I did find. It was just the grave that put me on to it. Look
here, Angela, I'll give you one hint ; you remember my saying
that the doctor was worth suspecting in this case, simply
because he *is* a doctor ? " [1]

" Heavens, you're not going to fix it on him, are you, after
all ? "

" That's not my point. What I mean is that my principle
was right. In a case like this, if you spot the expert, you spot
the person who's behind all the trouble."

It was a rather embarrassed tea-party that was convened in
the small sitting-room which the Bredons had adopted.
Bredon explained that there was no point in going into the
thing as yet ; they had an expedition to make, under cover
of darkness, before the last strands of the mystery were
unravelled. He admitted, too, that they were all going to
trespass on the Dorn policies. Mr. Gilchrist registered a severe
access of professional concern, and was only reassured with
difficulty when Bredon pointed out that the Hemertons themselves had implored him to treat the house and grounds as
his own for the purposes of his investigation. But the highest
pitch of general confusion was reached when Mrs. Wauchope
sailed in, identified the company, and proceeded to rally them
on their mysterious silence.

[1] p. 110.

" No, it's no good looking as if you were all going off to evening church," she said. " I can see it's a meeting of the Black Hand all right. Henry, you were much stouter when I met you last ; you must tell me some time how you do it. Meanwhile, I can't make out at all what you're doing here ; I thought you were going round singing carols at Gleneagles. Doctor, I shall have a seizure unless you all explain yourselves, and then I shall be on your hands for a fortnight."

Angela dealt with the situation in the only possible way. " Come on, Mrs. Wauchope," she said, " why shouldn't you be in at the death ? You don't mind, do you, Miles ? Well, it's like this," and Mrs. Wauchope became, thereupon, as wise as the rest of them. She went upstairs with Angela, and reappeared in a few minutes, formidably muffled up against the weather. They embarked in two cars, and took the road towards Pensteven, but turned off before long up a side-lane. which marked the nearer bounds of the Dorn estate. The long stone wall which defended most of it gave place, at one point, to a thick hedge ; in the middle of this was a stile, and the beginning of a mossy path, threading its way between dark trunks of fir. Here they stopped, and Bredon, assuring them that it was only a short walk which lay in front of them, led the way to the verge of a silent pool, buried away, some fifty yards from the road, behind a thick screen of covert.

" Blairwhinnie Pool," said the Major, looking round as if to take his bearings. " What made you look for developments on the farm road, Mr. Bredon ? "

" Well, you see, I found out that the garden car is kept at the farm. So anybody who—let us say—found the garden car on one of the drives would pass this way in taking it back to its shed. And, passing this way, if he happened to be looking out for a sheet of water, this is the one that would obviously occur to him. I had reason to think that somebody was doing this a little while ago ; so I thought I would come and look for traces of him here. As a matter of fact, I had luck. We might have had to drag the pond ; as it is, somebody has been good enough to provide us with ropes." And, kneeling at the further edge of the pond, he untied from an overhanging root the end of a long cord—that thick, rough cord which is often used for tying up packing-cases. The other end of it dipped and made moonlight eddies in the pool.

" Do you mind giving me a hand, Doctor ? " said Bredon.

" The weight's not much, but I want a steady pull, for fear of jerking the rope and breaking it. And if you wouldn't mind, Major, just standing by and gaffing the . . . the exhibits. No, there's nothing frightening," he explained, as Angela touched his arm.

The cord tightened and slackened, tightened and slackened, shining drops running down it and falling from it. You could see, from the angle, that the pool was of no great depth, and that their prize lay near the middle. It had to be dragged warily over stones and across hollows, but it was not long before a dark, billowing object began to show above the face of the water. The Major caught at it with the crook of his stick, and drew it nearer in ; it was a heavy great-coat, buttoned tight and so contriving to hang from the cord. The next moment, there was a heavier tug as the rest of the burden left the bottom of the pool. It consisted of two suit-cases, with the end of the cord passed through their handles and so tied.

There was no difficulty this time about identification. The two suit-cases were plainly marked " C. R." ; the overcoat actually had Colin Reiver's full name in it. Bredon pointed, with evident satisfaction, to the button-hole, from which still streamed the bedraggled relics of a paper flower. " Major," he said, " when was your hospital flag-day ? "

" Early last month ; can't remember the day. Rum, dashed rum. Still wearing it."

" That'll help you to believe," explained Bredon with a grin, " that I didn't throw the thing in here yesterday. Oh yes, Major, I know you don't trust me, and there's not much reason why you should. But it's genuine this time ; will you fish in the pockets ? It seems to be your right, somehow."

The contents of the pockets were laid side by side on a broad stone by the water's edge. They proved to be—a passport, a railway ticket, a book of coupons such as travellers carry with them abroad, a pipe, matches, a tobacco-pouch, a pair of gloves, and finally a flask—all but empty, yet containing a few drops of what was unmistakably brandy.

" Well," said Bredon, " I'm not very keen on exploring any further to-night. We had best put the coat and the suit-cases back in the water, I think, and just tie up the end of the cord here so that they can be retrieved when it's necessary. Meanwhile, I think we might take these smaller things back to the hotel with us. It's quite time you all had an explanation, but I thought I would like you to be witnesses, first, to my discovery. And I wasn't very keen on having any other witnesses, which is why I wanted to do it quietly, in the dark of a Sunday afternoon."

CHAPTER XXV

THE STIRRUP-CUP

" THAT PAPER FLOWER," reflected Bredon, " is a quite undeserved piece of luck. The first time one wears the coat after the day is over, one throws those things away. Colin Reiver just hadn't time to notice his before his overcoat was . . . disposed of. We know that he started out for his cruise in his tweed overcoat ; Mrs. Hemerton said so, and she had no reason to misrepresent the facts there. It looks, doesn't it, as if he never got very far on his cruise ? "

" It hardly looks as if he'd tried," suggested Mrs. Wauchope.

" As a matter of fact, he never meant to," Bredon explained. " He was still full of his idea of joining the Foreign Legion.[1] He would have left the boat at St. Malo (I think it was) and made across country to Paris. Naturally, he gave his family no idea of this, but he confided in a friend of his, Denis Strutt. I wrote to Strutt the day before yesterday, asking whether he knew anything of Colin's intended movements ; uncertainty on this point, I told him, was holding up the payment of his insurance money to the family. I had got Denis Strutt's moral theology taped all right.[2] He recognized no obligations except those of friendship, and would have carried the secret to his grave if I hadn't made him believe that he was doing the family a good turn by coming clean."

" My husband," Angela confided to the doctor, " has no mania for the truth whatever."

" Actually, everything went off quite otherwise. I can't be certain of the exact details ; there is one man living who could tell us about them, but it would be rather embarrassing work asking him. What I'm going to give you now is a reconstruction of Colin's movements, as nearly as 'they can be traced by conjecture. You must picture him setting off, on the night of January the seventh, in a fine glow of self-congratulation. He was going to make good ; to atone by a P. C. Wren existence for all the misfortunes of his past.

[1] p. 17.   [2] p. 15.

At the same time he was keeping his family in the dark about it; nobly, he thought. He had been at considerable pains to post a letter to the consulate at Madeira, which would come back to Dorn and convince them all, a month or so later, that he was indeed enjoying himself on a foreign cruise. Everything was for the best. He started up the garden car,[1] and slid down the drive. It was fairly late at night, and the gates of the Blairwhinnie Lodge were shut.

" His first impulse was to blow his horn. Then he wondered whether it would not be kinder to get out and open the gates for himself. Then he reflected who it was that would have to open the gates—Wishaw, the gardener, whose little son he had knocked over in his car. Was he funking a meeting with the aggrieved parent ? Would it not be better to have a final reconciliation before he left home ? A parting dinner, well washed down with port, had put him into a good temper with the world. In a haze of good-fellowship, he imagined himself convincing the gardener at last how beastly sorry he was.[2] There was plenty of time. He had recourse, unfortunately, to his now inevitable counsellor—the brandy-flask in his pocket. He was not the sort of man who goes off for a sea-voyage without filling up his flask at home. You saw for yourselves just now how much there was left in it.

" There was no rug in the garden car ; he took off his great-coat, and hung it over the engine to keep out the cold. Then he knocked at the door of the lodge ; he saw, framed there in the lamp-light, the grim figure of the man he had wronged. Wishaw's first impulse will have been to slam the door in his face ; then he had a second thought—was it one of kindliness, or of black malice ? God knows. He asked the young laird in, and offered him whisky, after the custom of the country. I say, we can only guess whether he meant the whisky to have the effect it had. Anyhow, when they had talked for a few minutes, he showed Colin to the door. And Colin—the cold air filling up the measure of his potations —fell flat on the door-step. He was dead drunk.

" Then, if not before, the devil entered into the heart of Hugh Wishaw. The man who lay before him had killed his child. All the country-side knew that he was drunk when he did it. But the Procurator Fiscal had palliated the offence ; had treated Colin's drunkenness as if it were the act of God. Was it not, equally, the act of God that he lay drunk there

[1] p. 20.   [2] p. 20.

171

now, on the threshold of the house into which he had brought mourning a few weeks earlier ? Was it not the will of God that he should lie there, as he lay, unbefriended ? You remember Clough's bitter couplet :

> Thou shalt not kill, but need'st not strive
> Officiously to keep alive.

Would it not be officious in Hugh Wishaw, of all men, to come between the hand of God and its projected vengeance ? Here, surely, was an ordeal of Divine Justice ; if it was intended that Colin should die, he would sleep his drunken sleep until death overtook him. Wishaw had read, all too well, his Old Testament. He shut the door softly and went to bed."

Bredon's audience, even Mrs. Wauchope, had sat hitherto in thrilled silence. It was only now that the Major was heard to murmur indistinctly : " Always said it was the men on the estate."

" Wishaw did not sleep late," Bredon went on, " even if the dubieties of his conscience allowed him to sleep at all. The first sight that greeted him when he opened his front door was a corpse ; the vengeance of Heaven had taken effect. Then panic seized him as he began to think of himself. The doubtful approval of his own conscience might be enough for him, but what view would his neighbours take ? How would his name stand in the country-side ? Was he even, perhaps, a murderer in the eye of the law ? It would be difficult to pretend that he had shut the door before, not after, his guest fell down in a stupor. No, it would be better to conceal the traces of what he had done ; and here too—you could see Providence still at work—he was in a position of strange security. Before the month was out, he would have gone off to join his relatives in America ; during that month, and still longer, the absence of Colin would occasion no surprise ; in the end, it would be supposed that Colin had gone on his travels and never returned from them. All that was needed was to hide the traces of the tragedy.

" As for the car, there was no difficulty ; he could drive it back himself to its shed, and nobody would think to enquire whether it had in fact been taken down to Blairwhinnie, garaged there overnight, and brought back in the morning according to plan.[1] The suit-cases and the overcoat could be

[1] p. 20.

172

sunk in Blairwhinnie pool, until such time as he could devise a safer hiding-place. The corpse must be buried; and there would be no difficulty for him, as head gardener, to arrange that part as long as time was given him; he could dig away where he would, and make sure that his subordinates were elsewhere. Only, for the moment, some accommodation must be found; and inevitably the ice-house suggested itself.[1] A key to it was officially in his possession; there was another up at the house, but the place was seldom visited, and not likely to be visited—the supply of ice had just been laid in, and there would be no occasion to use it, surely, till the summer began.[2] For the time being, then, he removed the body to the ice-house; he drove the car to its shed, and on the way dropped the coat and suit-cases, as we know, in the pool. All day, making sure that he was left alone in that part of the garden, he worked away at the grave; with a grim instinct of heraldry, he dropped a horse-shoe in it, the emblem of the Reiver family.[3] I pointed out to you this morning, Angela, that we ought to have known the grave for the work of an expert. No amateur digger would have worked so regularly, keeping the walls of the pit so squarely marked out.[4]

"But while he dug, and relaxed the concentration of his mind with the exercise, the fortress of conscious self-approval with which he had surrounded his action of yesternight began to crumble away. He saw himself, no longer as the impassive witness of a Divine judgment, but as a murderer; one who had betrayed his guest, taken advantage of a drunkard's weakness, perhaps plunged a soul into hell. That reproving voice must be stifled if he was to carry through his work without detection, nay, if he was to sleep again in the empty lodge. He had recourse to the same fortifying influence as his recent victim, achieving an hour of glorious drunkenness in the public-houses of Blairwhinnie. Even then he gave nothing away; his grim type does not babble in its cups. But the old grievance that had been preying on his mind found its outlet at last; and, in an access of berserk indignation against the laird and all his kindred, he defaced a public monument. You will remember the case, Major; I think you had to sit in judgment on it."

"Drunken scoundrel," agreed the Major, chewing the cud of judicial reminiscence.

"He must have been having a bad time in prison," Bredon

[1] pp. 9, 23. [2] p. 9. [3] p. 131. [4] p. 173.

pointed out. " You see, all his arrangements had been put out of gear, because they were still incomplete. At any time somebody might stumble, as Carstairs Wright did, upon the open grave in the garden. At any time some party of mischievous urchins might drag to light the accusing evidences he had sunk in Blairwhinnie Pool. And, though the summer was still far off, there was the chance that somebody would go into the ice-house and find there—so he must have been picturing the situation to himself—the mouldering body of Colin Reiver. There, of course, he was wrong."

" Did it not stay there, then ? " asked Mr. Gilchrist.

" It stayed there, but it didn't moulder. The doctor here will correct me if I am wrong, but I understand that a body left lying on ice is preserved, just as much as the South American beef you and I ate for luncheon." [1]

" That is so," agreed the doctor. " Always assuming, of course, that the death has been from natural causes, as Mr. Bredon tells us it was in this case. If there were wounds left by violence, they would show the effect of time. But here, you see, it was death from exposure ; the drink had lowered the poor boy's temperature and reduced his powers of resistance, but the death was a perfectly natural one. So the body would remain and did remain in the same state it was in when it was put there, until somebody moved it, of course."

" And then," added Bredon, looking away from the doctor's direction, " early in the morning of the Monday before last, somebody did move it."

" We'll have no more secrets," said the doctor briskly. " I'm grateful to you though, Mr. Bredon. You'll remember, Gilchrist, the night we were up at the house, when the laird was so bad. I wanted to go back to Blairwhinnie to fetch some ice, but Mrs. Hemerton said No, there was plenty in the ice-house, and she gave me the key and asked me if I'd just fetch it up in the car.[2] Well, the first thing I found when I got into the ice-house was the body of. poor Colin. It was half buried in the straw, with the idea of concealing it, and that helped to keep it from getting too cold, for a body that's to be preserved must be neither too cold nor too warm.[3] Well, I was busy with my ice-pack, so I just did nothing and said nothing at the time. It was curious, though, Gilchrist, you saying that to me about keeping Colin Reiver immortal, and

[1] pp. 20, 82, 139, 159, 168.   [2] pp. 23, 24.   [3] p. 85.

174

there was I just fresh from seeing his body preserved on ice.[1]
Well, you'll believe that I gave it more than one thought or
two when I got to bed. And the more I thought over it the
more two things stood out in my mind. The one was, that
this thing mustn't be hushed up any longer; for if it was,
we should be throwing dust in the eyes of the Insurance
Company. And the other was this—that it was no business
of mine to throw suspicions on anybody, when I was quite
unable to understand what had happened. I won't deny but
I wondered a little whether Mr. Hemerton hadn't been up to
something wrong. He's a man of great force of character.

" Well, that made it clear what I ought to do; I had to
move the body from where it was, in such a way that it would
be discovered publicly; but once I'd put it where it would
be found it was no business of mine to make it easy for the
police or anybody else to find out just how it got there. So
I took out the laird's invalid chair, very early in the morning,
and carted the body to the side of the road, where the first
car that came from Pensteven way would get a full view of
it. You'll imagine how puzzled I was when we went out to
look for the body and it wasn't there any longer; and you'll
see, Gilchrist, why I was so positive that MacWilliam was
speaking the truth when he said he had seen it.[2] Eh, and
I puzzled you more than a bit, I'm inclined to think, when
I told you the morning's doings put me in mind of a Greek
tragedy, but I wouldn't say which.[3] Did you ever read the
Antigone at college, Gilchrist ? "

The laughter of the Scot, if it comes late, is given in full
measure. Gilchrist rocked to and fro in appreciation of
the doctor's rather macabre humour; nor, being a Scot, did
he spare his audience a full exegesis of the pleasantry. " Eh,
to be sure, a man's dead body being carted this way and that
by his own sister ! Losh, and I never thought of that ! "

" Yes," said Bredon, " it was the Hemertons who took a
hand next. Vincent Hemerton carried the body off in his
car, under the very noses of the police ; he'd called them in,
I fancy, so as to convince the public that there really was
nothing to find. On the Wednesday morning, he produced
the body again, reconstructing the scene, though not quite
accurately, so as to set us all talking about MacWilliam and
his second sight. When Dr. MacLaughlin saw the body,
though it was in reality five weeks old, it seemed to him,

[1] p. 27.   [2] pp. 31, 32.   [3] p. 34.

naturally, as if it had only been dead a few hours. Because Vincent Hemerton, in his turn, had thought of the ice-house as the nearest and the handiest place for concealing a corpse; so it was on ice again from the Monday morning till the Wednesday. Doctor, you've been mighty close all through, but you just gave yourself away yesterday evening when I asked you that question about refrigeration.[1] I never guessed till then that it was in the ice-house you found it."

" I wonder," said Angela, " what the Hemertons have been thinking all the time ? Because of course it was all spoof, their pretending to think MacWilliam was second-sighted. Did they really believe, I wonder, in that story of Colin having lost his memory ? "

" I imagine so," replied her husband. " You see, they had no mystery to explain to themselves. If we make away with that overcoat and those suit-cases, both the Hemertons and Donald Reiver will go on in the belief that Colin started on his foreign trip, came back from Madeira when he heard his father was ill, then went soft in the head and died of exposure while he was wandering about the country-side."

" Mr. Bredon," said the Major awkwardly, " one thing I want to say. Y'know, I've been thinking most of the time you weren't handling this business properly. But you were right, huh ? Question was, what had happened to the dashed luggage.[2] You kept your head all the time ; thought there was foul play, but wouldn't go off on wild-goose chases. Glad you came into this business. Sleep sound at night now."

" It's very kind of you, Major. But really I don't think there's much for me to write home about. I ought to have spotted the ice-house from the first as the place where the body was hidden between Monday and Wednesday, and if I'd done that, ten to one I'd have cottoned on to the rest of the business too. I think it was really the doctor's interferences in the game—you must get him to tell you about that, Major —that distracted my attention too much. On the whole, I think it's easier to deal with consistent liars than with a person who really tells the truth."

" Meanwhile," complained Angela, " we haven't given any explanation to poor Mr. Carstairs Wright."

" Carstairs Wright ? " said Mrs. Wauchope. " He'll be in Wiltshire by now."

[1] p. 168.   [2] p. 61.

CHAPTER XXVI

WAS IT MURDER?

"And now," said Bredon, "the only question left is what we are going to do about it? We can hush it all up; or we can publish it all; or we can publish the main part of it and leave out the Hemertons. Personally, I'd sooner we said nothing about the Hemertons, because it would look as if I were making use of Mr. Reiver's private letter to me; though actually I shouldn't need to make use of that. But I rather question whether we do any good by dragging the whole thing into the light. I'd like to hear what other people think about that; you belong to the country, and know the people—I don't."

"I'm very glad you raised that point, Mr. Bredon," said the doctor; "it's what I was thinking over when you were talking to us just now. And I don't mind saying, for myself, that I'd like to see the whole story buried. It may be, of course, that I'm afraid of getting a bad name from it myself; it's difficult to keep me out of it. But I'm more concerned, if you'll believe me, about the poor fellow that's in jail now on a lesser charge, with this thing hanging on his conscience. If we publish the story, we break him; and whatever we think of him, I don't see why we would want to do that."

"He's a murderer," said the Major.

"Now, Major, it's no good clapping names to him and fouling the issues that way. It's true he could have saved a young man, his enemy, from dying when he did. But, if you'll excuse me as a member of the family, I'm very doubtful whether the poor boy's life was worth saving or not. He was a misfit from the first, we all know that—just something wrong with the make-up of him that we can't put any name to, but it stuck to him like a curse, and he was never happy inside his family or out of it. A psychologist might have made something of him, perhaps, but that would have had to be done months ago now. This last year or two, he'd taken to the bottle, and I don't believe it was in him at all to get the better of that vice. Well, it wouldn't have taken long for him to kill himself, the way he was going on. And the way I look at it is, if he was due to drop out of the ranks of society before long, there was not much to be gained by saving him from a painless death that night, when it would only have meant reserving him for all the horrors of a drunkard's end."

" Fat lot Wishaw cared about that, huh ? " interposed the Major.

" I'm just coming to Wishaw. I'd say that he wasn't very normal either, but with this difference, you see, that he was only suffering from a sort of temporary melancholia, due to his little boy's death ; and he'll be all right again if he's let down easy. There's a man that has some function in the world ; whatever way you look at it, he's a grand gardener. We know he did meanly ; he may have done worse ; but he wasn't, and isn't, of what you'd call a criminal type. Let him down gently now, and he goes back to what he was. Set the law moving against him, and you'll turn him into an enemy of society."

The little Major was growing more and more restive under this defence of anarchy. " Man's a murderer," he repeated. " Doesn't make a straw of difference whether Colin was fit to live or not ; point is, he killed him—as good as killed him, anyhow. Mind you, if he'd seen red when he opened that door, you know, up with his fists and gone for him and knocked him out altogether maybe, I wouldn't be hard on the feller. Stands to reason a man can't always control his temper, huh ? But that's a different thing ; done in hot blood. This was in cold blood ; my God, did you ever hear of anything more cold-blooded than going back into the lodge and reading his Bible, like as not, with that poor boy passing out by inches just outside ? Won't do ; can't make out that a fellow like that deserves any consideration. You'll have vendettas all over the place at that rate ; same as in Corsica. 'Sides, you've got to look at it another way—Wishaw'd been born and bred on the estate ; never earned a penny in his life that didn't come from our family. Lodge he was living in was our property ; hadn't a roof to his head, you see, without the family. Well, what I mean is, can you justify a feller like that leaving the heir of Donald Reiver to die on the mat ? Won't do ; destroys the whole structure of society, huh, if you can't trust your own men to look after you in a tight place. 'Tisn't just murder ; it's mutiny, that's what I say. Must show the feller up, for the sake of the example, that's how I look at it."

It was Gilchrist who took up the discussion ; you could see that his professional susceptibilities were severely tried. " You must excuse me, Major Henry, but if I understand you rightly it's legal action you want to take against Wishaw, and in that case it's just as well we should use terms in their legal sense. There's no law in Scotland, nor in England either for that matter, against allowing a man to die. As Mr. Bredon here says, it's possible that Wishaw gave the unfortunate young gentleman spirituous liquors which helped to deprive him of his faculties. But we've no proof of that whatever ; and if Wishaw denied it under examination it's hard to see that there's any way we could bring it home to him. And even if we could, it's doubtful if there was anything tortious about his action. There's no suggestion, apparently, that alcohol was the cause of death. As it was, death came from exposure, and could have been avoided if Wishaw, say, had just lifted him into his kitchen. We all agree, to be sure, that it was the part of a humane man to do that. But it's a very different thing to establish the principle that there was any legal obligation to do that. If Wishaw had been the guard of a train, say, or any other official employed in a public capacity, there's no doubt a court would have taken the view that he showed culpable negligence, and could be punished accordingly. But it's no business of the gardener, *sicut sponsus* and in his professional capacity, to see that the son of his employer sleeps warm. I'm not defending Wishaw, mind you, I'm only saying that I don't see how you'll get a verdict against him in any court, because I don't see you've any legal offence to allege against him. It's not a case I'd take up myself, anyway."

" Well, we don't seem to be frightfully unanimous," said Bredon. " What are we going to do about it ? "

" Obviously," suggested Angela, " we put it to Mrs. Wau-chope."

The suggestion was acclaimed ; and the Major himself, after some hesitations, consented to treat the voluble lady as a court of final appeal. She herself displayed no diffidence about the task allotted to her. " Of course, you're all wrong," she explained. " You're quite wrong, Doctor, in suggesting that it makes any difference to a murder, if it is a murder, whether the victim is a useful member of society or not. And you know you're wrong, because you spend most of your life curing people of diseases when you yourself say they would be much better dead. Your other plea, about Wishaw not

179

being responsible for his actions, has a lot more substance in it. Of course, I think we're most of us rather dotty, always have. And fatalists are the dottiest people of all, because there's a kind of method in their madness. Wishaw is a good Calvinist, and therefore for practical purposes he's a fatalist. Comes of reading the Bible too much, I think, when people are always seeing judgments everywhere, and treating it as a special mark of divine favour, don't you know, if they can sell their butter for twopence a pound more than it's worth. I've no doubt Wishaw thought that he was just aiding and abetting Providence in a rather appropriate piece of poetic justice ; but then nearly all murderers *think* they're doing the right thing at the moment. A man gets chucked by his young woman, and he works himself up into such a passion of righteous indignation about it that he really believes he's justified when he cuts the girl's throat. But Henry's quite right in saying you can't keep society going like that."

" Course you can't ; what I said," explained the Major.

" That's all very well, Henry, but, of course, you're talking drivel too. You can't make it out a case of *lèse-majesté* or desertion in the face of the enemy, just because Wishaw used to raise Donald's vegetable marrows for him. Wishaw was no more and no less bound to help a drunk man at his door than anybody else would be to help any other drunk man. And as for murder, that's all rot too. Incredible meanness, if you like, taking advantage of the man when he's down ; but it's not murder. How many drunks do you see in Pensteven at the New Year, and how many of them do you see home ? No, it's no more murder than it's theft to evict a tenant when he can't pay his rent."

" That's an admirable comparison, if I may say so," agreed Gilchrist.

" Yes, but where do you come in, Mr. Gilchrist, with all your legal jargon about whether things are tortious or not ? It's true we can't have the law of the man, but we can do much worse to him—turn the story loose in the world and let the world take its own vengeance on him. He wants to go out to America, but he'll never get his naturalization papers through if he has that reputation behind him. He'll come back to Scotland, probably to Blairwhinnie, and know, all the rest of his days, that mothers are pointing at him and telling their children the story of how Colin Reiver died. Oh, if we could have the man hanged, I'm not saying it wouldn't be a good clean end for him. But your law, you see, is a blunt instrument; it can't always hit the nail on the head—or is that a mixed metaphor? Colin kills a child, in act but not in intention, and the law can't get at him. Wishaw kills a man, in intention but not in act, and the law can't get at him And what I say is, if the law can't deal with a man, leave him to his own conscience, and whatever justice there may be on the other side of the grave. Don't publish his story, for all the world to punish him by cold-shouldering him. That only means envy, hatred, and malice, and all uncharitableness. I've talked more scandal than most women in my time, but don't I know the harm it does; don't I know how all our peace is wrecked by setting ourselves up to be better than one another? Leave the man alone, Henry; the brand of Cain's on him, let him wander where he wills."

There was no more room for dispute after this unwonted outburst of Mrs. Wauchope's. She had surprised herself by her own eloquence; " really, my dear," she told Angela, " I felt just like a minor prophet, only not nearly so obscure." It was the doctor who raised a practical point. " There's only one thing, Mr. Bredon; what way exactly will it affect the Insurance Company if we agree to hush everything up? Won't they be paying out money for a claim that's no business of theirs?"

" That's just the rum thing about the whole business," Bredon explained. " It's what always happens; I've served my Company too dashed well. I went all out to discover whether Colin died on Monday morning or on Wednesday morning, because in the former event my principals wouldn't be liable. All I've succeeded in doing is to prove that Colin died on the seventh of January. And that means that the Company is liable after all, because the premium wasn't due till the first of January, and we always give our clients a fortnight's grace as a matter of agreement.[1] So Donald Reiver gets his money. I may have to tell the full story to the directors, but they would gain nothing by publishing it. On the contrary, they will leave things just as they are, and take credit to themselves, publicly, for paying up an insurance that to all appearance wasn't due. The Hemertons will be happy; everybody will be happy except Hugh Wishaw. But as Mrs. Wauchope says, I don't see how we could make him happy unless we could bring him to trial for murder."

[1] p. 38.

" And what about the things that are in Blairwhinnie Pool ? " asked Gilchrist.

" I thought about that, and it seemed to me the best thing would be to get MacWilliam to dispose of them. He, if anybody, deserves to be told the whole story ; and I'd trust him, as I'd trust very few people, to let the story go no further. He has the gift of silence. He can fish out those things at his leisure, and drown them deeper or put them on an incinerator. And he will have to get that grave filled up, before the laird finds it."

" And what about the Devil's Dimple ? " asked the Major.

" Well, if you're round there, you might tidy up a bit, Major. But I don't think anybody else is going to piece out the story, even if the place is left as it is."

And so the concealment was arranged. Hugh Wishaw, on the day when ·he left prison, committed suicide ; or rather, lest Mr. Gilchrist should fall foul of the statement, let us say that he lay down on a railway-line just before a train passed ; so Mrs. Wauchope's judgment was vindicated. Donald Reiver came into possession of the insurance money, just in time to save a stupendous crash which was threatening Hemerton's firm, and it is not likely that the " Circles " will see much of his legacy when he dies. Major Henry is happy, because the family have allowed him to act as factor for the Dorn estate. And no trace remains of the mystery ; unless you care to climb up to the Devil's Dimple ; where you may still read, among the cynical and amorous legends that adorn the smooth rock at its entrance, the mysterious words :

C. R., XIII. ii. HERE HE LIES.

>>> If you've enjoyed this book and would like to discover more great vintage crime and thriller titles, as well as the most exciting crime and thriller authors writing today, visit: >>>

The Murder Room
Where Criminal Minds Meet

themurderroom.com

www.ingramcontent.com/pod-product-compliance
Ingram Content Group UK Ltd.
Pitfield, Milton Keynes, MK11 3LW, UK
UKHW040436280225
455666UK00003B/104